"Ready?" Jack asked.

The little flutter inside Darcy roared into full-blown excitement. Jack wasn't just any aviator. He was the absolute best, and he was taking her up in his plane. Darcy nodded and hastily secured her seat belt. She pulled the motor hood over her hair. Jack passed her a pair of goggles, and their hands touched. That same spark.

With a whir and a roar, the motor gained speed. The plane began moving forward, slowly at first, then bumping more and more rapidly across the field before it rose.

Darcy screamed. She was flying! In the air, above the earth, like the eagle. God had not created her to fly, but she'd done it. She had done it on her own—well, with the help of Jack Hunter—and it was every bit as wonderful as she'd imagined.

This was where she belonged. In the sky. Here, above the busy-ness of the world, she would make her place, and it would truly matter.

CHRISTINE JOHNSON

is a small-town Michigan girl who has lived in every corner of the state's Lower Peninsula. After trying her hand at music and art, she returned to her first love—storytelling. She holds a bachelor's degree in English and a master's degree in library studies from the University of Michigan. She feels blessed to write and to be twice named a finalist for Romance Writers of America's Golden Heart Award. When not at the computer keyboard, she loves to hike and explore God's majestic creation. She participates in her church's healing prayer ministry and has experienced firsthand the power of prayer. These days, she and her husband, a Great Lakes ship pilot, split their time between northern Michigan and the Florida Keys.

Soaring
HOME

CHRISTINE JOHNSON

Steeple
Hill®

Published by Steeple Hill Books™

STEEPLE HILL BOOKS

Steeple
Hill®

Recycling programs
for this product may
not exist in your area.

ISBN-13: 978-0-373-82848-7

SOARING HOME

www.SteepleHill.com

Printed in U.S.A.

Trust in the Lord with all thine heart;
and lean not unto thine own understanding.
In all thy ways acknowledge him,
and he shall direct thy paths.

—*Proverbs* 3: 5,6

For my husband, Eric, who encouraged me to fly
with my dreams.

Acknowledgments

First and most important, to God belongs the glory.

To the editors at Steeple Hill, especially
Emily Rodmell, thank you for guiding me
with skill, patience and encouragement.

To my pilot and nursing friends, thank you
for answering my many questions.

To the Writing Buddies, thanks for every ounce
of advice. Especially to my critique partners,
Jenna Mindel and Kathleen Irene Paterka.
You kept me on the sidewalk. Without you,
I wouldn't be here.

To the many writers, readers, family, friends and
teachers who have helped and encouraged—
thank you for believing.

Chapter One

1918 Pearlman, Michigan

Darcy Shea squinted into the bright September sky, trying to make out the rigid, oversized bird approaching Baker's field. Her pulse skipped and bounded. Could it be? Seven years since she last saw an aeroplane. Seven years waiting. It had to be, it just had to.

"Why did you stop?" Best friend, Beatrice Fox, pirouetted under her lace-trimmed parasol. "We're already late."

"Just wait a moment." Darcy stood still, listening.

The sun's heat shimmered off the baked road. Grasses rustled and crickets hummed, but no low drone of an engine. She absently tucked a loose strand of hair behind her ear. Perhaps she was mistaken. She sighed and resumed walking to the grange.

"Blake's cousin George from Buffalo is visiting this week," chattered Beatrice. She was lately engaged to the only son of the richest family in town, and every relation seemed to be paying respects. "You'd like him. Perhaps you could spend some time together."

Darcy cringed. Her friend was forever trying to create a

match for her, quite as bad as Papa. "What's wrong with the man?"

"Absolutely nothing." Beatrice wove an arm around hers. "He's handsome, intelligent and our age."

"Then why isn't he in the war?"

"Because he's studying to be a physician. A doctor, Darcy, a professional." Beatrice tugged slightly, urging Darcy to walk faster. "I have a thought. We can go on a picnic, all four of us. You can't object to a picnic."

Darcy did not want to go anywhere with a man she'd never met. "I don't know anything about him."

"Blake says he's a real sport."

"Blake would say that. It's his cousin."

Beatrice *tsked* her disapproval. "He's perfectly charming. And educated. There aren't many opportunities to meet eligible men, so if you want to catch one—"

"I don't."

Beatrice planted a hand on her hip. "Darcy, you must be reasonable. You're twenty-three. People are starting to talk. The war can only be an excuse for so long."

"I'm not using the war as an excuse. I don't want to marry. Ever." She shuddered at the drudgery of children and housework. "Better to fight for women's rights."

"Are you still following Prudy and her lot of suffragists? You'll get a bad reputation. Felicity says some people already wonder if you're one of those man-haters."

Darcy didn't care two pins what Felicity Kensington said, and she didn't see why Beatrice placed such stock in her uppity future sister-in-law. "I don't hate men. I just don't want to marry. I have things to do." Such as flying. She scanned the sky for the plane. Gone.

"Just meet him and talk a little."

"No."

"It's just a picnic, not marriage."

A faint drone froze Darcy. The aeroplane. Within seconds she located it low in the eastern sky, heading toward them.

"What is that sound?" Beatrice looked everywhere but up.

The plane dipped and veered toward town. It was landing. It had to be. No plane would fly that low if it wasn't landing. If only she could be onboard. If only she could fly. Darcy danced across the road.

"Where are you going?" Beatrice called. "We're already late from the nickel show. Your mother will be furious."

"No she won't." Which wasn't quite true.

"She'll make us roll extra bandages."

Darcy motioned for her to wait. "Just one moment longer."

The hum intensified until it sounded like a whole hive of bees. An aeroplane. Darcy hung transfixed at the edge of the field. She couldn't leave now. She hadn't seen an aeroplane since the 1911 Chicago air exhibition, the day she knew God intended her to fly. In the air, women flew alongside men as equals. That's where she belonged, not in lowly Pearlman, where not even the scent of an aeroplane could be found.

Until now. The biplane wobbled slightly as it descended, the left wing dipping before the pilot righted it at the last minute. It did not resemble the planes she'd seen in Chicago. This pilot sat farther back, below the upper wing, in a partially enclosed cockpit. The engine was located forward, giving the machine a sleek, fast appearance.

Beatrice shaded her eyes. "What is it?"

"The answer to my prayers."

The aeroplane headed straight toward them at low altitude. Beatrice shrieked and clutched at her impossibly flowered hat as the plane zoomed overhead and banked to make a run down the length of the empty field. The grass bent flat under the roar, and the turbulence sent Darcy's hair swirling. The plane swooped onto the field, bouncing once before mowing a wide swath through the grass.

"Whooee!" Darcy ran after it, and then, seeing as Beattie was still hunched on the ground, came back. "An aeroplane. Here, in Pearlman. Imagine." God had sent Darcy's dream on canvas-covered wings.

"Tell me it's gone," Beatrice whimpered.

"Of course it's not gone." Darcy peeled Beattie's gloved hands off her ears. "It stopped by old man Baker's empty barn." Already, Hendrick Simmons from the automobile garage and Dennis Allington from the train depot raced down the road on their motorbikes, twin trails of dust rising in the dry September air. "I wonder if something's wrong."

"I don't care, and neither should you." Beatrice smoothed down her dress. "I thought that horrible thing would kill us."

"It wasn't going to kill us. The pilot knew where he—or she—was going. Imagine! It could be a woman pilot." Darcy had to meet her somehow.

The beep of a motorcar horn sent them scurrying to the edge of the road. Frank Devlin, editor of *The Pearlman Prognosticator*, chugged past in his dusty Model T touring car. That was the answer. The newspaper. She could write a story on the plane and talk the pilot into giving her a ride.

"I need to talk to the pilot, Beattie." Darcy squeezed her friend's hand. "This story will make the front page, and I'm going to be the one to write it. Tell Mum I'll be late."

"We're already late. Your mother won't like it. She'll say your duty is to the Red Cross."

"My duty is to the people of Pearlman. Tell her I'll roll double the bandages tomorrow." Darcy itched to run. A plane. A pilot. Everything she'd dreamed the past seven years had come directly to her. She had to see it.

Beatrice clutched her arm. "Don't do anything foolish. Promise?"

Darcy pulled away and bounded down the road. "I'm going to ask the pilot to give me a ride."

"A ride?" came the cry from behind her. "You're going into the air in that thing? Stop, stop." Beattie panted, struggling to run in her hobble skirt and heeled shoes.

As much as Darcy loved her, Beattie was such a perfect Jane, all frills and lace. She'd faint from this much exertion. Darcy went back to her. "What are you doing? I said I'd meet you at the grange."

"You could die," Beatrice insisted breathlessly, "like that heroine of yours. What's her name? Harriet Quincy?"

"Quimby, and it was an accident. The passenger moved suddenly and threw the plane off balance. That's not going to happen here."

The pilot, dressed in knee boots and leather jacket, climbed out of the plane. A man. Too bad.

"How do you know disaster won't happen?" Beatrice insisted. "She fell a hundred feet."

A thousand, actually, but Darcy didn't correct her. Though silent now, the plane beckoned to her. The smell of burnt oil hung in the air. A sizeable crowd had gathered around the plane, and opportunity was slipping away. If the pilot had only stopped to fuel, he might be gone within the hour.

"Sorry, Beattie, but I have to go."

"But, your father. He won't like it," Beatrice huffed. "What will he say?"

Darcy knew exactly what Papa would say. No, with a capital N. Respectable young ladies don't fly aeroplanes.

But they did. They did.

"He doesn't need to know," Darcy insisted.

"He's your father."

"I'm a grown woman." Nothing and no one would keep her

from her dream. "And if he doesn't know, he won't be hurt. Promise me, Beattie."

Across the field, the pilot had returned to the cockpit and the crowd was turning the plane, readying it to fly off. Her future was about to disappear into the pale blue sky.

"Only if you promise to go on the picnic with George."

Darcy gritted her teeth. It was extortion. "All right, but only if I reach the plane before it takes off." Without waiting for confirmation, she hitched up her skirts and ran across the field. The wiry grass tangled around her ankles. She stumbled on the uneven ground.

Dennis Allington pulled on the propeller. The engine coughed and rumbled to life.

No time. No time.

Darcy gasped for air, her lungs burning. She couldn't run any faster. She couldn't get there in time. Her whole future was flying away.

Her hair tumbled from its pins as the plane inched forward. Then the motor spluttered, choked and died. A thistle caught her shirtsleeve. She tore loose as the men gathered along the back of the wings. They pushed. She stopped, gulping for air, as the machine coasted into the barn.

Thank heavens. She composed herself and twisted her hair back into a knot, so she'd look professional for the interview.

By the time Darcy slipped through the open barn doors, Devlin, Allington, Simmons, old man Baker, and half of the supposedly employed men of the town had gathered around the aeroplane in a big semicircle. Darcy tried to wedge through, but they stood like a fence between her and the plane.

She circled around, looking for a gap, and spied Hendrick Simmons. Her childhood friend would let her through. She made her way toward him as the pilot climbed out of the cockpit. He tossed his goggles into the forward seat before jumping to the barn's dirt floor, still seeded with trampled bits of straw.

"Should be a matter of two, three days at most," the pilot said to Baker, who was doubtless calculating precisely how much rent he could weasel out of his new tenant. "Do you have a telephone?"

"Don't need them newfangled contraptions," Baker said, his lower lip drawn over his upper, due to the few teeth he had left and his general disinclination to spend money on luxuries like false teeth.

"There's one in town—" Darcy began, but Devlin cut her off.

"Closest one's at the *Prognosticator* office." He stuck out his hand. "Frank Devlin, managing editor of our fair city's most highly esteemed publication. I'd be glad to loan you the use of our telephone."

Oh, no. Devlin was going to beat her out of the story and steal the pilot, too.

"Jack Hunter." The pilot shook Devlin's hand. "I'll take you up on that offer."

Mr. Jack Hunter ruffled his sandy-colored hair with the luxurious ease of a cat rising from a nap. Standing perhaps six feet tall, Hunter had the confident manner to be expected in a pilot. And he was handsome. Easily as athletic and dashing as Douglas Fairbanks. Every unmarried woman in town would swoon over him, but not Darcy. Darcy Shea did not swoon.

"Tell me what fair city this happens to be," Hunter said.

With one quick thrust, Darcy burst through the circle of men. "Pearlman," she said before Devlin could answer. "Pearlman, Michigan."

Jack Hunter took notice, his gaze traveling up and down Darcy's frame, as if sizing her for a dress, but if he thought he would unnerve her, he was sorely mistaken.

She stared back. Square between the eyes.

One eyebrow rose. "Pearlman? Never heard of it. Anywhere near Chicago, Miss…?"

"Shea. Darcy Shea. And yes, about a hundred miles, less by air."

"That so?" Hunter chuckled as he fetched a cap from the cockpit. He tipped it slightly. "Many thanks, Miss." He turned to Devlin. "With any luck, Burrows—he's my mechanic—will have reached Chicago by now."

"Let's get going, then." Devlin shoved the stump of a cigar back into his mouth. Frankly, it was a wonder he'd bothered to take it out. He never did at the presses, and the stench of the thing overwhelmed even the smell of ink and grease.

Hunter turned to old man Baker. "I'll be back later to check on the plane."

Darcy had to act now. If she was going to have any chance at this story and her plane ride, she had to be with Devlin and Hunter in the motorcar, not hanging back in Baker's barn. She curled behind the bystanders, who pressed closer to the aeroplane.

"Don't touch anything," Hunter warned, when one of the kids climbed on the lower wing. "Any damage, Mr. Baker, comes out of the fee."

That put Baker into action, rousting everyone from the barn. It also gave Darcy opportunity to slip past unnoticed.

"I'm a mechanic…" Hendrick Simmons said weakly as Hunter strode by, but the pilot didn't hear him.

Poor Simmons. He was a nice guy, forever tinkering with motors, and talkative enough when you asked him how stuff worked, but he hadn't an ounce of gumption. Darcy, on the other hand, had plenty. Devlin was not going to steal Hunter away from her. She raced to the Model T and slid into the backseat, keeping low so Devlin and Hunter didn't spot her.

"Cora can place the call while you settle up at Terchie's," said Devlin, opening his door. "That's the hotel here."

Darcy smothered a laugh. Terchie's was nothing more glamorous than a boardinghouse.

"Want to bring your bag along?" Devlin asked. "It'll save you the trouble of hefting it into town later."

Jack Hunter dropped into the passenger seat. "Don't have a bag."

Darcy could see his reflection in the windshield. Even teeth and a boyish grin, just a little lopsided. And his eyes. She sighed. Oh, his eyes. Bright as cornflowers. If she did happen to be interested in a man… Darcy shook her head. What was she thinking?

"Didn't expect to need it," Hunter said. "My things are with Burrows on the train."

He sat so close Darcy could touch him. She could smell the warm leather and faint scent of soap. No starch or stiff collar in his shirt. The black tie hung loose, as if he didn't care what people thought. And his jacket was soft and brown and buttery.

"Well, I might be a tad larger," Devlin said, rubbing his expansive gut, "but I could loan you—what on earth?" He'd spied her. "Shea. What are you doing in my car?"

"Uh…" Darcy scrambled for an explanation and spotted Beatrice approaching, red-faced and out of breath. "You do give rides to ladies, don't you?"

"Ladies?" he spluttered. "Out!"

Hunter grinned at Darcy, and she nearly melted. Those blue eyes. The crooked smile. The strong jaw.

"I don't see why we can't give Miss Shea a lift," he said. "We're going that direction anyway."

In that instant, Jack Hunter won her gratitude. Now, if he would just give her a plane ride.…

Devlin didn't share Mr. Hunter's generosity. "I don't have time to ferry girls around town."

"I'm hardly a girl," Darcy noted for Mr. Hunter's benefit, "but that's not the point. We're tired and hot."

"We? I see only one of you."

Darcy waved to her friend who had reached the barn. "Beatrice. Here. Mr. Devlin is giving us a ride into town."

Poor Beattie looked overheated and frazzled from the rapid walk, but somehow that made her more beautiful. Unfortunately, Jack Hunter noticed. He hopped out of the car and opened the rear door.

An irrational wave of envy swept over Darcy as he helped Beatrice into the seat beside her. Why not her? Darcy wasn't as beautiful as Beattie, but she and Hunter shared an interest in planes.

"Good afternoon, Miss—?"

"Fox. Miss Beatrice Fox." She folded her parasol, tucking it daintily beside her.

So proper. So pretty. So engaged. Darcy throttled her petty jealousy and apologized. "I'm so sorry. I didn't mean for you to follow."

Then Jack Hunter flashed that smile at her. Her. Darcy Shea. Not Beattie. Not any other woman. Her. She fanned herself with the notepad. My, it had gotten hot.

Beatrice was staring at her. "Do you feel all right? You look rather flushed."

Darcy touched her hot cheek. "I'm fine." She cleared her throat and tried to remember why she'd gotten in the motorcar in the first place. It certainly wasn't to lose her head.

While Devlin cranked the engine, Hunter worked his charm. "Tell me what brings two lovely ladies to a dirty old farm."

"I'm a reporter," Darcy said, getting back her wits.

"Ah." His eyes narrowed. "And you, Miss Fox?"

She blushed. Beatrice always blushed. "Nothing very important."

"It had to be important to walk all the way out here."

Beattie's blush deepened, and Darcy nudged her friend to remind her that this little encounter was all about getting a plane ride.

"Not really," Beattie warbled, glancing at Darcy. "I'm with Darcy. She wanted to see your aeroplane, but we're supposed to go to the grange hall to roll bandages for the war effort."

The car chortled to life, and Devlin shuffled back to the driver's seat.

"A noble effort," Hunter said as Devlin got in. "Our boys overseas will thank you."

"And what do you do for the war effort, Mr. Hunter?" Darcy asked, holding up a pencil so he couldn't mistake her intent.

Hunter noted her writing implement and answered dryly, "I train recruits to fly."

Train to fly. The words flashed through Darcy like electricity. He could not only take her up in an aeroplane, he could teach her to fly it. She could be up there, in the blue expanse, looking down on all creation. She could proclaim to every man on earth that women were capable of doing anything. She could change the world.

"Aren't you going to write that down?" Hunter asked.

"Oh, yes." Darcy started to write, but Devlin chose that moment to put the car in gear and drive through the biggest pothole in the barnyard. She flew forward and had to brace herself against the back of the seat or she would have smashed right into Devlin.

Beattie had bounced forward also, and Mr. Hunter steadied her until she settled back in the seat. He smiled, not just any old smile, but warm and welcoming. With a sinking feeling, Darcy realized he must have meant it for Beattie. Beatrice was the beauty, not her.

Darcy squeezed the pencil tight and pretended to survey

the passing scenery. She reminded herself that she was never going to marry. It didn't matter if no one found her beautiful. She would be fine by herself. After all, marriage meant being shackled to a man's will.

On the other hand, from a purely aesthetic sense, Mr. Jack Hunter had a certain dashing charm. His jacket was of an excellent cut and style, though worn pale at the edges. No pomade, thank heavens. Though oiling the hair was all the rage, Darcy despised the smelly stuff. She imagined sinking her fingers into his thick hair. The soft tug. Silky smooth.

"Did you have another question?" he asked.

Darcy gulped, feeling the heat lick up her face. She must have been staring at him.

"Uh, where are you from?" she asked. Ridiculous question. Devlin must be laughing.

"New York." He smiled in a most disconcerting way before resuming his conversation with Devlin.

"Are you sure you're all right?" Beattie asked.

"Fine." But she wasn't. Jack Hunter was turning her into a fool, making her forget what she really wanted. Just spit it out. Tell him she wanted a plane ride. But her mouth refused to form the words. Her mind went blank every time he looked at her.

The car flew down the road toward the newspaper building. More than once they bounced off the seat when it hit a rut. Beattie clung to the door frame, but Hunter took the jolts in stride. Maybe he was accustomed to bumpy rides in his aeroplane. Baker's field couldn't have afforded a smooth landing.

Devlin didn't apply the brakes until they'd passed the Kensington Mercantile, two doors from their destination. He pointed the motorcar straight at the hundred-year elm outside the press's front window. With a screech, a squeal and a grinding jolt that threw everyone forward, the automobile shuddered to a stop, bumper just touching the elm.

"Oh," hiccupped Beatrice, her eyes wide. "Oh."

Devlin rolled out of the vehicle. Now was her chance.

"Mr. Hunter." Darcy tried to tap his shoulder, but he moved just out of reach. "Mr. Hunter, if I might have a word." Since she couldn't get past Beattie, she jumped out her side. "Excuse me. I have a proposition."

Devlin's head snapped toward her. "Miss Shea, I'm not buying any stories."

"But this will be spectacular, and something only I can do, seeing as I'm a woman."

"That might be debatable," Devlin grumbled.

She scooted around the back of the motorcar, only to find Hunter helping Beatrice out of the backseat. The streak of jealousy flashed through her again, but she shoved it aside. He was doing what any man would do. He would have done the same for her if she'd stayed in the vehicle.

"Why thank you," Beattie said. "You are such a gentleman. Just like my Blake."

"It's easy around two lovely ladies." He smiled broadly.

Darcy coughed to settle her mind. He could not disarm her with a mere smile. Devlin was sidling near. She had to act.

"Take me up," she said without explanation.

For a moment, Hunter looked surprised. "Take you up on what?"

"Oh, no," Beattie said, aghast. "Darcy didn't mean anything improper. She's not that kind of woman."

Darcy felt the heat rise again in her face. "Up in the aeroplane." Her voice squeaked. "I'll write about it for the newspaper. It'll be the highlight of the year. Remember my articles on the Chicago aviation meet, Mr. Devlin? You sold out and had to make another print run."

"Those were for a school project." Devlin's ill humor

soured. "Besides, you were the only one from Pearlman at that meet. You go up in that thing here, and everyone will know about it. No news. No story."

"But they won't be able to experience it—assuming Mr. Hunter isn't giving rides. But if you are, just wait until the article comes out, and people will line up around the block."

Hunter shook his head. "No one is going up in that plane. The motor is locked. Frozen. Won't run."

Devlin guffawed, and the two men started toward the newspaper office door. Men. If they thought a simple dismissal could stop her, they were dead wrong.

"Yes, I know you need to make repairs. But after it's fixed," she said, tagging along, "you could take me up. On a ride," she added, so there'd be no repeat of the last misunderstanding.

Jack Hunter stopped on the steps. "In case you're not aware, Miss Shea, the government has restricted civilian flights due to the war."

His words slapped hard. She did know it. She'd just forgotten in the heat of opportunity. "But *you* must have permission."

"To test new aircraft for possible military use."

Darcy's head throbbed. Her dream sat so close she could touch it, but Hunter kept pulling it just out of reach.

"You'll need to test the repairs," she suggested.

"Not with a civilian passenger, and definitely not with a woman. Good day, Miss Shea. Miss Fox." With that, he and Devlin went inside. The door banged shut behind them.

Darcy stood before the closed door. She would get that ride. She didn't quite know how at the moment, but Darcy O. Shea was no quitter. She'd find a way.

Chapter Two

While Jack waited for the telephone operator to ring back, he stood lookout at the grimy front window. Devlin and Miss Shea had him trapped. Inside the newspaper office or outside, he faced an interview.

Devlin pulled open drawer after drawer in his paper-buried desk, looking for cigars. "They're in here somewhere."

"Don't put yourself out," Jack said for the third time. "I don't smoke."

Miss Shea still hadn't left the front steps. Something about that woman sent common sense into a tailspin. He could hardly take his eyes off her, and paying extra attention to her friend hadn't helped.

"What brings you to Pearlman?" Devlin asked from behind the mounds of paper.

Direct and to the point. No dodging about. Jack could respect that, but he still wouldn't give an interview, even the easy kind Miss Shea wanted to conduct. He blew on the window and rubbed a spot clean with his elbow. If he wasn't mistaken, the lovely Darcy Shea had finally left with her friend. One threat gone.

"Heading for Chicago?" Devlin said.

"I'm not giving an interview."

"Did I say anything about an interview? Just a little friendly conversation."

Jack didn't believe that for a minute. "I thought any interview belonged to Miss Shea."

"Humph." The newspaperman grunted from below the heaping desktop. "It takes more than desire to write for *The Prognosticator*. It takes a level head and a certain flair with the written word. Miss Shea...well, let's just say her ambition outstrips her talent."

Devlin's dismissal of Darcy rubbed Jack wrong. "Ambition goes a long way toward success."

Devlin's head popped up. "What's your interest in the inimitable Darcy Shea?"

"No interest." He couldn't let Devlin see how the woman affected him, so he sauntered across the room and peered into the print shop, where, near as he could tell, no one was working. "Just wondered how many reporters you have on staff."

"Enough to do the job. Aha." Devlin held up a fat cigar and then ran it under his nose. "Sure you don't want it? Next best thing to Cubans, at half the price."

Again Jack waved it off. Accept a cigar; accept the interview. He had to keep this story out of the newspapers. His bosses at Curtiss weren't going to be happy when they heard about the locked engine. A sensational news story would put an end to long-distance test flights and tie him to the airfield.

"So the plane's a prototype." Devlin puffed to light the cigar. "Military use, eh?"

Jack preferred Darcy's questions. She just wanted a ride in the plane. Impossible, of course, but he admired her tenacity.

"What's it going to be used for?" Devlin propped his feet on the desk, sending papers tumbling to the floor. "Bombing? Scouting? Reconnaissance?" A cloud of smoke followed each word.

Such questions from Darcy would be called persistent. From Devlin they were just annoying.

"I can't tell you any more than I could tell Miss Shea." When Devlin frowned at the mention of her name, Jack realized he'd struck proverbial gold. He could turn the conversation away from the plane and toward her. "Speaking of Miss Shea, is she from here?"

"Born and raised." Devlin pulled down his feet and leaned forward. "Is the army going to use the plane in the war? Advantage in the air is advantage on the ground, I say."

Jack ignored Devlin's question. "I expect everyone was born here. This is the kind of place a person would hate to leave. She married?" He could not believe he'd just asked that.

"Definitely not." Devlin chuckled before returning to his questions. "Is the plane destined for European or North African duty?"

"Can't say." He wished Devlin had explained that little laugh. What was so funny about Miss Shea not marrying? Most women did. "Her friend is engaged?"

"To the richest bachelor in town."

"You don't say." Jack didn't care about the pretty blonde. His thoughts clung to the bundle of fire who insisted he give her a plane ride. Spirited. Determined. Fearless. All the qualities of a top-notch aviator. If she was a man.

"For which company do you fly?" Devlin asked.

Jack, still contemplating Darcy's attributes, answered without thinking. "Curtiss Engineering."

"That the same as Curtiss Aeroplane?"

Jack choked. He shouldn't have said that. No one was supposed to know about the scout plane. "This model is just in testing. There's a long way to go before it's ready for production—if it's ever produced." He was digging himself out of a job. If the powers at Curtiss discovered he'd talked to the press, he'd be fired before he climbed out of the cockpit. "That's strictly off the record. Can't jeopardize the war effort."

Devlin just grunted.

The newspaperman was not going to forget this. Confidential information would end up on the front page if Jack didn't come up with a bigger story. He ran a hand through his hair, clueless how he could patch up this fiasco.

Thankfully, the telephone rang. Unthankfully, Devlin got to it first.

The newspaperman listened a long minute before saying, "Yep, got it Cora." He hung the receiver on the wall hook. "Your man's not there."

"Not there?" Jack checked the time. Four-thirty. Burrows should have arrived an hour ago.

"Cora talked to the hotel manager. Seems your mechanic hasn't checked in."

Things were getting worse. If Burrows hadn't arrived in Chicago yet, he wouldn't get to Pearlman until late tomorrow at the soonest. Another day's delay. Jack blew the air out of his lungs slow and steady. "Guess I'll send a wire."

"Should have said so while I had Cora on the line. She sends the cables around here."

"The same person?"

Devlin scowled. "Pearlman has every advantage of the largest cities."

"Good." Jack glanced at his watch again. "I'd better hurry. Get there before she closes. Thank you for your hospitality."

He fled the office before Devlin resumed the interview. At the bottom of the steps he met a well-dressed man better suited to the streets of Manhattan than a country village. The young man doffed his hat, revealing dark hair that gleamed like engine oil. Jack instinctively mistrusted the type.

"Blake Kensington." The man extended his hand with a surprisingly open smile. "You the pilot that landed in Baker's field?"

Jack couldn't hide his surprise that the news had already spread around town. Nonetheless, he grasped Kensington's hand and completed the introduction.

"Buy you a soda?" Kensington's quick, almost imperceptible lift of one eyebrow told Jack the invitation involved more than a simple beverage.

"I need to send a wire first." One soda couldn't hurt. He'd hear the man out, and if he proved a pompous fool, beg off.

"The drugstore's just across the street from the telegraph office. I'll meet you after you're done." Kensington leaned close and whispered, "Back door. Knock twice, wait a second, and then knock three more times." He clapped Jack on the shoulder and yanked open the door. "Devlin?"

Jack's flutter of unease blew into a gale when he overheard Kensington say, "I told you front page. Make it right or you'll hear from my father."

Jack hurried down the sidewalk past Kensington Mercantile and Kensington Bank and Trust, trying to come up with an excuse to get out of that soda. He idly noted the emptied racks inside Kensington Bakery and the tidy desks inside Kensington Farmer's Insurance Company. Did that family own the whole town?

On the next corner stood a weathered storefront with a freshly painted sign proclaiming it the communications hub of Pearlman, as well as the town's official United States Post Office.

He pushed open the door, and a woman in her thirties popped up from behind the heavy oak counter. Her small eyes, snub nose and generous rump gave her an unfortunate resemblance to a sow. Cora, he presumed.

"You must be Mr. Hunter." She beamed. "Beatrice Fox was right."

"Miss Fox? About what?"

"Never mind," Cora giggled.

Jack had lost patience with tittering single women. He had a problem to fix and little time to do so. "I'm here to—"

"—place a wire. What did you want to say in it?"

Small towns. Too nosy. Too personal. Better to live in the city, where a man could blend into the teeming sidewalks. But instead of snapping at Cora, he forced a smile.

"Send it to the Palmer House hotel in Chicago, care of Dick Burrows." He made out the cable, paid the fee and tucked his wallet inside his jacket.

Cora didn't budge. She also didn't send the wire. She stood at the counter, twisting a dull brown curl around her index finger.

"Did I give you the correct amount?"

"Oh, yes," she sighed without blinking.

"I need it sent right away."

"Fine," she huffed. "I'll do it now." But her glare made it perfectly clear that she would not send the wire while he waited.

Jack stepped back. What sort of town was this? He couldn't get out of here soon enough. He turned and found himself face-to-face with the last person he wanted to see.

"Miss Shea."

Her hair was coming loose again, and her skirt sported dozens of burrs, but she was just about the prettiest woman he'd ever seen.

"Mr. Hunter." She jutted out that determined little chin.

He stepped aside, but she moved in the same direction.

"Excuse me," he said, attempting to get around her. His mouth had gone dry and that soda sounded better every minute. "I'm meeting someone. At the drugstore."

Her eyes widened and her lips curved into a frown of disapproval.

He wished he'd kept his mouth shut. "Just for a soda." Why did he say that? She didn't need to know every detail of his day.

"What you drink is none of my business," she said with far too much self-righteousness. She moved to her right just as he moved to his left, and they collided. "Excuse me. Oh."

Her embarrassed laugh warmed Jack right to his toes. A hint of pink tinged each cheek, making her unbelievably attractive. The heady scent of violet wafted past. He had a terrible urge to kiss her.

"Excuse me." Her curt tone destroyed the urge. "I need to check the post."

"Of course." This time he stood still and let her make the move, which she negotiated without further difficulty. He tipped his cap. "Good afternoon."

Her delicate neck lifted, and her head turned until those deep brown eyes gazed at him again. "And to you, too."

My, she could take a man's breath away. Strong yet vulnerable. Plus she had no idea how beautiful she was. Jack took a deep breath and eased out the door, somehow managing to get to the sidewalk without stumbling.

The street was busy. Horns honked. Harnesses jingled. A dozen passersby could have witnessed that little scene. Cora certainly had. He walked as fast as he could toward the drugstore, dodging a slow-moving Packard and an even slower-moving horse and buggy. He jumped to avoid a fresh pile. Horses! Why didn't this town join the twentieth century?

"Mr. Hunter." Miss Shea's words pierced through him with the efficiency of bullets. She no doubt wanted to pester him about flying. He quickened his step.

"Mr. Hunter."

Didn't she know she was creating a spectacle? Didn't she

care? Maybe that's why Devlin laughed when he asked about her. Maybe that's why she still wasn't married.

He ducked his head and nearly barreled into a matron dressed in an outdated gown, oddly reminiscent of a ruler-wielding schoolmarm from the turn of the century.

"Sorry, ma'am." He dropped into a deep bow.

She was not at all amused. "Watch your step, young man."

"Yes, ma'am."

With a nod, the matron dismissed him and marched across the street. "Darcy Shea, where have you been?"

Jack whipped around.

"Mum." Miss Shea's disappointment hung in the air with the stench of manure.

Mum? The schoolmarm was Darcy Shea's mother? For a second he felt sorry for her. He even wanted to stand up for her, but then common sense returned. Jack Hunter didn't belong in decent society. With his family background, no self-respecting mother or father would welcome Jack's attentions to their daughter.

He had to put an end to this fantasy now.

Once he knew Darcy was watching, he strode to the back door of the drugstore. He knocked as directed, and before entering caught Darcy's shocked expression. Good. That's the way it had to be. Women like her could have nothing to do with men like him.

Darcy's stomach refused to unknot, even after she was back in the privacy of her bedroom. She plopped on the bed with the hand-stitched quilt, but couldn't lie still. Jack had gone into Mrs. Lawrence's blind pig, the illicit drinking house that everyone in town knew about, yet law enforcement completely ignored.

Thank heavens Mum hadn't seen that. Her opinion of the

man would have sunk even lower. And Papa? If he found out, she'd never get that plane ride.

She pressed a damp cloth to her cheeks to cool them. If she appeared at supper all flustered, her parents would think something had happened. But nothing had, other than that little encounter with Jack at the post office, and that meant nothing. No, she could hold her head high and maintain cool detachment when it came to Jack Hunter.

Her sole objective was to get a ride in his aeroplane. To do that, she needed to persuade him to her point of view. But how? What could she give Hunter that would make him grateful enough to offer her a ride? He'd already shot down her story idea. By tomorrow afternoon his mechanic would arrive. She needed to convince him tonight, but how?

She chewed on her fingernails and tapped her foot, waiting for inspiration to come. Her parents wouldn't allow her to go out after dark unless accompanied by someone they trusted. Beatrice wouldn't do. She was dining at the Kensingtons' tonight. She needed someone else, but who?

Oo-gah. A car horn sounded below. Darcy raced to the window. Of course. Hendrick Simmons. He would do anything for her, and even Papa couldn't object. They'd been friends since childhood, climbing trees and riding bicycles and repairing motors.

Repairing motors. Of course. She and Simmons could fix Jack Hunter's broken engine. He'd be so grateful that he'd give her a plane ride. It was the perfect plan, pure genius.

The clock struck the six o'clock hour. Darcy donned a clean white waist, brushed the dirt off her skirt, and twisted her hair into a tight knot before going down to supper.

A massive, claw-footed walnut table dominated the Shea dining room. Mum favored pressed Irish linen and delicate English porcelain, but Darcy thought it looked out of place, like a top hat on a miner.

Papa set aside the newspaper and downed his daily medicinal of Dr. Caldwell's Syrup Pepsin, beet juice and vinegar. Mum glanced up as Darcy entered. Her grim expression told Darcy this wouldn't be easy.

Darcy slipped into her chair. "Sorry I'm late."

A platter of roast beef sat in the center of the table, surrounded by bowls of potatoes, green beans and carrots from the garden. None of it tempted her.

After Papa said grace, Mum served the beef.

"We missed you at the grange today," Mum said.

"I'll roll double tomorrow afternoon. I promise."

"Tomorrow is too late. You know we ship the bandages out in the morning. Darcy Opal Shea, this wild behavior has to stop. You're nearly twenty-four, too old to make a spectacle of yourself. Your hair. Your skirt. I was embarrassed. Dermott, did you know your daughter went running through Mr. Baker's field?"

Papa looked up from the newspaper, clearly only having heard the part of Mum's harangue that came after her utterance of his name. "Baker's field? I hear a plane crash-landed there. Did you see it, Darcy? Dennis Allington said it was quite loud."

"It didn't crash," Darcy said. "It had to land due to engine trouble."

"Is that so?" Her father snapped the paper and folded it against the crease. "Perhaps I'll go over there and have a look."

Oh, no. She did not need Papa meddling. "It'll probably be gone in the morning. I don't know for certain, of course, but I could ask. Someone in town must know. Hendrick Simmons, for instance. If the plane needed fuel or had a problem, they'd have to go to the motor garage. I could ask him after supper."

"But it will be dusk," Mum pointed out.

"We'll walk there together," Papa suggested.

Worse and worse. "No reason to waste your time, when I can run over in moments and report back." A twinge of guilt rushed past Darcy's conscience too quickly to pay it much mind. With her plan, everyone would gain. Simmons would get the business, Mr. Hunter's plane would get fixed and she would get her plane ride. It was the perfect solution.

Papa gave her a long look. "You spend too much time with that Simmons boy."

"He's just a friend."

"Exactly," said Papa. "If you loved him, well, then we'd need to discuss things."

"I don't." Darcy didn't elaborate. Papa would never understand her refusal to marry.

"Speaking of prospects," said Mum, "I understand someone new is in town." She paused dramatically, waiting for Papa to ask who it was. When he didn't, she proceeded to enlighten him. "Dr. George Carrman, from Buffalo. I ran into him while I was out. He seems a very pleasant, likeable young man."

"You met him?" Darcy's mother had an almost miraculous ability to run into any eligible bachelor who happened into town.

Papa furrowed his brow. "We already have Doc Stevens. There's no need for another doctor—and a young, inexperienced one at that. That's the way it is these days. The young people get an education and think they can take away a man's job."

Mum laughed off his concerns. "George Carrman is not here to take away Dr. Stevens's job. He's just visiting."

"And he's not a physician yet," Darcy added. "He's still studying."

"Carrman, you said?" Papa pulled his attention from the newspaper. "Don't know the family. Who's he visiting?"

"He's a Kensington cousin." Mum clearly took pleasure in this announcement. "Must be on Eugenia's side."

"Kensington, eh? And a doctor. Don't suppose he's married."

"No, he's not married," snapped Darcy. Better to get it over at once. "And don't worry, Beatrice has already arranged a picnic so I can meet him."

Father removed his reading spectacles and set them on top of the newspaper. "I'm glad someone is looking out for your future."

"I'm not interested," she said.

Mum shook her head.

Papa ran his thumbnail down the newspaper's fold, creating a knife's edge. "Don't go into this with a closed mind, Darcy. He may be a fine young man and deserving of your attention."

Darcy toyed with the green beans on her plate, separating the two halves and rolling out the little beans.

"Your mother and I only want what's best for you," her father continued. "A good marriage will ease our worries. You're what? Twenty-three? Your sister was already married and had her first child by that age. It's time to settle on someone." He unfolded his spectacles and put them on again.

The front door opened, ushering in a tumult that could only be Darcy's sister, Amelia, children in tow. "Hello, Mum, Papa." Her greeting trailed through the house.

Darcy had never been close to her older sister. Besides the eight-year difference in their ages, they had nothing in common. Amelia loved clothes and babies. Darcy wanted to be a great explorer. They hadn't fought—well, not that much. They simply didn't like the same things.

"I must tell you. I simply couldn't wait." Amelia winged into the dining room, coat and gloves still on. Pale and willowy where Darcy was short and dark, Amelia had commanded numerous beaus before settling on Charles Highbottom, a local dairy farmer with enough income to buy the fancy hats and gowns she favored.

The girls, aged five and eight, ran to Grandmum while ten-year-old Freddie went straight to his grandpapa.

Darcy's father broke into a wide smile. "How's my Frederick? Find any treasures lately?"

Ordinarily shy Freddie dug in his pocket and extracted a handful of dusty baubles, which he dumped on the table.

"Let's see what we have here." Papa bent over the treasures while Freddie explained where he found each one.

Meanwhile, Mum doled out one piece of taffy to each girl. Darcy pushed aside her plate, appetite gone. Amelia was the pretty one, the smart one, the good one. She knew how to carry herself. She knew her place. Darcy had heard the comparisons all her life.

"Papa." Amelia tugged off her gloves in irritation. "I have news. Are you listening?"

Papa looked up from the army of treasures. "Darcy, do you remember that bear claw I gave you? Wouldn't that be a fine thing for young Frederick?"

Darcy's mouth dropped open. The bear claw? Papa had given it to her. That claw was his prize, taken from the grizzly bear he killed years ago on his grand adventure. Give it to Freddie? He'd only ruin it.

"Papa!" Amelia stomped her foot.

"Forgive your father, dearest," said Mum. "He's partial to his grandson. Dermott?" Mum managed to capture Papa's attention. "Your daughter has something to tell you."

Amelia's porcelain complexion had turned faintly pink. "It's terrible timing, what with Charles having to sign up for the draft tomorrow, but that can't be helped. You're going to have another grandchild."

Mum and Papa stared, dumbfounded.

"I thought you didn't want any more children," Darcy said.

Amelia hugged her gloves to her chest. "Well, Papa? Aren't you pleased?"

"Oh, my dearest Amelia," Mum gushed. "We are. Of course we are. It's just that it's such a surprise."

Papa rose, brushing crumbs from his gray waistcoat. "Amelia, my dear. Good job." He enveloped her in a hug.

"Congratulations," Darcy said, though an unreasonable peevishness smothered any true celebration. Marry. Have children. Would nothing else please her parents?

"Good girl." Papa beamed, pride elevating him an extra inch. "Let's make it another boy."

Another boy. There were more important things than having babies. Any woman could bear children, but precious few had the nerve to travel to the ends of the earth. Tears stung Darcy's lids as she slipped out of the house. She would make her mark. She would do something no one had ever done before. Yes, she would.

Extricating Jack Hunter from the blind pig, or illegal saloon, had seemed like a good and noble idea at the time, but as Darcy approached the drugstore's back door, the nerves set in. Her hands sweated, and she shivered in the cool evening air. She hadn't exactly told Papa she'd be going here.

Since the state had gone dry two years ago, Vanesia Lawrence had run her saloon out of the back of the drugstore. Papa called it the blight on the apple of Pearlman, but his opposition hadn't begun with prohibition. He had drilled the evils of drink into Amelia and Darcy from an early age, their Aunt Meg, who'd married a drunk, serving as his primary example.

Now Darcy stood at the door of a saloon, calling on a man, a drinking man, a man she barely knew. If Papa found out, he'd yank her home by the ears and never let her step outside again.

Dark and damp descended on the narrow alley, trapping the smells of rotted cabbage and horse dung between the brick buildings. Darcy hesitated outside the plain wood door, gathering her courage.

"Shouldn't be here," Simmons muttered.

He was right, of course, but Darcy couldn't back down now, not when she stood this close to her dream. She turned the cold iron knob. The door didn't budge. "It's locked."

"Good, we can go." Simmons edged away. "I didn't wanna come in the first place."

"No, no. We can't give up yet." She knocked.

"What're you doing?" Simmons hissed, tugging her away from the door.

"Finding Mr. Hunter."

"We should get outta here." Simmons glanced each way down the alley.

"Please stay, Hendrick. I need you. You're the ace mechanic who can fix Mr. Hunter's motor."

"If you say so." He drew a circle in the dirt with the toe of his shoe.

"Don't worry. Remember your dream. Hendrick Simmons, aeroplane mechanic. You'll have your own shop."

"Garage."

"Garage. Your name in big letters on the sign over the door. You can go places, Hendrick."

"I don't want my name up in big letters, and I don't wanna go nowhere else. Them kind of dreams are fine for you, Darcy, but I'm a simple kinda guy. I like Pearlman, and I like my life fine just the way it is."

Darcy sighed. Squeezing ambition out of Hendrick Simmons was tougher than getting Cora to stop listening in on telephone conversations. "Pearlman is fine, but maybe your children will want more. You could leave them an inheritance. You could be the Henry Ford of aeroplanes."

Simmons rubbed his brow against his shoulder, somehow managing to smear black grease across his forehead in a faint echo of his sparse mustache. "Aw, Darcy, I don't even have a girl. There's no sense talking about children."

"You'll find someone." It might be true, if he ever got up the nerve to ask a girl out. "She'll appear one day, and you'll know she's the one. Who knows, maybe she'll fly in on an aeroplane. But if a plane's to come here, there needs to be a mechanic. You could be that mechanic. Imagine, she'd step out of that aeroplane and sweep you off your feet."

"Aw, Darcy," he mumbled, burying his hands in his trouser pockets. "I don't think…"

Mrs. Lawrence—though to Darcy's recollection there'd never been a Mr. Lawrence—threw open the door. Music and laughter emanated from inside, but Vanesia Lawrence's orange silk gown filled the doorway. Even on tiptoes, Darcy couldn't see past her.

"What do you want?" the proprietress said.

Darcy squared her shoulders. "Mr. Jack Hunter. Is he here?"

Mrs. Lawrence hesitated long enough that Darcy knew he was. "Now why would he be here, sugar? I don't even know the man."

"I saw him come here this afternoon."

Mrs. Lawrence smiled lazily. "You must be mistaken. Now run along home to your papa."

Darcy fumed at being treated like a child, but she couldn't think up a deserving retort.

"Let's go," Simmons whispered. "He's not here."

"Yes he is." Darcy faced off against Mrs. Lawrence. "I know what I saw, and I know what your business is, so you can stop pretending. Either you fetch Mr. Hunter now, or I write an editorial about your little establishment."

Mrs. Lawrence's artificial smile curved slightly, the blood red of her lips garish against the orange gown. "A threat, Miss Darcy, needs teeth to be effective. Our newspaper would never print such a piece."

Which meant Devlin frequented the place, too. Darcy set her jaw. Vanesia Lawrence might block her now, but Darcy would not give up. "Then I'll find him myself." She darted past Mrs. Lawrence, but got only three steps into the dark, smoky hallway when she ran into something very solid and very alive.

"Back you go, Miss Shea," said that all-too familiar voice.

A second later, Jack Hunter deposited her in the alley beside a wide-eyed Simmons, who looked ready to bolt. Mrs. Lawrence calmly closed the door, leaving Darcy alone with both her bait and her quarry.

"What do you want?" Hunter sounded almost bored.

"A moment of your time." Darcy gave him her broadest smile.

"Couldn't it wait until morning? This is no place for respectable ladies."

"I know that, but—" she began, but he'd already turned on Simmons.

"You should know better than to bring her here."

Simmons backed away.

She was going to lose Hendrick unless she talked fast. "I have a proposition for you, Mr. Hunter."

"Is that so?"

"A business proposition," Darcy clarified. She dragged Simmons forward as witness to her honorable intentions. "We only need a few minutes."

Hunter looked faintly amused. "I already told you I'm not giving rides in my aeroplane, not to you or to anyone."

"I'm not talking about a plane ride. I'm talking about solving your problem. We can repair your motor."

To his credit, he didn't laugh. "I have a mechanic. He'll be here tomorrow."

"Late tomorrow," she emphasized. "We can save you time, get you on your way more quickly."

"And you, out of pure goodness, want to help me leave as soon as possible." The shadow of the doorway masked his expression. "That does run counter to your goal, doesn't it?"

"I do want to help you. Mr. Simmons here is a mechanic. He can fix anything."

"Good for Mr. Simmons."

She disregarded the sarcasm. "We can begin now."

"Listen Miss, didn't you hear what I said before? This is a prototype. The motor isn't like anything you have here. We need the correct parts. No matter how good you are," he nodded at Simmons, "you just don't have what that plane needs."

Simmons hung his head, but Darcy dwelled on the meaning behind Hunter's words. "Then you know what caused the problem."

"I'm not a mechanic."

"But you have an idea. Pilots do know their planes, don't they?"

"It's a prototype. I didn't build it. Now if you'll excuse me, Miss Shea, I'd like to return to my business conversation." He rapped twice on the door.

Darcy very much doubted she'd interrupted business. More likely he wanted his drink, making him a man of dubious morals. Still, that didn't disqualify him as a flight instructor, providing he didn't imbibe before flying, and she'd seen no indication of that.

"Conversation will not get you in the air, Mr. Hunter. Your job, if I understand correctly, is to test this aeroplane and get it in top working condition for military use."

"Very good. Apparently something I said is getting through to you."

Darcy wanted to toss back his sarcastic jibe, but that wouldn't get her in the air, so she pasted on a smile that would make Beattie proud. "Everything you've said, Mr. Hunter, is getting through to me. In fact, I'm so concerned for your mission and helping our boys overseas that I want to offer my assistance. Mr. Simmons is perfectly capable of machining a part if need be. If that is not to your satisfaction, at least you'll have the motor apart so your mechanic can repair it quickly. Considering how anxious you are to leave Pearlman, you should be pleased."

He took a moment. "You aren't going to leave me alone until you get your way, are you?"

Darcy curbed her triumph. "That's right."

"If Burrows tells me you made it worse, you'll pay for the damages."

She agreed with a nod. Papa *would* be furious.

"And how do I know you have the money?"

Simmons finally found his voice. "Her father's the banker."

"The banker, eh? All right, you have a deal. Eight o'clock tomorrow morning."

"Eight o'clock." She stuck out a hand to shake on it.

Hunter hesitated before grasping ahold. When he did, it was with a firmness and warmth and duration that sent a shock through her. She tried to breathe. She considered letting go, but couldn't. She'd stalled, gone into free fall, and the whole world narrowed to just the two of them. Gone were the streets of Pearlman. Gone the moon. Gone Simmons.

Then he smiled, the kind of smile he'd given Beattie, the warm one, the one that said she was beautiful, the one that sent every thought fleeing from her head.

She opened her mouth, but nothing came out.

His smile curved back into a grin, but his hand still held hers.

"Uh, it's late," Simmons said.

"That it is." Hunter finally let go, but as he did, his fingers brushed her palm.

Her hand tingled. "We have an early start." *What a mindless thing to say.*

But he didn't point out her lack of wit. He smiled softly. "So we do."

Once again his gaze lingered, and she could not help but return the look. In the light of the half moon, she saw something besides the callous adventurer. He had shown consideration for her reputation. He'd acted honorably. He couldn't be a complete reprobate.

But then, with a nod of the head, he went back inside and ruined every good thought.

Darcy touched the cold, wooden door. Half of her wanted to follow him. Half knew she should go home. Jack Hunter was no good. He was a drinking man.

She had no business even thinking about such a man.

Chapter Three

Jack sat at the dining table the next morning with a thunderous headache. Didn't seem fair, considering he never touched alcohol. He took a gulp of coffee, hoping the strong brew would clear the pain. He, of all people, knew better than to go into a saloon, but it had seemed the right choice at the time.

He unfolded the newspaper and blinked repeatedly to focus his eyes. He could swear that was a photograph of his aeroplane spread across the front page with the one-inch headline: PLANE CRASH-LANDS.

Jack slammed the paper to the table. *That illiterate, no-good newspaperman!*

Four sets of eyes fixed on him.

Jack nodded at the other boarders. "Sorry."

He had to get out of this town before the damage got worse. Curtiss hadn't wanted the prototype scout plane to leave Long Island, but Jack and Burrows had insisted a distance test was required. Chicago and back, that was all. Two days, three at most. But Jack had not counted on disaster. An emergency landing and a missing mechanic added up to one major headache.

"Dzien dobry. Good morning." The stout Polish pro-

prietress set a plate of runny eggs before him. Though his stomach turned, he managed a nod of thanks.

The other boarders—a salesman type, a meek professorial fellow, and two gray-haired gossiping hens—watched with interest, no doubt waiting for the introduction he didn't intend to make. Boardinghouses attracted the misfits of society, those without the comfort of family, and Terchie's was no exception.

Jack shielded himself with the offensive newspaper. He had an uneasy suspicion he'd agreed to something last night, but he couldn't remember exactly what.

"Are you the pilot who crashed?" one of the ladies asked.

Jack grumbled an excuse, gathered his coffee and newspaper, and went to the porch. The open windows let in fresh air as well as the sounds of motorcar horns, people yelling and birds squawking. Better than gossiping hens.

He settled into the overstuffed chair farthest from the windows, and opened the paper to read what that newspaperman had written about him. It took only a moment to get the gist.

Tripe. One hundred percent tripe.

Jack tugged on the ring he wore on a chain around his neck. It had belonged to his grandmother and was his only link to a happier past. He fisted his hand around it. That Devlin fellow had spilled everything, calling the plane a secret military model. If this spread outside Pearlman, Jack would lose his job.

He crumpled the paper in disgust, and then shook it out again when the two gossips approached. Couldn't a man get a moment's peace? He scrunched down in the chair, seeking solitude behind the newspaper.

Every printed word battered him: "hapless pilot," "frozen motor," "lost mechanic." Mechanic. Oddly, the word conjured someone other than Burrows. A woman. A pretty woman with dark hair. Darcy Shea. He hoped that promise he vaguely remembered making didn't have anything to do with her.

Bam! The impact of the door slamming shook the porch and rattled Jack's raw brain.

"Hey, careful," he said. "Some of us are trying to rest."

"Rest? It appears that's all you've been doing. You were supposed to be at the barn over two hours ago." The woman herself stood three feet away, hands on hips. Darcy Shea. Lovely and irritated.

Jack winced and drowned the pain in another gulp of coffee. "Good morning." He forced a smile.

"Oh. I see. You forgot." She plopped down in the chair opposite him.

Jack groaned. He did not under any circumstances want her to stay. "I'll be there shortly. Go ahead. Get started without me."

"Mr. Baker won't let us in the barn without your permission."

Figures. Not only had he found the pushiest woman in town, he'd stored his aeroplane with the most conscientious price-gouger.

"Fifteen minutes," he said, hoping she'd leave. He waved her away, but she didn't move. His head pounded, and every word took effort.

"Fifteen minutes isn't going to be enough time." She managed to say it without the usual feminine condemnation. "You need a powder. I'm sure Terchie has some."

With that she blessedly went inside, taking her head-piercing comments with her. Jack struggled to his feet and headed for the staircase. If he could get to his room before she returned, he'd be safe.

He got to the third step.

"Here you are," said Miss Shea, waving a packet.

Not quick enough. Jack leaned his forehead on the rail. "Look, Miss—"

"—Darcy."

"Look, Miss Shea, I appreciate your assistance, really I do, but the best thing for me right now is bed. I feel a fever coming on."

"All the more reason to take the powder." She jammed it into his hand.

"You aren't leaving until I do, are you?" He had a feeling he'd said those words before.

"I'm not leaving until you go with us to the plane."

"Us?" Jack tapped the powder into his mouth and washed down the bitter stuff.

"Me and Hendrick Simmons. The mechanic."

He remembered it all: the touch of her hand, her ridiculous request and his even more ridiculous response. What had he been thinking? Burrows would have his head if he let anyone touch his baby.

"Look, Miss Shea, only the company mechanic can work on that plane. It's a test model. Do you understand?"

"Of course. I'm not a fool."

"Then you know this is not something for amateur mechanics. So be a peach, and hurry along to whatever normally occupies you at this hour of the day. I'm going to get some rest. It was a pleasure meeting you. Goodbye."

He headed up the stairs, but the fool woman followed him. He faced her. "Where do you think you're going?"

"Up in that plane with you." She said it as if it was the most natural and possible thing in the world.

Jack had occasionally met a woman eager to fly just to say she'd done it, but this was beyond reason. This woman was like a hound chomped onto his ankle. She reminded him of…

He shook his head. No. Sissy was stuck in a hospital,

whereas Darcy bubbled with life. Yet something about Darcy reminded him of his sister. Spunk? No, stubbornness. Once Sissy made up her mind, nothing could change it.

"Look, I explained everything yesterday. I have government permission to fly this plane. I do not have permission to take passengers. There's nothing I can do."

"You can convince them."

"It's not in my control."

She dug in, jaw thrust out. Her full lips pressed into a determined pout. Her wide dark eyes demanded an answer. Yesterday's attraction rushed back. He should pull away, but he leaned forward, drawn into her snare. The tilt of her neck. The curve of her chin.

Just in time, he caught himself. "Excuse me, I need to rest."

"Don't go." She caught his hand, and her touch hit him like a hundred volts of electricity. "Not yet. You haven't heard all the advantages. If you teach me to fly—"

"Teach you?" The words exploded in his brain. *Never.* Jack Hunter would never teach a woman to fly. "I thought you only wanted a ride."

"And while we're there, why not give me a lesson?"

"No, absolutely not."

"It will be a coup for the company. They can tell the military that the plane's controls are so simple, even a woman can manage them."

"No," he growled, keeping his voice low so he didn't draw the attention of the gossips.

"You haven't heard me out. The military has to train raw recruits, right? What better selling point? It's a sure bet, good for both sides. The army can train all the aviators they need in minimal time, and the company sells hundreds and thousands of planes."

She held her head high, doubtless expecting him to agree

or even applaud her logic. Though her argument made some sense, the answer was still no. Even if he was willing, the Curtiss executives would never agree to it. Women didn't fly in the war. They sure didn't test warplanes.

"It's not possible," he said. "Sorry." Best to crush her hopes now.

"You promised."

Those two tiny words smashed through every argument Jack could devise. He'd promised. With painful clarity, he recalled the exact moment. It did not include flying.

"I promised to let you and your mechanic friend work on the engine." He rubbed his aching head. Never let it be said that Jack Hunter reneged on his word. "I did not agree to give you a ride or lessons."

If she was disappointed, she didn't show it. "Very well. That's why I'm here."

"Give me an hour." With luck, he could stretch that to two and prevent this woman and her friend from damaging his plane.

"One half hour, and I'm waiting right here."

"Suit yourself." Stubborn was too mild a description for Darcy Shea. Before entering his room, he made sure she understood. "Under no circumstances will you be flying."

"But—"

He bolted for his room before she could finish protesting.

Jack should have known this little project would end in disaster. He shouldn't have given in to those pretty eyes, but Darcy Shea had a talent for talking him into doing precisely what he didn't want to do.

Thus, one day later the motor lay in pieces on the ground, with Burrows due on the three-thirty train. Jack did not want to witness the explosion when Burrows saw his motor torn apart. He hoped Darcy's powers of persuasion also worked on fiery mechanics.

"I don't suppose you can finish before three-thirty," he asked Simmons, who was standing on a ladder propped against the fuselage.

The kid grunted and pulled a valve out of the number three cylinder. He handed it to Darcy, who then placed it in order on the white sheet she'd spread on the barn floor. Rows and rows of parts, each carefully cleaned and labeled.

She stepped back to survey Simmons's progress. "Don't worry, we'll have it apart by then."

"And repaired?"

Darcy blinked slowly, taking it in. "You said not to fix it. Just take it apart. That's what you said."

Her voluminous overalls left everything to the imagination except two delicate ankles, and her hair had been braided and coiled so tightly that she looked like a spinster, but her smile could charm a dead man. It sent prickles across his skin.

"Are you listening to me?" she demanded.

Jack nodded.

"Well, don't change your instructions halfway through the project."

"Yes, ma'am." He was tempted to salute. She certainly acted like an officer. "I'm just anxious to finish."

She cocked her head. "It would go faster if you helped."

"I'm no mechanic."

"Neither am I, but I'm helping." Her long eyelashes brushed the top of her cheek when she blinked.

"You're doing fine without me." He nodded up at Simmons. "Besides, three's a bit crowded."

The Simmons kid glared, reinforcing Jack's opinion that he had eyes for Darcy. Anyone could see it. Except Darcy.

Jack downed the last bit of coffee from his vacuum bottle and checked his watch. Nearly one o'clock. He yawned and stretched. Maybe he should help. But then he'd miss watching Darcy.

Simmons suddenly cried, "Found it." The kid climbed down the ladder and waved the oil screen under Jack's nose. "Plugged."

"Huh." Jack didn't dare comment, or he'd give away that he knew more about the motor than he'd let on.

"What Hendrick means is a plugged screen stops the oil from flowing," Miss Shea explained with unnecessary pertinence. "Without lubrication, the engine locks up."

"Leave it for Burrows," Jack snapped, irritated at being tutored like a novice. He'd been flying almost ten years. He knew more about planes than the whole population of Pearlman put together. "I'm going to get some lunch."

Simmons stood dumbly staring at his feet, as if he expected something more.

"Repairs have to be made by the company mechanic," Jack explained. He screwed the top on the vacuum bottle. "Thanks for the help."

Simmons gulped and nodded, but Miss Shea braced her hands on her hips, oblivious to the grease she was depositing there. He could tell by the set of her mouth that she was angry.

"What is it?" Jack asked.

Her lips worked a full minute. "You know what." She nodded toward Simmons, who was packing up his tools.

He hated when women assumed he could read their minds. "Humor me."

She whispered, "Hendrick Simmons put in a lot of time on your plane, when he could have been working at the motor garage. He deserves some…compensation."

"Why didn't you say so?" Though it irritated him that she expected payment when they'd volunteered, he pulled out his wallet and settled with Simmons.

"Want a ride, Darcy?" asked the kid, pocketing the money.

She shook her head. "Brought my lunch."

Simmons hesitated. Clearly, he didn't want to leave Darcy alone with Jack, nor should he.

"I'm locking the barn." Jack put on his cap. "I'm afraid you can't stay, Miss Shea."

Jack's words spurred Simmons on his way, but Darcy took her time gathering her lunch basket. "I'm going to eat under the big oak. I brought roast beef sandwiches. There's enough to share."

"Share?" Jack wasn't so sure that was wise.

"What's wrong? You don't eat beef? Or is it the company you find objectionable?"

"Not at all." He searched for an excuse. "I wanted something hot."

"I can set your sandwich in the sun."

He had to double-check, but sure enough, Darcy Shea was teasing. It had been a long time since a woman had teased him, and it felt good. "That won't be necessary."

"Then you'll join me?"

"After an invitation like that, how could I refuse?"

She unpacked the basket beneath the big oak: sandwiches wrapped in paper and a mason jar filled with a pale yellow liquid that had to be lemonade. His mouth watered. He hadn't sipped a lemonade in years.

"What else do you have in that basket of yours?" He made sure he stood a good ten feet away.

"Dill pickles, boiled eggs and blackberry pie, but you'll have a hard time eating them from there." She plopped to the ground and pointed to the grassy expanse in front of her. "Plenty of room to sit."

He dropped to the grass and bounded right back up. The

ground was littered with thousands of acorns. "I don't suppose you remembered a blanket and wine."

"It's lunch, not a picnic. Besides, Michigan happens to be dry, Mrs. Lawrence's notwithstanding."

"I know that," he said, though he found the tone a bit too temperance for his liking. Jack didn't drink alcohol for personal reasons, not due to some self-righteous cause. He brushed the acorns away so he could sit with reasonable comfort.

"How do you know Michigan's dry? You're from New York."

A wet state doesn't need blind pigs, Jack wanted to say, but that was a conversation Jack did not care to have, so he turned its direction. "I live and work on Long Island, but I grew up in Buffalo."

She gave him a peculiar look. "Buffalo? You're from Buffalo? How odd. Everyone seems to be from there these days."

"Who is 'everyone'?"

She shrugged. "No one important."

After an awkward silence during which the ants made progress toward the lunch basket and Darcy fussed with her napkin, Jack ventured, "Did you make the pie?"

"What if I say I did?"

"It's not a competition. I don't care who baked the pie. I'm just making conversation."

"Oh." A lovely, dusky blush rose in her cheeks. It was nice to know Miss Darcy Shea could be embarrassed. "I thought, well…never mind."

He stretched out on the grass, leaning on one elbow, and tipped his cap back so he could watch her every move. If she'd give up that defensive shield she put around herself, she'd be downright attractive.

She unscrewed the lid on the mason jar. "We'll have to share, unless you still have coffee."

"Tough luck. It ran out a half hour ago."

"I suppose I have enough for two." She set the jar between them and took a bite of her sandwich. She even looked attractive chewing.

He checked the sandwich. Beef and mustard. Homemade bread, with its rich, yeasty aroma. It had been ages since he'd eaten anything other than bakery bread.

"What happens when your mechanic arrives?" she asked while he was chewing. "Will he have the replacement parts? Does he know what to bring? What did you tell him when you talked on the telephone?"

Jack choked down the food. "Is this an interview?"

This time no blush, just an enigmatic twist of the mouth. "I'm just curious."

Jack ripped his gaze away. "He'll bring everything he can. But if he doesn't have a replacement part, we'll have to wire the factory."

It looked as if she perked up, but maybe it was his imagination.

"Where is the factory?"

He poured some lemonade into his coffee cup. "Do you have a cup? I'll pour."

"Oh, yes." She dug around in the basket and came up with a glass.

While he poured, she repeated her question. "So where is the factory?"

"The main plant is in Buffalo, but all the prototypes come out of Long Island, under the direct supervision of G.H. himself."

"G.H.?"

"Curtiss. Don't tell me you've never heard of G.H. Curtiss."

"Of course I have," she said rather quickly, and for a second he thought she was lying, but she followed with a litany of facts that would impress anyone. "Flew the Rheims Racer to the Gordon Bennett trophy at Rheims. Winner of The Scientific American Cup and the *New York World* prize for flying between Albany and New York in less than a day. Maker of the JN biplanes."

"All right, all right. I don't need a history lesson."

"So he designed this plane?"

"At least in part." He sampled the lemonade. Tart but refreshing.

"I'm guessing it's designed for distance flight."

What was she getting at? "The plane's ultimate use is not my concern."

"You just fly them, right?"

"That's right." But there was something about the brightness of her eyes that got to him, that made him say things he shouldn't. "This flight was a special test."

"For distance." She leaned forward. "It had to be. How far can it go on one fueling?"

He shrugged and picked up a hard-boiled egg. "Farther than here."

She laughed at his joke, but he could see her calculating. "To Chicago and back is a long way. Hundreds of miles in each direction. How many miles can a gallon of fuel go? Not that many. Oh, my. That's a lot of fuel. The military must be spending a fortune on this."

He rolled the egg between his hands. "I wouldn't know."

"Do they know you're here?" she asked breathlessly. Her lips parted, moist from the lemonade. She couldn't possibly know what that did to him.

He blinked, trying to remember what she'd asked. Oh—if his bosses knew he'd been forced to land here. "The proper people know."

"Do you think Mr. Curtiss is anxious?"

She was assuming he had a greater knowledge of Curtiss

than he did. He'd met the boss a few times. It wasn't as if they were friends.

"Maybe a little," he said with a wink, glad to see she followed with a smile, "but I can handle it."

She leaned toward him, and a curl drifted across her brow. He resisted the urge to brush it aside.

"You mean your mechanic can handle it," she said.

He laughed. "Touché."

For a moment she stilled, deep in thought, and he wondered if he'd somehow offended her. Then, slow as a propeller starting to turn, her eyes widened. He wanted to believe that glow in her face was for him, but he'd only be kidding himself. She had hit on something, something important.

"I want to do it, what you do," she breathed, rising to her knees and sweeping her arms to the open sky. "I want to fly. Ever since the Chicago air meet, I knew that one day, no matter what it took, I would fly."

He could have looked at her all day, but he had to open his mouth. "But you didn't."

She lowered her gaze to meet his, jaw set with determination. "I will."

Jack began peeling the egg. He knew what she meant, that he could be the one to fulfill her dream. This was the danger point. Rushing in was easy. Getting out wasn't. Especially with a banker father lurking in the background.

"There are good flight schools around the country," he said carefully. "Chicago would be closest."

She sat back on her heels, deflated. "They're closed. The war."

"They'll reopen after the war."

"I don't want to wait. Who knows how long the war will last. You're an instructor. You could teach me."

The desperation in her voice made him want to help, but he couldn't. "I teach recruits."

"I know. But what's one more person? They'll hardly know I'm there. I'm not meant to be here, in this small town. I want to do something, set a record, go places no woman has ever gone. Someday I will be the first to fly over the North Pole."

Jack gagged on the lemonade. "Excuse me?" Her intensity was thrilling, but he had to set her straight. This wasn't a little jaunt she was talking about. "Do you have any idea how much funding and preparation it takes to make a flight like that? Plus there's no money in it. Now, be the first to make the transatlantic flight in one hop, and you'll get yourself fifty thousand dollars. That's a prize worth going for."

She didn't blink. She didn't breathe. "That's what you want to do, isn't it?"

He ran his thumb around the rim of his cup. "It's not possible."

"Not now, with the war, but later, after it's over, you can do it. You can be the first."

She was so close he could see tiny drops of perspiration on her upper lip.

He cleared his throat. "Others have the jump on me, and the planes aren't capable of that distance yet." Though true, his excuse did nothing to break the charge between them, so he joked, "I can't even make New York to Chicago without engine failure."

If she thought it funny, she didn't laugh. She didn't move an inch. He was uncomfortably aware of the smells of violet and petroleum, not to mention the heat she generated.

"That's a test flight with a new plane," she said, seemingly oblivious to the electric moment. "Take an aeroplane you've tested and run for hours, one you know inside and out, and you can do it."

"First I need to get *this* plane running again." He cleared his throat, but it was too late. She'd noticed its rough edge.

"Let me fly with you when it's fixed," she said, looking at the open field. "I want to know. I *need* to know what it's like to fly, even if it's just for a minute."

This was what he knew had been coming, but the faraway gaze, reddened cheeks and desperate hope undid him. Memories rushed back. He and his little sister, twenty years ago, playing in the sunlight. The river rushing past. Sissy laughing. *Come along, Jackie. Are you afraid?* He'd gone with her to the riverbed and look what happened.

He shook his head, banishing the past.

Miss Shea looked at him with the same eager eyes and tense anticipation. Such desire could not be crushed by one refusal. If he didn't give her that plane ride, she would find another plane and another pilot, likely less scrupulous and willing to risk her life for money or a cheap thrill. Jack wouldn't see the disaster, but it would be his fault all the same. But if he gave her a ride, he would be in control. He could scare her just a little and rid her of these romantic notions once and for all.

"Promise you'll tell no one?" He would regret this.

She brightened. "I do, I do! Oh, thank you." She clapped her hands together, her cheeks flushed with excitement.

His boss would kill him if he knew what he was doing. "That means no newspaper stories. No magazine stories. No stories at all. Promise?"

She nodded. "Absolutely."

"It also depends on the weather," he cautioned.

"I know."

"And it has to be early in the morning, at first light. I want you here at four o'clock, the morning after the plane is repaired. Wind, rain or storms, and the flight is called off."

"I understand. I'll be there." She impulsively squeezed his hand. "Thank you."

"Thank me later." After he'd scared her enough that she'd never fly again.

* * *

Two days later, Darcy stomped her feet in the cool morning air, while Burrows tinkered with the aeroplane's motor. They'd rolled the plane out of the barn well before dawn, but the engine wouldn't stay running. By now the horizon had lightened to pale gray rimmed with gold. Jack said they had to fly at first light. If this took much longer, the flight wouldn't happen.

She glanced toward town. No one coming yet, but the longer this took, the better the chance she'd be spotted. Soon Mum would rap on her bedroom door to wake her. When she didn't show for breakfast, they'd know.

She nipped her lower lip.

"Be patient," said Jack, hands buried in the pockets of his jacket. "You don't want to fly unless everything's perfect. Haste leads to crashes."

"That and weather." Darcy hoped she sounded informed. The Chicago newspapers had blamed the 1911 aviation meet fatalities on high winds. "Today is dead calm."

"Perfect weather, if it warms up."

She tucked her hands into the folds of her skirt, wishing she had thought to wear gloves, and watched Jack work. He looked so assured talking to Burrows. This was his element. He belonged in the air.

Excitement tugged at her. If only they'd go.

Jack walked over to her. "You cold?"

She balled her hands and shook her head.

He fetched her a scarf from the cockpit. "It gets colder the higher you fly. Wrap this around your neck and tuck it in. Don't let the ends come loose or you'll be flying that plane alone."

"What?"

"This girl has dual controls," he explained, "and if your

scarf gets tangled in the controls, you'll find yourself with one hard to handle lady."

"That won't happen," she said, tucking the ends into her coat and trying not to be nervous. "I promise."

His lips snaked into that lopsided grin.

"What's wrong?" she asked. "Is there an end loose? Do I look foolish?"

"Not at all." But his gaze lingered a little too long.

"Something's not right."

He shook his head. "You'll have a time of it climbing into the cockpit with that skirt. Tuck it tight around your legs once you're settled or it'll blow into your face and my field of vision. You should have worn the outfit you had on yesterday."

Darcy inched up her skirt a little. His eyes widened as she revealed overalls.

"Harriet Quimby had a flying suit that could convert from bloomers to a skirt," she said. "I thought such an arrangement might prove practical today, given the circumstances."

He whistled, long and low and with obvious appreciation. "Miss Shea, you surprise me sometimes."

"Darcy," she insisted. "If I'm going to put my life in your hands, you should call me Darcy."

The warm notes of his laughter resonated deep within her. "Is that all you think of my ability to pilot this plane? Well Darcy, let me tell you a little secret. I have never wrecked an aeroplane, and I don't intend to start today."

The little flutter inside her roared into full-blown excitement. He wasn't just any aviator. He was the best, the absolute best—and he was taking her up in his plane.

Burrows hopped down and indicated the plane was ready to go. At last. Hunter confirmed a few last-minute details while Darcy gathered her skirt and climbed aboard. From atop the lower wing, she could see clear to town. No one coming.

"Forward cockpit," Jack said.

"I know." Once in the cockpit, she stretched her legs past the rudder bar and eyed the wheel. Good heavens, she could actually fly the plane from here. She placed her hands on the wheel and closed her eyes, imagining for a moment what it would be like to be in control.

"Ready?"

Darcy's eyes popped open, and she hastily secured her seat belt. She pulled the motor hood over her hair. Jack passed her a pair of goggles, and their hands touched. That same spark. She jerked away and fumbled with the eye gear.

"Remember, we won't be able to talk in flight," he said while she retrieved the goggles, "so a thumb down means you want to land."

Darcy nodded.

Jack shouted to Burrows, and the mechanic gave the propeller a tug. With a whir and a roar, the motor gained speed. The plane began moving forward, slowly at first, then bumping more and more rapidly across the field. The Baker house and barn vanished behind them, and the village approached. She could see Terchie's and the roof of the bank. Papa.

A wave of regret washed over her. She hadn't exactly told him what she was doing. He'd only forbid it. But still, it was wrong. *Forgive me,* she prayed.

The end of the field loomed closer and closer. She gripped the edge of the cockpit. If they didn't get in the air soon, they'd clip the trees. She could end up like so many aviators: dead or severely injured.

"Watch out," she yelled, though there was no way Jack could have heard her. She wished they could stop now, wished she'd gotten her father's approval, but it was too late. Soon she'd be smashed to bits.

They hurtled toward the trees. Then, when it seemed certain they'd crash, the bumping stopped and the plane rose.

Darcy screamed. The icy air blasted her face and made her

shiver, but as soon as she looked below, she forgot how cold she was. Trees and houses shrank below her until they looked like toys.

Jack banked to the right, toward town. Pearlman looked so small, so insignificant from above. There stood her house, the kitchen window lit. Maybe her parents would hear the noise and look out, never suspecting their daughter was flying overhead.

She was flying! In the air, above the earth, like the eagle. God had not created her to fly, but she'd done it. She had done it on her own—well, with the help of Jack Hunter—and it was every bit as wonderful as she'd imagined.

From this height she could see how rivers and roads and railways connected the scattered houses one to the other in a great web. *This was how God had made the world. How He watched over it.* She leaned back, letting the air flow past her face, and gazed straight into the heavens.

This was where she belonged. In the sky. Here, above the busy-ness of the world, she would make her place, and it would truly matter. She'd show the world that women deserved to be treated equally. Same wages, same voting privileges, equal stakes in marriage. She would change the world.

Then the engine coughed. It almost died before racing madly. The plane accelerated.

Darcy looked back.

Jack was frantically working on something in the cockpit. He wasn't watching where they were going. He wasn't even steering.

She grabbed the wheel and tried to hold it in place.

Then the engine died.

It grew deathly quiet, with only the whistle of wind rushing past.

The wheel yanked in her hands. She held on tighter.

"Let go," Jack yelled.

She released it like a hot stove iron. The village, once so far away, was coming nearer and nearer in great swooping circles. They'd stalled and gone into a spin. Spins were fatal.

"Do something!" she yelled.

"I am."

But the buildings and trees kept coming closer. They were going to crash.

"Brace yourself," he yelled.

She bent low. An exposed head could be snapped off if the plane tumbled end to end.

In the eerie silence she heard Jack moving around behind her. Why wasn't he bracing himself for impact?

Then, as she offered a fervent prayer for undeserved forgiveness, the engine sprang to life. The plane shot upward, leaving her stomach on the ground.

Her scream trailed across the dark-edged sky. Were they really going to live? She looked back. Jack stared at the controls. She checked below. Yes, the ground was where it belonged. She gulped in the sweet air, but she couldn't stop shaking.

Jack circled, lined up the field and brought the plane down. It bumped and hopped over the uneven earth, bouncing her brain against her skull. But after the plane came to a halt and the propeller turned slower and slower until it stopped, a fierce ache took hold.

She'd flown, had faced the worst that could be endured and had lived.

She swallowed as Jack tapped her on the shoulder.

"Sorry about that. Little problem with the engine. You all right?" He'd already taken off his helmet and goggles, and his sandy hair gleamed gold in the rising sun.

She nodded and pulled off her goggles and hood. The flight might be over, but her dream was not. It had only begun. This experience only confirmed that God had destined her to fly.

She climbed out the far side of the cockpit and pulled down her skirt. By the time she rounded the plane, half the town was streaming toward them.

"Thank you." She threw her arms around Jack. "It was wonderful."

"Stop that." He extricated himself. "Remember, you never got into the plane. You had nothing to do with that flight."

"I know, I know." She shoved the motor hood into her pocket, but she couldn't so easily wash away her disappointment. "I was just congratulating you on an excellent flight."

Jack glanced from Burrows, who was climbing down from the wing, to the gathering crowd, clearly worried.

"Just a kink in the fuel line," said Burrows. "I'll check it over, fill her with gasoline and oil, and we can be on our way."

"I'll get the oil." Jack sprinted to the barn.

Leaving? Right now? How could he fly off, after what had just happened? Jack Hunter held the key to her dream. He could teach her to fly. He couldn't leave. She started after him.

"Miss Shea?" The wiry mechanic caught her arm. "A word of warning. Jack Hunter is not the marrying type."

She pulled away. "Who said anything about marriage?"

"I just thought..." he let his voice trail off as Jack reappeared with an oilcan.

Burrows was wrong. Despite Jack's admittedly attractive qualities, she had no intention of marrying. She had to fly first. Her interest in Jack Hunter was strictly professional.

She caught Jack's arm. The leather was cold and dead, but the man beneath it was not. "Take me with you."

He stared, a mixture of shock and wariness that sent her spirits tumbling.

"I'll earn my way," she said, words spinning out faster and

faster. "I'll work. I won't be a financial burden. I have to fly. I will do anything to fly. Anything. Please?"

Jack looked disgusted, and for a second she saw herself through his eyes—a pathetic, pleading woman so consumed with her dream that she'd throw away propriety.

"Darcy?" Papa's gruff voice shivered down her spine. He'd heard. He'd heard everything. She looked for Jack, but he was climbing into the cockpit. Burrows pulled the propeller.

No! The cry wailed deep inside, but she dared not let it out, not when she stood face-to-face with judgment.

Excuse after excuse whirled through her mind in time with the propeller's revolutions. The din spared her from answering her father immediately, but once the plane sped down the field and arced into the air, sun glinting gold off its wings, the reprieve ended.

"What was that about?" he asked.

She fought the horrible deflation. "It doesn't matter anymore." She swallowed, but the pain would not diminish. "It's over. All over."

The aeroplane grew smaller and smaller until it vanished.

Chapter Four

All Darcy's efforts had come to naught. Jack flew away, and she returned to dull, normal life. Papa must have sensed her despair, because he didn't lecture. He waited until she spilled the whole story. When the tears subsided, he accepted her apology and requested she devote her free time to worthy causes like the Ladies' Aid Society and the war effort. No social functions except Beattie's picnic. Even that came to a dismal end, when pouring rain sent everyone scurrying.

The tedium turned days to weeks. Summer slid into autumn. Though her dream felt as dead as the maple leaves tumbling to the ground, Darcy caught herself looking for Jack around every corner. She gazed for hours into the empty sky. She devoured the newspaper, hoping for word of him. She checked the post every day. Nothing.

Occasionally she'd catch a whiff of a saddle or harness and snap around, looking for the familiar leather jacket. At night she prayed for his return and gazed at the million stars, wondering if he saw the same ones she did.

"I'm so tired of this town," she complained to Beatrice as they painted signs for the November election. "I need to do something. I need to go somewhere."

The grange hall bustled with activity, from women

preparing voter lists to men setting up tables. Damp wool coats and hats steamed above the clanking radiator. The leaky roof dripped steadily into the tin bucket at the end of their table. The room smelled old and musty and worn.

"You just have the blues," said Beattie, swathed in an old shirtwaist and apron. "A little sunshine will set you right again."

"It'll take more than sunshine." Darcy dipped a brush in blue paint and laid a wavy streak on the V of the VOTE HERE sign.

"You'll think of something. You always do."

Darcy wasn't so sure. In the past, she would have thrown all her energy into the election. Since this one would give women the state vote, she should be excited, but the old spark had died.

"Maybe I'll run away," she mused.

"Stop being a goof. You can't run away. You have responsibilities. Think of your parents. And Amelia's expecting."

Though deep down Darcy knew Beattie was right, she still wished she could recapture the thrill of flying.

"Besides, where would you go?" said Beattie, carefully keeping her paint within the penciled lines.

To Jack's airfield, of course, but she didn't want to make it public knowledge yet. Mum stood across the room, talking to Prudy. No one else was near. She could risk telling Beattie. "New York. Long Island to be exact."

Beatrice's eyes widened. "Where Jack lives?"

"This doesn't have anything to do with Jack Hunter. I need to learn to fly, and New York is the only place I can do so while the war's still on. Besides, that's where Harriet Quimby learned. New York." She savored each syllable.

"New York?" Felicity Kensington flounced near, her brunette hair adorned with diamond-studded combs. "I'm going there next week. If there's anything I can get for the wedding, Beatrice, do let me know."

"There's nothing, thank you." Beattie concentrated on the sign.

"Your dress is finished already? Usually Benton's takes forever."

Poor Beattie's cheeks flamed. The Foxes could never afford a New York dressmaker, least of all Benton's. Mrs. Fox, a skilled seamstress, was making the dress herself.

"Don't trouble yourself, Felicity," Darcy said. "If Beattie needs anything from New York, I'll fetch it."

Felicity's lips pursed into a frown. "I was just trying to help."

"Thank you." Beattie smiled at her future sister-in-law, which was more than Darcy would do.

"Shouldn't you be helping with the voter lists?" Darcy suggested.

Felicity sniffed. "My work is done."

"Then you can help us paint." Darcy stuck the wet paintbrush inches from Felicity's serge suit.

Felicity jumped back. "Be careful. Do you know how much this suit cost? My mother would be furious if I showed up at the Ladies' Aid Society meeting with my dress ruined."

Darcy was tempted to flick paint at her.

Felicity looked down her nose. "You are attending, aren't you? Mother said it's mandatory."

Darcy gritted her teeth. "If I'm done here."

"Well, we shall somehow manage without you." She flounced directly to Cora Williams, to whom she'd undoubtedly divulge Darcy's itinerary.

"That ungrateful simp," Darcy said.

"Now Darcy, don't be unkind."

"As if she wasn't."

"The Bible says we're to turn the other cheek, remember?"

"I know, but some people make cheek-turning mighty difficult."

Beatrice giggled, and Darcy was glad to hear her friend laugh. A wedding was supposed to be a joyful time, but lately Beattie had been terribly overwrought, and Darcy could guess the cause.

"So," Beatrice said, a knowing look on her face. "You're going to talk Jack Hunter into giving you lessons?"

Darcy completed the V with a quick swipe. "He's an instructor, and I'm a pupil, nothing more."

"Nothing more." Beattie laughed. "Um-hm."

"It's true." But her glowing cheeks betrayed her.

"I hope you succeed," Beattie said more seriously. "Did your father give you the money?"

Darcy squirmed. "Not exactly, but I have an idea. I'll talk Devlin into paying for the lessons in exchange for daily correspondence to the newspaper. That's how Harriet Quimby paid for flight lessons."

"Do you think he'll do it?"

"It's to his advantage, isn't it? He'll sell more papers."

"Then why don't you ask?" Beattie nodded toward the door where the newspaperman gathered his hat.

"Oh, uh," Darcy stuttered. "Not here. Not now." She hadn't had time to think this plan through.

"Why not?"

"He looks busy."

"Looks to me like he's leaving. Hurry, and you can catch him."

Though Darcy gave her friend a scathing look, Beattie was right. If she was going to learn to fly, she needed money. The only way to get money was to act. She scooted across the room, arriving just as Devlin grabbed the door handle.

"Mr. Devlin." Darcy slipped between him and the door. "I wonder if I might have a minute of your time."

"Not now, Shea. I'm on deadline."

She pressed her weight against the door. "All I need is one minute."

He glanced at his watch. "Sixty seconds."

"I have a stupendous idèa. Imagine this headline: 'Local Woman Learns To Fly.'"

Devlin snorted. "No news there, Miss Shea, though I'll consider an announcement in the ladies' column when you pass your licensing exam." He reached for the door.

"It's not just about learning to fly," she said, searching for something that would impress him. "I plan to go for a record."

"Sure you do. Record for what? First woman over Baker's barn?"

"First woman to cross the Atlantic," she blurted out. Never mind she still needed to learn. Jack had mentioned something about a transatlantic attempt. She'd convince him to do it and take her along. "That's where you come in. The *Prognosticator* can sponsor me."

"Transatlantic?" Devlin nearly choked on his cigar. "You?"

"Yes me," she said with growing confidence. Fulfilling a dream first required believing in it. "Of course, I need to take lessons."

"Aha, we're back to that. And I suppose you want me to pay for those lessons."

"In exchange for stories. Every day."

"No, Miss Shea."

"The readers will love it, and when I make the transatlantic attempt, the *Prognosticator* will have an exclusive."

"No, no, and no." Devlin spat a flake of tobacco on the floor. "Your sixty seconds are up."

"But I can do this. I can take lessons in New York—"

"No, Miss Shea. That's my last word." Devlin pulled the door open and left.

That man didn't have an iota of common sense. No wonder the *Prognosticator* hadn't increased its circulation in ten years. It takes risk to succeed.

"Darcy?" Mum walked up and gently touched her sleeve. "What did Mr. Devlin say to you? You seem upset."

She shook her head though her heart was breaking. When would she ever see Jack again?

"I thought I heard you say something about New York," Mum said.

Darcy steeled herself. "It was just talk." Mum would never understand her need to fly. Long ago, when Darcy was young, Papa would have understood. He might even have encouraged her, but that all changed when she grew up.

Mum looked ready to burst. "I know how much you love to travel, dear. That's why your father and I have been talking." Her eyes shone.

"About New York?" Darcy hardly dared to believe.

"We think it might raise your spirits." Mum brushed a lock of hair from Darcy's forehead, as if she were still a little girl. "You do so love the museums and shows."

"We're going to New York City?" Hope rose from the damp ground of despair.

"New York City? Heavens no, we're going to visit your aunt in Buffalo."

Buffalo? Darcy's spirits instantly deflated. She couldn't learn to fly in Buffalo. Jack lived hundreds of miles away. Buffalo got her no closer to her dream. She might as well stay home.

"Now?" She struggled for an excuse. "But don't you want to be here for Amelia?"

Mum patted her hand. "Bless you for thinking of your

sister, but Charles's sister can help, should anything arise, which is unlikely. She is only four months along. Now is the perfect time."

Darcy knew better than to argue. It was settled. They would go to Buffalo, and Darcy's plans had to be postponed again.

Buffalo in November chilled to the bone. The wind blew constantly off Lake Erie, rattling the bare elm branches. The constant drizzle threatened to turn to snow.

The war's end raised Darcy's spirits briefly. With no army pilots to train, Jack might return home. She checked the street in front of Aunt Perpetua's overstuffed Victorian twenty times a day. Though the odds were slim he'd walk that neighborhood, it was possible. Darcy dwelt in the faintly possible. She volunteered to go to the market. She rode the streetcar, she walked downtown—all in the hope she'd see Jack—but when the days turned to a week, hope dwindled.

One afternoon, she looked out the parlor window while Mum and Aunt Perpetua took tea. The streets were lifeless. Barely one motorcar had passed in the last half hour.

"A dinner party would be just the thing," Aunt Perpetua unexpectedly said, the enormous feather on her scarlet turban bobbing up and down. "I realize this is more to Amelia's tastes, but a grand party, with all the finery, might cheer even Darcy."

"I don't need cheering." Darcy ran a hand across the steamed pane to clear her view.

"We could invite a young man," Perpetua suggested.

Darcy instantly thought of Jack, but Mum had other ideas.

"I understand George Carrman is finishing his studies right here in Buffalo. Eugenia Kensington gave me his address."

Darcy inwardly groaned. *Not George Carrman again.* "I'm not interested in a dinner party."

"Then what would suit you, dear?" Mum asked.

To go to Long Island. To see Jack Hunter. But Darcy couldn't say that.

"Going out to retrieve the newspaper," Papa called from the other room. The front door opened, sending a rush of chilly air through the parlor.

Darcy shivered as she watched her father, bundled in wool coat, bowler and scarf, trudge to the gate where the newsboy had left the daily paper.

"I gather you don't care for Mr. Carrman," Perpetua said.

"He's pleasant enough," Darcy conceded for her mother's sake, "but I've already told him I'm not interested in a serious relationship."

"Darcy," Mum exclaimed. "You don't say such things to a man you just met."

"Would you rather I gave him false hope?"

"Of course not, dear, but you didn't give him a chance."

Mum was right. She hadn't given George a chance, but how could she when there was Jack? No other man had ever sent her emotions whirling so.

"It's not him," Darcy conceded. "George Carrman is a nice enough sort of man, but the fact is, I don't care to marry at all."

Mum choked on her biscuit.

"Extraordinary." Perpetua set her cup on its saucer. "What would you do instead?"

Darcy hesitated. Papa had made it very clear that respectable young ladies did not fly aeroplanes. They married. But Darcy couldn't marry without love. That left just one option. She needed a career. "I've written articles for the local newspaper."

"Journalism is a worthy pursuit." Perpetua's dark eyes glittered. "I would like to see more fire though. A true calling demands passion."

The mere mention of passion sent heat to Darcy's cheeks. Jack. His touch. Those cornflower-blue eyes.

"Ah, you *are* passionate about something. Or is it *some-one?*"

Darcy turned back to the window, but Perpetua was not going to let this go. "A young man?"

"I have my dreams," Darcy said quietly.

Perpetua placed her cup on the end table. "You are a young woman of talent. Set your goal and do it."

Why not? The simple words, so obvious and clear, turned her jumbled thoughts into a clear path. That path didn't include George Carrman, or even Jack Hunter. She wanted to fly. Jack Hunter wasn't the only flight instructor in this country. Now that the war was over, there'd be hundreds of aviators willing to teach her.

"I would like to—" Darcy began, but was interrupted by cold air whooshing through the room when Papa opened the front door.

Mum called out, "Close the door, Dermott. You're letting the chill in."

Darcy heard the click of the front door followed by her father's fumbling at the coatrack.

"Continue," urged Perpetua. "You were saying?"

Papa entered with the newspaper and sat down. Darcy couldn't say she wanted to fly in front of him.

She shook her head. "I forgot."

Perpetua frowned as Papa unfolded the paper. The large headline made Darcy gasp.

CURTISS AEROPLANE PLANT TO CLOSE

Curtiss Aeroplane. Jack's company. He said the main plant was in Buffalo. He worked out of Long Island, but if the main plant closed, surely the subsidiary would, too. Jack would lose his job. *Then* where would he go? She scoured her memory for some clue. All he'd mentioned was being born in Buffalo, but a pilot wouldn't come here in winter. He would go south or west, so far away that she'd never find him.

"What's wrong dear?" asked Mum. "You look like you've gotten a terrible shock."

Darcy pressed her lips together to squelch her fears. Jack gone. What would she do? Since the moment they met, she'd dreamed of flying with him.

"Darcy?" Mum rose, concerned.

"It's nothing. Don't worry." She turned to the window, which had fogged up again. This time she didn't bother wiping off the steam. The answer could only be found within. As much as she hated to admit it, her dream didn't require Jack. It required that she learn to fly. If Buffalo had been a center of aviation during the war, surely it would be afterward.

"Aunt Perpetua, do you know where the Curtiss aeroplane factory is located?"

"End of Elmwood Avenue, I believe. Why?"

Because they'd know where the flight schools were located. "Do you know if it has an airfield?"

That flummoxed her. "An airfield?"

Mum voiced her displeasure. "Darcy has been preoccupied with flying since she went to the Chicago air show with her father. That was how long ago, eight years?"

"Seven," Darcy said. "And I'm not preoccupied. I want to learn to fly." There. It was out. With the words came strength. The melancholy that had consumed her for weeks dropped away.

Mum's lips tightened. "It's not safe. Mott, didn't you say that two fliers died at that meet?"

"Didn't I what?" asked Papa from behind the newspaper.

Darcy corrected Mum, "Those pilots were attempting dangerous feats. Aeroplanes are much safer now, and I promise I won't try any tricks."

"Then do it, my dear," said her aunt. "If that's God's purpose for your life, then surely nothing can stop you."

Her words resonated in Darcy. God's purpose. Hadn't she known all along that God wanted her to fly? If it was God's will, she shouldn't let anyone stop her.

"Lessons cost a great deal," said Papa, showing he'd been listening all along.

Perpetua raised a hand. "Money is a poor excuse when Darcy has an aunt ready to help."

Darcy's jaw dropped. "You will pay for lessons?"

"Of course. I can think of no better use for my money. Find a flight school, and I'll fund the lessons."

"Perpetua," Mum cautioned, "this is not your affair."

"Darcy is a grown woman. She can make her own decisions."

"Thank you, oh thank you." Darcy enveloped her aunt in a hug. "How can I ever repay your generosity? I will though. I'll write articles about the experience and sell them to the newspapers or ladies' magazines. Oh Aunt, how can I ever thank you?"

"This is not settled," Papa said. "Darcy's welfare is her parents' concern, Perpetua, not yours."

"Nonsense. This is a new era, Dermott. We must not hold our young people back. It may frighten us older folk, but the world is changing, and Darcy must change with it."

Papa frowned. "Her safety—"

"Safety? That sounds more like the banker than the outdoorsman I remember."

His color deepened. "Flying is a pursuit for men, not girls."

"Women," Perpetua emphasized, "drive motorcars. We ride bicycles and row skiffs. We play tennis and jump horses.

And yes, we fly aeroplanes. We have for nearly a decade. If it is God's will…" here, she looked at Darcy, who nodded affirmatively, "then who are we to stand in the way?"

"I don't see what God has to do with this." He rose and threw the newspaper onto the vacated chair. "Flying is dangerous."

"Please, Papa. I promise I'll follow every safety precaution. I'll check every wire and screw. I'll never fly in bad weather. I'll be as careful as Marjorie Stinson."

His eyebrows rose at her mention of "the Flying School-marm." "Planning to open a flight school, are you?" he said with the faintest smile.

Darcy hadn't really considered the result, but why not? Marjorie Stinson had run one. Why not her? "Maybe I will."

"That's the spirit," said Perpetua.

Papa cleared his throat. "Just promise me one thing."

"Yes, Papa."

"Promise you'll give every man a fair chance."

"At what?" Darcy instantly thought of Jack.

"Marriage."

It was the last thing she wanted now, but Darcy was smart enough to realize she wouldn't get flight lessons without this promise. "I will."

"Good." He picked up the newspaper and shook it out. "You can begin by inviting Mr. Carrman to that dinner party."

The army closed the training airfield when the war ended. It didn't need aviators without a war. That left Jack unemployed, so he contacted his old buddy, Dwight Pohlman, who happened to have a job for him in Buffalo.

"Stay here," Burrows urged as they left the Long Island plant.

"You know I can't." The icy breeze sent a chill down Jack's spine. He wouldn't miss the fence, the gate, the security. Dried-up leaves tumbled across the brick-hard ground. Lately he'd found himself longing for a simpler life, more like what he'd seen in Pearlman.

"There's a big project underway," Burrows said in a low voice, "exactly what you've been waiting for."

"What project?" Jack hadn't heard a thing about a new project.

Burrows grinned. "What's your dream, old sport?"

For a second, Jack allowed himself to remember. Transatlantic flight. Claim the *Daily Mail* prize. Fifty thousand dollars and enough fame to put him on the lecture circuit for years. Until recently, only Burrows and Sissy knew about that dream. Then he told Darcy. Darcy. That gal would have attempted the crossing in a minute, ready or not.

He chuckled to himself. She had crazier dreams than he did. Worse, she actually believed they were possible. Fly over the North Pole. It was insane, but he remembered the sparkle in her eyes, the way she made him believe. Women like that were rare.

"Whoa." Burrows yanked Jack sideways. "That's one powerful daydream."

Jack scowled. He'd nearly walked into the gate. That was precisely why he shouldn't care about Miss Shea. Flying and romance did not mix.

They showed their passes to the guard. Considering the armistice, Jack was surprised the tight security continued. What had Burrows said? That something big was afoot? Suppose Curtiss was going for the big prize.

"Curtiss is attempting the transatlantic crossing?"

"Shh," hissed Burrows. "Don't go telling the world."

Jack stared. "You're not joking?"

"Never. Stay on here. I'll put a word in for you. Just think, you'd be in on something big, and we'd be working together again."

Jack couldn't deny the appeal. It *was* his dream, but it came with a cost. A man taking such a risky flight should have no personal entanglements. That meant no girlfriend and no dependents. He could control the first but not the latter.

"I'll think about it." But he knew it was an impossible dream. Sissy needed him.

"Don't think too long," Burrows urged.

"I'll give you my answer in a week." That was long enough to determine if Pohlman's offer was legitimate.

The next day, Jack flew his plane to Buffalo and landed at the flight school's airfield. He roared down the field and pulled up to the building, without seeing another plane in the air. Odd. Even though it was late in the season, snow hadn't fallen yet. Students should be practicing maneuvers.

Jack climbed out of his plane and looked around. No one. Not a sound. He had a bad feeling this was going to be the shortest job interview in history. He wandered into the hangar. "Anybody here?"

A tall, clean-cut man popped out of the office. "Jack Hunter? Imagine seeing your worthless behind here. I wondered who had the audacity to land on our field unannounced."

"None other."

Pohlman laughed and pumped his hand. "How's it going?"

Jack met the question with a grin. "Never better." There was nothing like a fellow pilot to raise a man's spirits. "You said you had a position open?"

"Going straight to business, eh? Fine with me. Let's talk. Coffee?"

"Why not?"

They strolled across the concrete-floored hangar to Pohlman's office. Nearly all the training planes were parked inside, grounded. On past visits the place had buzzed with activity.

"Business slow?" Jack asked. If Pohlman needed an instructor, where were the students?

Pohlman poured a cup of muddy brew. "Up until last Saturday I had a full house. Then news comes in the Kaiser abdicated, and an hour later we get the wire to cut loose the recruits."

"Tough luck. We didn't hear until Monday." Jack stirred five spoonfuls of sugar into the coffee to make it palatable. "What about civilians? Interest was wild before the war."

"Four signed on, one a woman."

"You'd teach a woman?"

"She was really interested. Asked a hundred questions. Besides," Pohlman rubbed his fingers together, "money's money. Can't afford to hang onto old prejudices."

"But women aren't suited to flying. You'd endanger her."

Pohlman laughed. "Same old Jack. Haven't changed a bit, have you?"

Jack ignored the jab. "Only four students? I thought you needed a flight instructor."

"I do." Pohlman raised his cup in a toast. "I'm off to Florida."

"No kidding. The Curtiss school there, or some other venture?"

"School, naturally, and my girl."

"You have a steady girl?" Jack was astonished. Dwight Pohlman had never dated seriously. Was the whole world turning upside down?

"Two years."

Two years. Jack felt a flash of envy. To have someone love you enough to stay with you two whole years. "Getting married?"

Pohlman nodded. "January."

"You? Hooked?" He made a choking gesture.

"All the way. You should try it, Jack. Far better than we made it out to be."

"Not for me." Women were fragile. Women got hurt. Women had families and banker fathers. "You can have it."

"Just you wait. The right one will come along and you'll change your tune. It happened to me, it'll happen to you. Which brings me back to this place. I need someone to take over. It'll be slow at first, with winter on its way, but that'll give you time to recruit students."

"Recruit?" This sounded like a lot of work. "I'm not a recruiter."

Pohlman thumped him on the shoulder. "You're just the man to do it. Your charm will bring in the ladies, and your track record will grab the men."

"Ladies?" Jack balked at the idea of teaching women.

"Paying customers."

Burrows's idea sounded better all the time. If the team accepted him, he'd have a steady income and a shot at fame... if he survived.

That was the problem. Sissy was his responsibility.

"What's the pay?"

"Small stipend, plus a percentage of sales." Pohlman outlined everything the job entailed. It would take a lot of effort, but with a good-sized class, he could make a decent living.

"Sounds workable," Jack said, "though I'd rather not teach women. Unless her husband approves, that is."

"You are so old-fashioned. Even the boss taught the gals."

Though Jack knew G.H. Curtiss had taught women, he held his tongue. Once Pohlman left, he couldn't tell him what to do. "There's just the one, right?"

"One who's already paid."

"In full?" No one paid the whole fee in advance.

"In full. You'll be living off that this winter, so you might want to reconsider."

Jack set down the unpalatable coffee, his stomach soured.

"In fact, she might still be around here." Pohlman motioned for Jack to follow. "Wanted to write a story about the school for the local paper. I told her to go ahead. It'll be good publicity."

Jack was getting a very bad feeling. "I don't suppose she has dark hair and a pushy attitude."

"Don't know about the attitude, but you're dead on with the hair coloring."

They'd reached the hangar.

"Miss Shea?" Pohlman called out.

Impossible. For seven weeks he'd tried to forget the woman.

"Yes?" She rounded the fuselage of the trainer, and the moment she saw Jack, she fumbled her notepad and lost her pencil. It clattered to the concrete floor.

Jack couldn't seem to move. He wanted to run to her and sweep her into his arms, but Pohlman was watching. Jack ran a hand through his hair, unable to believe what he was seeing. Darcy. The fine ankles. The dark eyes that sparkled with life.

Every nerve ending sizzled. The propeller could have cut off Jack's arm and he wouldn't have noticed.

"Ja-ack," she said with the slightest hitch.

That little break in her voice brought sense rushing back. She was vulnerable. She didn't belong in a plane. His ears rang. His stomach churned. What had he gotten himself into?

He had to teach Darcy Shea to fly.

Chapter Five

"You two know each other?" Pohlman asked.

"We've met." Jack couldn't take his eyes off her. The thick, dark hair. The curve of her jaw. The stark, almost masculine dress that managed to make her look more feminine. He drew in a ragged breath as she stooped to pick up the pencil.

"Allow me." He touched the pencil first, and her fingertips grazed his. He handed it to her.

"Thank you." She kept her gaze fixed on the floor, as if she were shy.

Shy! Jack could safely assume that term had never been applied to Darcy Shea.

"Then you won't have any problem teaching her," Pohlman said.

Jack glared. "I certainly do."

"He's already given me a plane ride," Darcy offered.

She wasn't supposed to tell anyone about that.

"He did?" Pohlman chuckled. "Seems our Jack has dual standards."

"Is that anything like dual controls?"

Pohlman laughed at her joke, which only irritated Jack more.

"Flying is dangerous," Jack insisted. "I've seen students lose nerve and crash."

She set her jaw. "I have strong nerves."

True, she'd been eager to continue after his attempt to frighten her. He tried again. "A student needs a fearless disposition."

"That's me."

"Along with an even temperament." He had her there.

She cocked her head. "You don't think I can keep my head, do you? Well, I've grown a bit since you last saw me, Jack Hunter. Trust me, I can keep my head."

"I recall you screaming in terror."

She crossed her arms. "I might have screamed, but it wasn't in terror. Even if I had, no one would blame me. You put the plane into a spin."

"A spin?" Pohlman said. "That would frighten anyone, me included."

Jack knew he would ultimately lose this argument, at least with Pohlman, but Darcy wasn't an ordinary student. She was a woman, and, well, she was Darcy. Her father would have his head if something happened to her.

He lobbed that bomb. "Does your father know you're doing this?"

"Of course."

Jack didn't believe that for a minute. "And he approves?"

"He agreed." She tapped her toe impatiently. "Are we going to begin or not?"

"Now?" Jack wasn't certain he was officially hired. He certainly wasn't ready to teach her.

"No time like the present."

Jack looked to Pohlman, who struggled to suppress a grin.

"Go to it, old chum. It'll give me an opportunity to assess your abilities."

Pohlman had to be joking. "I've been teaching for years. More than two hundred recruits passed my course."

Pohlman clucked his tongue. "But no women."

"Last I checked, there are no women in the military." Jack looked to Darcy. "Though I suppose you'd like to see them there."

"If they want to join, why not?"

He had to be attracted to a feminist.

She tucked the pencil behind her ear in a very alluring way. "So where do we start?"

Jack stalled. "Ordinarily, I begin by having the student disassemble and reassemble the motor."

"But I've already done that."

"You have?" Pohlman looked impressed. Apparently anything Darcy said impressed him.

"She *helped* disassemble a motor and had nothing to do with reassembling it," Jack clarified. "Motor disassembly is where we'll start."

"Can't we do that once the weather turns? There's so little time before winter."

Her reasonable request put him in the gun sight.

"She has a point," said Pohlman.

Jack gave his friend a "don't interfere" look. "It's too windy today."

Darcy looked to Pohlman, hoping for more support, but this time the man backed him. "I'm afraid Jack is right. No student flying at ten knots or higher." As her smile fell, he added, "but it could die down. I'll keep an eye on it for you."

"You do that," Jack said. At least that would get one troublesome person out of the way.

Pohlman laughed. "I know when I'm not wanted."

Jack waited until Pohlman walked into his office before addressing Darcy. "What on earth are you doing here?"

"Taking flight lessons." She stuck out that determined little chin again. "And you?"

"That wasn't what I meant, and you know it. I didn't expect to see you here."

"And I didn't expect to see you. The last I knew, you were on Long Island. Of course that was ages ago, and I never heard from you in between."

Jack recognized an accusation when he heard one. "I didn't hear from you, either."

"How was I supposed to write when I didn't even know what city you lived in? Long Island is rather large."

Jack crossed his arms and headed for safer ground. "I meant, other than flying, what brought you to Buffalo?"

Her expression softened a bit. "I'm visiting my aunt. And you?"

"A job. As you see."

"You said you were from here. I thought you might have family."

"Just a sister." He wished he hadn't said that. It would only lead to more questions.

"Where does she live?"

Jack needed to change the topic and quick. He knew only one way. "There's enough time to show you the aeroplane controls."

She bit off whatever retort she was going to toss at him, and said gently, "I'd like that."

Demands could make a man do things he must, but a soft voice led him to do things he resisted. Jack took her to the nearest trainer, an older model with minimal horsepower and tremendous gliding ability. He started students on these. They couldn't climb far, and forgave many errors.

"Unlike the prototype you saw, this model has stick controls."

"And the cockpit is different," she observed.

"Tandem, so the instructor can work beside the student." He helped her into the cockpit. "Take that seat, and I'll familiarize you with each control."

It didn't take long for the old banter to return. By the time he was demonstrating how to move the ailerons, she'd made him forget that he didn't want to teach her.

"How are ailerons used?" she asked.

"For turns, in conjunction with the rudder," he patiently explained, and when she screwed up her face in puzzlement, he asked for her pad and pencil and drew pictures demonstrating the airflow for the various maneuvers.

"But the best way to learn is to do it." He regretted the words the minute they left his mouth. "Sorry. I forgot about the wind."

"It'll calm down." Her eyes glowed the way they had when she talked of that crazy North Pole flight, and for a moment he thought she was going to grab him the way she did just before he left Pearlman.

"*If* the wind calms," he said stiffly.

She must have recognized his discomfort, for the soft reticence returned. "I'm so glad you're teaching here."

Her words sucker-punched him. He didn't want to teach her. He couldn't let her take the controls. With her impulsive nature, it would end badly. He should have taken Burrows's offer: stay on Long Island and hope to make the transatlantic team, if there was still room for him.

"I might not stay," he cautioned.

"Why not?" A shadow crept across her face.

Though it hurt to crush her hopes, he had to do it. "I have a chance at the transatlantic attempt."

She gasped, eyes widening. "Where? When?"

"I can't give details."

"Do it." She grabbed his hand with unexpected fervor. "Whatever it takes, be on that flight."

"It's a bit more complicated than—"

"Why? Anything is possible if you try hard enough." She bubbled with excitement. "Oh, Jack. God brought us back together for a reason. I know it."

God had nothing to do with it. Fate, maybe, but not God.

God had abandoned him long ago. Jack reiterated the part she seemed to be forgetting, "I might not stay."

Her smile never wavered. "I know."

It took a moment, but Jack was no fool. He saw clear through her. She thought she was going, too. *Never.* He shook his head, ready to correct that misunderstanding, when Pohlman interrupted.

"Tell me, Miss Shea, should I give him the job?"

Darcy looked startled. "Jack doesn't work here?"

"He will, if you give him a good recommendation." Pohlman sounded entirely serious, though Jack knew better.

"Of course," she said. "He's the best instructor in the world."

"Well then," said Pohlman, "the lady makes the call."

No, she doesn't. Despite the wild desire to be near Darcy, Jack was going back to Long Island. He couldn't watch her fail. He couldn't let her get any closer. He would take his chances with Curtiss, if Sissy agreed.

St. Anne of Comfort Hospital looked grand from the outside, with its turreted stone edifice, but the interior reeked of vomit, urine and bleach. Jack didn't know how Sissy stood it. The colorful pictures she pasted on the wall and the flowers he sent each Monday couldn't mask the scent of disease.

"What happened, Jackie?" Her pinched smile revealed concern.

"Nothing." He settled into the chair at her bedside.

His sister appeared normal, except for the withered, stiff

legs. Polio. It hadn't taken her life, but it might as well have. It had crept far enough up her spine that she had to live in the hospital. Jack wished he could buy her a home and full-time nursing care, but that would cost tens of thousands of dollars. He had less than a hundred dollars.

"You can't fool me, big brother." Fragile and pale as a porcelain doll propped on pillows, she smiled readily. Cecelia— "Sissy" to him—loved to laugh.

Jack did not want to talk about Darcy. That impulsive woman would rush into the most dangerous ventures without so much as a backward glance. He couldn't talk, so he gave Sissy his gift.

"For me?" Her eyes lit up as she tore open the paper. Sissy always acted as if every trinket was the first gift she'd ever received. She held up the silk shawl. "Oh, Jack, it's beautiful."

The dark blue silk glimmered in the light, the lavender flowers bright against her pale skin. Sissy loved anything colorful.

"I'll wear it all the time." She wrapped it around her shoulders and held out first one arm then the other to see how the light reflected off the fibers.

Shame rippled through him. Sissy had nowhere special to wear such a shawl. No trips to the theater or opera. No concerts or lectures. It was a thoughtless gift.

"Now, don't think you can distract me." She shook her finger. "I can tell something's bothering you." She leaned forward, her eyes animated. "Is it a woman? Have you met someone?"

He forced a laugh, trying to appear nonchalant. "Maybe little sis is wrong for once."

She countered with the light and tinkling laughter that made everyone love her. "Little sis is never wrong. What is it?"

Jack looked at his dusty boots. The toes were nearly worn

through, but he couldn't afford new ones. Neither could he afford to tell her about Darcy. He knew what Sissy would say: "Spend time with her, see if she feels the same way, marry her. If it's meant to be, it'll work out." Sissy was such a romantic.

"Nothing. Would you like your hair done? I could have someone arrange it, or whatever you ladies have done. Put it in the latest style."

"The latest style?" She laughed. "Why would I need the latest style? There isn't a patient or nurse who cares one whit what I look like."

Another thoughtless comment. Jack scrubbed his chin. He needed a shave. "I thought maybe you'd like it."

"I know when my brother is avoiding something. What happened?"

He rose and opened the window blinds. "You should look out more. There's a fine view of the lake."

"It's gray and dismal and I don't want to look out."

She sounded just like Darcy. Headstrong. Stubborn. Jack pressed his face to the cold windowpane. He'd come to get Sissy's permission to run back to the Island, but it didn't seem like such a good idea anymore.

"Stop trying to hide things from me," Sissy said. "You know I always worm it out of you."

"There's no reason to worry you—"

"There's no reason not to." Like always, Sissy persisted until she got what she wanted. "I'm a good listener."

Jack sighed. He might as well spill everything. She would keep at it until he told her. Given the choice between Darcy and work, he chose the latter. "I've taken a job at the flight school here."

"Here?" She clapped her hands. "Oh, that's wonderful."

"It has its drawbacks. Lack of students, for one. Income will be a little tight this winter."

"I see." Worry furrowed her brow. "I don't need a private room. And Dad might do more."

Dad would not do more, but he couldn't tell Sissy that. "Don't worry, I have prospects. There's someone—" this was getting dangerously close to telling about Darcy, "—who is going to write some newspaper articles. Hopefully, they'll spur business. If not, I can always go back to exhibition flying."

"No Jack. Not stunts. They're too dangerous."

"They pay well."

She pursed her lips. "There must be another way you can use your skills. Surely people won't stop flying."

"They might. The army closed the airfields. The flying boat I told you about ran its distance test last week, but no news on what's next."

"It did? That's wonderful. What was the flight like?"

"I didn't fly it," he said carefully, steering clear of his resentment.

"Why not?"

"Not my project. Mine was the long-range scout plane. Now there's no need for it."

Sissy was quiet for a long while, and he could tell by her expression that she was working out a solution. "Surely, peacetime commerce has a need for long-range aeroplanes. They could transport businessmen between cities, carry packages."

Jack sighed. "No one wants to look ahead. I don't know if it's due to the war, but they're just not interested. Not the military. Not civilians. Not anyone." Except Darcy.

She tilted her head. "It will work out. God always works things out for the best."

Jack choked back a retort. Sissy clung to faith like a bit of wreckage in the wide ocean, but God wouldn't save her. He hadn't cured her when He had a chance. He'd left her an invalid. If that was how God worked things out, Jack wanted nothing to do with Him. But he couldn't sink her faith, so he broached the possibility of returning to Long Island.

"Something is afoot, but it's top secret."

Sissy's eyes widened. "I promise not to tell a soul, not even Nurse Margarete."

"Not even Margarete?" he teased, remembering he was supposed to cheer her up, not vice versa.

"Cross my heart."

He leaned close and spoke in a conspiratorial tone. "Word is, the flying boat will make an attempt at the transatlantic flight."

"Oh, Jackie," she squealed. "It's your dream!"

"Quiet," he urged. "Top secret, remember?"

"Yes, of course. It's just that I'm so excited for you." She paused a second, long enough to see the holes in the plan. "But why wouldn't they have had you make the test flight?"

Jack cleared his throat. "The navy hasn't officially committed yet. It's just speculation, now that the war is over." Jack didn't list the possible options. She would know. The project could be over. Or it might transfer to civilians.

"Oh, Jackie, I hope it happens and you're the pilot. It has to be you." Her eyes shone with tears. She wanted this flight as much as he did.

"It's risky."

"Of course."

And you need me alive and well. He sent most of his earnings to her care. Without him, what would happen to Sissy? She was his responsibility. They'd played together that fateful day, but only Sissy got polio. He'd vowed to always take care of his sister. That meant giving up risky dreams. That meant staying in Buffalo.

He rose to say goodbye.

"Do you have to leave so soon?"

The words knifed through him. Bad enough that he visited so infrequently, but he seldom spent more than an hour with her each time. Coward.

"I'll be back tomorrow. I promise."

"You're busy. Don't worry about me." She didn't beg or try to hold him back in any way, though she, more than anyone, had absolute claim to his time.

"I'll always take care of you," he choked out. He would visit tomorrow, and for more than an hour.

"I know, Jackie. You always have. You and Dad."

Jack's gut wrenched. He didn't know how she could be so loyal to the drunk.

"Love you, sis." The words, though automatic, hurt.

"Do the transatlantic flight," she said. "Do what it takes to follow your dreams. I'll be right there with you. I will. Not in body of course, but in spirit."

The pain wound its fingers around his lungs, squeezing until he couldn't breathe. "I'm sorry," he whispered.

"Oh, don't be morbid—and give me a hug."

He gave her a quick and admittedly insufficient embrace.

"Follow your heart," she said. "Wherever it leads you."

But of course he couldn't. Not to Darcy and not across the ocean.

Darcy studied Jack's drawings until she saw them in her sleep. She would pass any test he threw at her. She'd show him she belonged in the air.

The next morning she stood in the frosty hangar, wrapped in a thick sheepskin coat, wool scarf and gloves. Apparently, Pohlman didn't believe in heating the vast space. She puffed little clouds of breath while Jack drilled her.

"In straight and level flight, where do you move the ailerons?"

"You don't," she answered. "You're trying to trick me."

He grinned just a little, marked something on his pad, and moved on to the next question and the next. When he finished, she waited for him to tally the results.

"Congratulations, you passed."

She shrieked and danced and nearly hugged him, but the expression on his face told her that that sort of contact would not be acceptable. But a little old hug couldn't be that bad, could it?

"Passed, but not perfect. You missed two questions on rudder and elevator function."

"Ugh." She couldn't believe she missed them. "Show me what I got wrong."

He rubbed his chin. "Maybe a demonstration would work better."

"We're going to fly?"

"*I* am going to fly," he said, "and *you* are going to listen. Understand? And we're not going very high. Everything you need to learn can be demonstrated ten feet from the ground."

"Oh." She bit back her disappointment. Though she wanted to learn everything right away, she had to trust Jack's method. He'd trained dozens and dozens of pilots. He must know what he was doing.

She tried to concentrate while he explained the controls, but he sat so close. His legs nearly touched hers, and the petticoats and bloomers weren't quite thick enough today. The smell of leather. The warmth he generated. She could barely keep her mind on his instruction.

In the air, she fought the urge to hold onto him. She could see the ground between her feet. Only a few strips of wood stood between her and the ground. The engine kept splattering oil on her goggles.

"Are you paying attention?" he chided.

She snapped to attention. "Yes, sir."

"Then tell me what this lever does."

"Um, when I pull back, the plane lifts into the air?"

He then demonstrated, bringing the plane up a short distance then taking it down for a landing.

After the machine rolled to a stop, she tried to demonstrate that she'd heard some of his instruction. "That stick controls the elevator and that one the ailerons."

He hopped down. "Exactly."

She sat stock-still. "We're not done, are we? That was only a few minutes."

"All initial flights are short. I demonstrate one control or maneuver, which you then practice until you get it correct every time."

"May I practice now?"

"Not today." He held out his hand. "Watch your step. The oil spray from the motor can make the frame slippery."

Even through the gloves, the touch of his hand gave her shivers. She pulled away the moment she reached solid ground.

"What's next?" she asked as they walked to the classroom.

"That depends on tomorrow's weather. If it's not good for flying, we need to familiarize you with every inch of the plane."

"Tomorrow? But it's only one o'clock." Somehow, she'd thought the lessons would last all day. She had so little time before winter set in, and she didn't want to waste a perfectly good afternoon.

"I have someplace I need to go," he said.

"An errand? I can go with you."

The shutter he pulled closed whenever she got too close

clapped shut again. "It's something only I can do. Study up, and I'll see you tomorrow."

Dismissed. And without a reasonable explanation. She didn't believe his excuse for a moment. She'd done better than he expected, and he didn't want to teach her more. At every step, he fought her. She thought maybe he'd changed. Apparently not.

She grabbed her handbag and walked out onto the street. A chill breeze slid its icy blade down her neck, but she was too hot to care. If Jack Hunter wanted professional, she'd be professional.

She'd reached downtown before she quite realized where she was walking. People hurried down the sidewalk, intent on where they were going. Unlike Pearlman, no one greeted one another. They kept their heads down, eyes averted and mouths closed.

Darcy dawdled in front of shop windows. Better than afternoon tea with her aunt and mother. They'd pepper her with questions about her lessons. Things would be easier after her parents left on Saturday, following the dinner party.

The dinner party. Oh, dear. She was supposed to deliver the invitation to George Carrman yesterday. It was still in her bag.

After asking directions to St. Anne of Comfort Hospital, Darcy rode the streetcar to within a block of the huge, stone edifice. The hospital's manicured grounds invited strolling, but the weather kept most patients indoors.

Darcy walked up the sweeping approach lined with parked motorcars and bare oaks. Acorns crunched underfoot while leaves skittered along the ground on the breeze. An ambulance raced past, drawing only the slightest notice from visitors with dark coats and even more somber expressions.

She stopped to determine the best entrance, and a familiar figure caught her eye. Brown leather jacket. Sandy hair.

Brown cap. No, it couldn't be. What was *he* doing here? He drew closer, shoulders hunched and head down. Jack.

Her heart stuck fast in her throat. People only went to the hospital for illness, so why on earth had Jack Hunter just walked out of St. Anne's?

Chapter Six

Darcy couldn't ask Jack why he'd come to the hospital. He'd think she had followed him. So she asked the nurse at the registration desk.

"I will give your message to Dr. Carrman," the woman said firmly, taking the invitation from Darcy's hand, "but we do not share information about patients."

So Jack *was* a patient. But for what?

Darcy stumbled out of the hospital without noticing the ambulance attendants returning to their vehicle. She blindly boarded the streetcar, and then missed her stop and had to walk ten extra blocks to her aunt's house.

At supper Mum and Aunt Perpetua babbled on about Amelia and the coming baby. Who cared about Amelia when a life was at stake? Darcy picked at the stuffed pheasant, unable to stomach the rich meat.

"You're quiet tonight, Miss Darcy," Perpetua noted.

Mum scrutinized her. "Do you feel ill?"

"I'm fine." But not Jack. She heaved a sigh.

"Ah, you're sorry Mr. Carrman can't attend Saturday," her aunt said, handing her the gravy to pass to Papa.

"He can't?" For an instant, her spirits revived, but then she remembered Jack. Such a brave man, never letting on that he was ailing. No wonder he kept to himself. No wonder he'd never written. He didn't want to encourage a relationship that couldn't last.

She choked back a sob.

"It's good of you to feel so for your sister," Mum said with a pat of the hand.

Darcy looked up, bewildered. Apparently the conversation had returned to Amelia, but what was wrong?

Mum interpreted her confusion as concern. "Don't fret, dear. Amelia always has these early pains. They'll pass."

Oh. That was all. Darcy sipped her mulled cider. The cinnamon tingled her nose.

Mum sighed, "Though with Dr. Carrman unable to attend the dinner party, I am tempted to return home."

"We can leave at any time," Papa seconded. "I should return to the bank."

"Nonsense, Lovina, we shall simply make the best of it." Perpetua passed the mashed potatoes to Darcy who then sent them to Papa. "As it says in the Good Book, when the invited guests refused to come, the master sought others. Perhaps Darcy could invite her instructor."

Darcy choked on the cider. Jack at a dinner party with her parents? She hadn't exactly told them that he was her instructor. Then again, they hadn't exactly asked. "I don't think that's a good idea."

Papa disagreed. "I would like to meet the man."

"Very well, it's settled." Perpetua rang the bell for her cook, who appeared at once. "You may bring the dessert now."

"Yes, ma'am."

Darcy struggled to find an excuse. She couldn't bring Jack here. Mum would recognize him at once. "I don't know. It is rather last-minute. He might have other plans."

"It can't hurt to ask," Mum said. "A good meal might be exactly what this poor man needs."

"He's not poor, Mum." But compared to them, he was. And ill. Her heart ached.

"We are all poor sinners in the eyes of God," said Perpetua. "Invite him to our table. Who knows but that this isn't God's will? He does have a way of turning plans to His own purpose."

Darcy had never been so nervous. Her hand shook as she opened the door to the hangar the following morning. Part of her hoped Jack wasn't there, but most of her wanted to hug him close and tell him it would be all right.

She waited for her eyes to get accustomed to the dim light.

"Good morning." Jack hopped down from the wing of the trainer they'd flown yesterday. "Today you can hold the controls."

"We're flying?" She scanned him, looking for some sign of illness.

"That is the point of lessons, but don't get any ideas. My hands stay on the controls."

He pulled open the big hangar doors. Outside, the November sun shone crisp and white. He looked the same as always. Same leather jacket, same worn boots, same confidence.

"Grass-cutting first," he said, "and then, if you do well with that, we'll attempt a few hops."

"What's grass-cutting?"

"On the ground. No elevator. Then short up and down hops, just a few feet off the ground." He tossed her a pair of goggles and a leather helmet.

"That doesn't sound fun."

"You're learning to fly, not have fun. Aviation is serious business. Pilots who think otherwise end up dead."

Dead. Maybe that's why he could be so sure in the air. He knew death lurked around the corner anyway.

He smiled reassuringly. "Don't worry. You're not going to crash while I'm with you."

"I'm not worried, at least not about flying." *Ask him. Just ask.* The words pounded in her head, but she couldn't get them out her mouth.

"What's wrong? I thought you wanted to fly."

"I do."

"Then get your head gear on. You can pull the propeller. In this cold weather, better give it a couple of turns." He settled into the cockpit. "Be sure you stand clear of the blade."

She dragged her feet. "I was just wondering."

He looked up from the controls. "Wondering what?"

"If everything's all right."

"The plane checks out. Ran through it already."

"No, with you."

"What do you mean?" Jack's words resounded in the huge hangar, and she instantly regretted saying anything. This was personal, and she had no right to pry.

"I'm sorry. It's nothing." Her face was burning.

"Obviously it is something. Out with it, Shea."

She took a deep breath. He'd asked. "Your health."

"My health? What about my health? My health is fine. Why on earth are you asking about my health?"

Thank God. Now she did feel the fool. "I—I," she stammered. "Well, I happened to see you leave St. Anne's Hospital yesterday."

He stared. "Were you following me?"

"No! No. I had to deliver an invitation to…well, a doctor there. George Carrman, a cousin of Blake Kensington's. My aunt invited him to dinner, but it turns out he can't come anyway, so we're one short." The words spewed out faster and faster, but she couldn't talk her way out of this embarrassment. "You're all right then?"

He turned back to the controls. "I'm fine."

"Then you were just visiting someone," she gushed, relief making her silly, "just saying hello to an old friend or fellow aviator."

"Are you ready now?" He pointed to the propeller.

Conversation over. She pulled on the helmet and goggles and spun the propeller. On the fourth revolution, the motor sputtered until it evened out to a mellow chug. She climbed aboard and the lesson began. Jack was all business, and the awkwardness between them disappeared. After they taxied onto the airfield, Jack reviewed the controls, making her confirm each one.

"I wondered if we'd fly today, considering the breeze," she said, "but I can't feel it here."

"That's because the buildings block it. If we were going higher it would be a concern, but for grass-cutting it's fine."

He sounded normal. He acted normal. He was even letting her fly.

"Thank you," she said impulsively.

"Why?"

"For teaching me. And trusting me."

"What makes you think I trust you?" he said with the old lopsided grin. He throttled up and waited for the propeller to get up to speed. "Put your hand below mine on the elevator control."

She did as directed, and her thumb rested against his little finger. Even through the gloves she sensed his strength. This man was not ill. He held tightly to the things he dearly loved.

Jack released the brake and they were off. He applied the elevator just a little, so they skimmed the surface, and then brought it back down. He slowed and turned the plane to go back down the airfield. "Now you try."

For each maneuver, he talked through the procedure and had her place her hand below his on the controls. Soon she reached for the correct stick without coaching. They moved in concert. She had never felt so alive.

She soon noticed he would look at her when he thought she was busy. And he smiled. When she laughed, he echoed it. When she shrieked over a mistake, he told her she'd done fine. Soon she could make a perfect pass.

"May I try a hop?" she asked as they taxied toward the end of the field. "You can correct me as I go."

"Make no mistake, I *will* correct you."

"Then may I try?"

He nodded and they were off. She worked the elevator and ailerons the way he had during the flight in Pearlman.

"Whoa." He checked her ascent and brought them back down to a lower altitude. "Little hops, not flying to the moon."

She had to laugh. Too much yet again. She held at level flight until he indicated she should descend.

"Back off the throttle," he yelled. "Watch the elevator."

But it was too late. They bounced off the ground and back into the air. Darcy shrieked and let go of the stick.

Jack seized the controls. "Let me bring her down."

"I'm sorry."

His face was tense. "Never let go of the controls. Ever."

"I won't. I promise." Why, oh why, had she ruined things by trying to do too much?

After they'd landed and taxied into the hangar, she apologized again. "I'll never do it again."

He wiped oil splatters off his face. "Yes you will. Everyone does. That's how you learn. Just make sure they're not big mistakes."

"I will. I promise." She reached for the rag, but instead of handing it to her, he gently wiped the oil from her cheeks.

"You're freckled."

She sucked in her breath. "Big black freckles."

He tipped her chin, and she nearly stopped breathing. "Tell me what you did wrong."

She struggled to get her mind back on flying. "I used too much throttle and attempted too steep a descent."

"A little off-line, too," he said, letting her go. "You want to keep your target dead ahead. This airfield is forgiving, but in most places you need to navigate around trees and structures."

"Like Baker's field."

He nodded, and she latched onto the small encouragement.

"Good ascent," he said. "A little hesitant, but that will smooth out with practice."

She let the praise sink in while she wiped her goggles. "How long does it take to fly like you?"

"I've been flying almost ten years now."

"Ten years?" She didn't have ten years. She needed to make her big flight now, before Papa married her off.

"But it only takes four or so hours of flight time to get competent."

"Four hours, and I've had what? One?"

He chuckled. "Five minutes."

"Is that all we were up?"

"That's how much time you had the controls."

"Oh." She unbuttoned her coat as they approached the classroom. "How many hours does a transatlantic flight take?"

Jack didn't answer right away, and she worried that she'd steamed too far ahead again. "Twenty hours, more or less. Of course, it all depends on the speed of the aircraft, if there are any winds assisting, the load and a million other factors."

"That long. Is that why the plane has dual controls, like the one you landed in Pearlman? So one pilot can fly while the other sleeps?"

"There's no sleeping on a transatlantic flight. The second cockpit is for the navigator. And yes, if the pilot needs to do something away from the controls, the navigator can take over."

"But you flew the scout plane by yourself."

He ruffled his hair before replacing his cap. "It's not that far from the Island to Chicago."

Then he'd need a navigator to make the transatlantic distance. "Do you have a plane?"

He blinked. "I, uh, how did you know?"

"You're an aviator. You must have a plane." Maybe even one that could fly across the Atlantic.

He responded with boyish enthusiasm. "Do you want to see it?"

"Of course."

He dragged her back outside to go over every inch of his plane, from the dual controls to the two-hundred-horsepower engine. He led her from point to point with a gentle touch to the arm or small of the back. She drank in every touch and syllable.

"It's a lot like the one you landed in Pearlman," she said when he finished.

He proudly surveyed his plane. "Very observant. It's an earlier model, with some personal modifications."

"Then it's made for distance."

"Possibly." The wariness returned.

She knew she was pushing, but she had to ask. "Could it fly twenty hours straight?"

His eyes narrowed. "No. Never. Not enough load capacity."

"But it could be adapted."

"No, no, and no. I know what you're thinking, and it's not possible. For one, it would take too many modifications. Secondly, a transatlantic attempt is a huge venture."

She swung on a wing strut. "Worth fifty thousand dollars."

"Just getting the plane ready would cost thousands. Then there's the transportation, the crew, the supplies. I don't have that sort of money."

But other people did. "I know someone who might be interested. My aunt is holding a dinner party Saturday, and there are bound to be interested parties, well-off interested parties. You're invited. Come and talk about it."

Jack looked skeptical. "Interested parties like your father?"

"Goodness no. My aunt, for one. She's paying for my lessons, except for what I make on my newspaper articles. I'm sure she'd contribute to the attempt, especially because it's my calling."

"Your calling?"

"What God has called me to do."

Jack laughed. "You're not serious."

His reaction stung. "Of course I'm serious."

He looked at her like she was loony. Once again the shutter slammed closed. "I'm sorry. I already have a dinner engagement that night."

"With your sister? She can come, too. Your whole family can come."

If anything, his expression hardened even more. "Thank you, but dinner is impossible."

What had she done? They were getting along so well.

"Then perhaps you could join us for Sunday worship. We always have a nice supper afterward."

Jack turned away and fiddled with the plane's controls. "I'm busy."

The moment crumbled. Somehow she'd offended him. The intimacy of flight vanished, and once again she stood alone and apart, knowing no more about Jack Hunter than before.

Darcy knew she'd barged ahead too quickly. It was one of her worst flaws. She bitterly confessed as much in her nightly prayers. But she just couldn't contain her enthusiasm. She wanted it all: flying, the transatlantic prize, and Jack. If she'd just stop rushing, she might stand a chance.

With the dinner party called off, her parents returned home. That left Darcy to fly and to write about the experience. Each morning she raced to the flight school. At night she wrote. Each day brought her closer to Jack. She kept her enthusiasm in check, and he warmed to her, at least in the plane.

She finished typing the first article the following weekend and brought it with her Monday morning. Jack would be pleased. She had painted the school in a very positive light.

With Pohlman gone, Jack was now in charge of the school. She entered the building, expecting things to look livelier, but the hangar was dark and deathly quiet.

"Jack?" The word echoed off the cold brick walls.

He didn't answer, so she searched until she found him in the classroom. He stood at the front reading a piece of paper. He didn't look pleased.

Darcy hesitated. "Is something wrong?"

He glanced up. "Oh. Darcy. No, nothing." He shoved the paper into a folder on the battered oak desk. "Today we'll cover the preflight check. We're a bit out of order, due to the weather."

She held out her article. "Could you read this first and tell me if there's anything I should add or subtract?"

"What is it?"

"My story on the flight school. If it meets your approval, I'll take it to *The Courier* tomorrow. They've already promised to print it."

"The Buffalo paper? I thought you were writing for that Pearlman paper."

She shook her head. "Mr. Devlin wasn't interested."

"His loss."

Those two little words warmed her through and through. Jack believed in her.

While he read, Darcy took off her coat and tidied the room. Apparently, Pohlman had not been a stickler for neatness. The tables could use a good scrubbing. A hundred greasy hands had left black fingerprints on the light gray paint.

"That's good." Jack tapped the article. "Very good. Other than noting our hours of operation, I can't think of a thing to add."

Darcy was relieved to see him smile. He'd looked so worried when she first saw him that she wondered again if he was ill. That paper could have been a report from his doctor.

"Yep, this is just the thing to bring in new students." His grin melted her fear. "I tell you Darcy, we make a great team."

She could hardly believe it. He not only loved the article, he enjoyed working with her. "Then you accept that women can fly?"

"Whoa, don't go that far. If it were up to me, I wouldn't teach women, but I might not have a choice."

"What do you mean?"

He opened the folder. "Seems the other students aren't as dedicated as you. I've had two cancellations and one postponement. I suppose I should have expected that, with winter setting in."

So that was all. Darcy could barely hide her relief. "I thought it was something serious."

"It is serious. I can't live all winter on one student's tuition."

She gasped. "Don't you get paid?"

"That's not your concern." He slapped the folder shut. "Your task is to learn to fly."

"I can rewrite the article to say that classroom work begins in the winter with flight training in the spring. That allows for certification by summer and gives the adventurous flyer the entire season in the air." She finished with a flourish, trying to draw a smile from Jack.

She got only a shake of the head. "You're not really going to write that. It sounds like an advertisement."

"So it is. We're selling the public on the glorious sport of aviation. You know it's wonderful. I know it's wonderful. We only need to tell the world, and they'll come flocking to learn."

"The world?" he said wryly. "I wish I had your optimism."

"Why not? Who would have thought three months ago that I'd be flying an aeroplane, but here I am. Believe it and it will happen."

He shook his head. "All right, Miss Optimism. It's time to do some work. We'll begin by examining every wire and screw on the plane."

"Every one? There must be hundreds."

"Every one. If it was good enough for your heroine, Miss Quimby, it's good enough for you."

They spent the next four hours in the cold hangar, checking every inch of the plane. Darcy suspected Jack had deliberately loosened several screws and stays to see if she found them. When she did, she then had to tighten them properly. Jack demanded perfection when it came to planes. She suspected he demanded the same of himself, at least when he was flying. For a second she remembered his visit to Vanesia Lawrence's saloon, but thank goodness she'd seen no indication of drink since.

"Did I pass?" she asked when finished.

Jack jumped off the wing. "The only way to know for certain is to survive the flight. No one's going to take care of a plane the way you do. It's your life. Never forget that, and you'll live a lot longer."

"You're just trying to scare me." At least she hoped he was. He was certainly succeeding. She checked a couple of stays again.

"I'm spelling out facts. Flying is dangerous. So far you've had me along, but that won't always be the case."

Darcy had never quite thought about Jack not being there. In her mind, flying and Jack went hand in hand, but of course, he was correct. Once she received her license, she would leave the school and fly alone. That idea had lost a great deal of its appeal.

They'd reached the dreary classroom where she'd left her coat and bag. The lesson was over, but she didn't want to leave.

"Come to supper," she said impulsively. "It's just my aunt and me, but we'd love to have the company."

He looked leery. "I shouldn't."

"I promise not to mention the transatlantic attempt."

Still he hesitated. "I'm not certain it's proper."

"My family always invited teachers to supper to thank them."

"Then this is nothing more than professional gratitude?"

"Right." Though it hurt to say so.

"I wouldn't want anyone to think otherwise." Yet, he hadn't stopped looking at her. Just like that night in the alley.

Her mouth went dry. Her fingers tingled. She could barely breathe.

"I promise," she whispered.

"In that case…" His voice drifted off.

She wanted to run to him, to throw her arms around him and feel his around her, but that would not only be far too forward, it was sure to fail. He'd made it clear she couldn't rush him about anything. *He* needed to set the pace.

So she waited. And he stood silent, eyes locked with hers.

"Um-hum." Someone cleared her throat.

Darcy jumped. Jack pretended to review the folder on his desk. It was Aunt Perpetua, dressed in black.

"Excuse the interruption." Perpetua planted her cane on the concrete floor. "When no one answered the door, I came in, in search of my niece."

Darcy inhaled deeply until her head cleared. "Why?"

Perpetua watched her carefully. "I just received a telephone call from your mother."

"Mum placed a long-distance call? She never…" That was the problem. She never placed a long-distance telephone call. It must be serious.

"Your sister has taken a bad turn," Perpetua said, "and the doctor ordered her to bed. Your mother needs your help with the children."

But flying… And Jack. Darcy looked to him for support, but he agreed with Perpetua.

"Winter's almost upon us. There's not much more we can do before spring."

"But what will you do?" He couldn't survive with no students.

He waved off her concerns. "Don't worry about me. I'll be fine. Go home to your family."

"I know it's a trial, child," said Perpetua, "but Mr. Hunter is correct. Family comes first."

Darcy's thoughts tumbled. How, when she was so close to her dream, could it be snatched away? She thought God wanted her here. She thought this was His plan. If so, why call her away? And why did it have to be her sister?

Wasn't this just like Amelia? If Darcy didn't know better, she'd think Amelia had planned it. She knew it was wrong, but she couldn't stop the rush of anger. Amelia had always managed to steal Darcy's moment away. Darcy's twelfth-birthday trip to Buffalo had to be postponed because of Amelia's wedding. Her trip to San Francisco got changed to Chicago when Lizzie was born.

"When do I have to leave?" she asked, hoping for more time.

"I've packed your things and hired a cab. We can still get you to the station for the evening train. I realize this is a setback, but God always has His reasons, even if we can't see them at the time."

Darcy could see no reason. Charles could hire a housekeeper. His sister, Grace, could help. Why did it always fall to her? "But she's not due until April."

"I'm sorry, Darcy," said Perpetua. "Your help is needed now."

She had no choice. She had to go.

Darcy opened the heavy door for her aunt and took one last look back. Jack stood in the center of the hangar, hands in his pockets.

"I'll be back in the spring," she promised.

He nodded before walking back to the classroom.

She let the door swing closed.

Chapter Seven

The following weeks passed in a blur of routine. Darcy rose before sunup and walked the quarter mile to Amelia's house where she cooked breakfast and dressed the children for school. She brought Amelia's meals upstairs and received unwanted instruction on how to properly fulfill every housekeeping task. Though her sister ended these directives with thanks, Darcy could not shake her resentment.

After the children left for school, she tackled laundry and ironing and cleaning and baking. Though Amelia had a motorized washtub, Darcy still had to crank the wringer. Then the clothes had to be hung and taken down and pressed with the electric iron, which was more trouble than it was worth, since it tended to scorch collars and handkerchiefs.

When the children returned, she had to feed them, bathe them and put them to bed. By the time she returned home, she was so exhausted that she fell into bed, too tired to undress.

"I'm not made for this," Darcy complained to Beatrice. She'd taken the afternoon off to help her friend tie bows for the wedding. After the last of dozens, Darcy never wanted to touch satin ribbon again. She lay on Beattie's bed facedown, stretching her aching muscles. "I don't know how Amelia manages. All right, I do know, because she tells me how every single day. But I can't seem to make it work. Freddie and Lizzie won't listen, and Helen refuses to come out from under the stairs."

Beatrice placed the last of the bows into a big basket. "Remember, they're her babes. It's always different with your own."

"Well, you can have married life. It's not for me. After this is over, I'm going back to Buffalo to finish flight lessons."

"What if your mother still needs you?" That was Beattie's delicate way of asking what she'd do if something happened to Amelia.

Darcy refused to consider that possibility. "Everything will go fine. It always has in the past. By April, I'll be back in the air." She pantomimed steering a plane with the pillow as the wheel, but Beattie snatched the pillow from her.

"Stop being silly," she huffed.

Darcy sensed trouble. "What's bothering you? The wedding?"

Beattie traced the embroidered flowers on the pillowcase. "Do you think of Jack often?"

A sharp pang shot through Darcy. Hearing his name aloud somehow hurt worse than thinking about him. "Sometimes."

"And you miss him?"

Darcy couldn't acknowledge her feelings, not when he'd made it clear he didn't want to get involved. "He's my flight instructor, nothing more."

"Then there's nothing between you." She heaved a sigh. "I'm so glad. I was worried you'd pine for him. When Blake was at the university, I could hardly get through a day. Even now, when we're together, it's never enough. I always knew he was the one, and I was so afraid you felt that way about Jack."

Darcy swirled Beattie's veil, edged with satin rosettes that her mother had made. "Don't worry about me. I have plenty to keep me occupied." She placed the veil on Beattie's head and spread it over her shoulders. "Gorgeous."

Beatrice examined her reflection in the mirror. "Don't misunderstand me, I hoped you'd fall in love. It's wonderful and amazing and life-changing, but when you had to return, well, I worried."

Darcy hugged her from behind. "Don't. Flying comes first for me. There's no room for romance."

"I can't imagine Jack believes that."

"It's true. If we were romantically involved, Jack would refuse to teach me. He said so. He claims women don't have a strong enough constitution."

"Maybe we don't."

"Beattie! I'm every bit as capable as a man, and so are you. I flew well. Jack said I did. But if we were involved…" she paused, mind whirling at the thought, "he could forbid me to fly. That's why romance is impossible."

"Isn't romance better than flying?"

"Romance leads to marriage, and marriage to husbands making every decision."

Beattie clucked her tongue. "What odd ideas you have. Marriage is a melding of two into one, a sacred union. If the woman follows her husband's guidance, it's only because both have agreed it's the best course. You can't possibly have two persons acting independently and call it a marriage. It would be like the lower half of the body deciding to walk somewhere that the upper half doesn't want to go."

Darcy shook her head. "If the lower half walks, the upper has no choice but to follow. I believe you've confirmed my point." Beattie looked so shocked that Darcy had to laugh.

After a pause, Beatrice began to giggle, too. Then Darcy joined her until they both collapsed on the bed in a fit.

"Wait, wait, you'll ruin your veil." Darcy helped untangle the delicate fabric.

"I know this has been difficult," Beattie said after they stopped giggling, "but think of all you're learning."

"Like how much I despise housework."

"Like what you really want."

Darcy had always known what she wanted, but she hadn't foreseen how much she would feel for Jack. Unfortunately, she couldn't have both. Flying had to come first. She'd remember that when she returned in April.

She plucked a white satin bow from the basket and plopped it on top of her head. "This is as close as I'm going to get to a bridal veil. Do you like it?"

Beatrice's wedding day arrived bright and sunny. Though Christmas had passed, the ground remained bare. Darcy knew her friend had hoped for snow, but if Beattie was disappointed, she didn't show it. The way the bride and groom looked at each other struck a chord of regret in Darcy. As the two spoke their vows before God and the congregation, she wondered what it would be like to have Jack standing beside her at the front of the church. How would it feel to have him slide a wedding band on her finger, to hear him promise before God to love and protect?

She bowed her head. That would never happen. Even if the impasse between them cleared, Jack had never mentioned a church home. He'd scoffed when she told him God led her to fly. A match with him was impossible in every way. So why did she still think about it?

The wedding dinner took place at the grange. The old hall had been transformed into a fairy-tale land, festooned with pine boughs, holly and mistletoe. Yards of white lace hung around every window and doorway, topped with the ribbon bows. Beatrice glowed in her ivory satin gown, overlaid with French batiste.

Darcy, on the other hand, had to endure George Carrman, who'd been paired with her at both the ceremony and reception. The poor man had bravely endured her family's constant attempts to match him with Darcy. Bland and doughy, with a crop of brown curls, he simply didn't suit her. No humble scholar for her. She preferred the adventurer.

After dinner, George led her onto the floor for the ceremonial dance. He proved a good dancer, but that didn't make this any more comfortable. Of all the dances Beattie could have chosen, why did she pick a waltz? Darcy kept as much distance as possible.

"How are your journalistic endeavors faring?" he asked.

"Not well, I'm afraid, not since Buffalo. Did you see my article about the flight school in *The Courier*?"

"Ah, yes, Blake told me you're learning to fly. I even looked into taking lessons myself."

"You? When? How?" Darcy could hardly believe her article had worked. She hoped Jack had signed dozens of students, and the school was now profitable. Then she realized dozens of students meant Jack would spend more time with them and less with her. It wouldn't be just the two of them anymore.

"I start in the spring," George was saying. "I don't intend to actually fly, but I wanted to learn the principles."

Darcy scrunched her nose. "You're not going to fly? Then why take lessons?" But she had a bad feeling she knew. He wanted to impress someone. A woman, most likely. A woman who wanted to fly. She changed the subject before he could answer. "Have you finished your studies?"

"I complete my internship next month, and then I'll be able to write the license examinations."

"Then you'll start a practice?" Darcy would rather endure

the boring details of medical education than hear whom George wanted to impress by taking flight lessons.

"No," George said, sweeping her toward the corner. "I've decided to pursue research in polio. They're close to finding the cause. I want to be in on it and make sure no one ever has to suffer again." His passion surprised her. The cherubic face glowed with excitement, and for the first time she realized an intellect hid beneath the shy and pudgy exterior.

"Why do you care so much?" she asked. "Was someone in your family afflicted?"

"No, but I met someone."

She could not believe the man was blushing. "You like her?"

He suddenly halted, and she nearly tripped over his feet.

"Why did you stop?" Then she noticed his attention was fixed on the doorway. She turned and caught her breath. A very familiar man stood in the entrance. Brown leather jacket. Sandy hair. Brilliant blue eyes.

Jack.

She stumbled toward him. He'd come back to her. He'd traveled all the way from Buffalo to see her.

She waved, but he didn't see her. He kept scanning the crowd. She waved again, but he started walking toward the opposite corner. She wove through the dancing couples, struggling to reach him.

"Jack." She stood just ten feet away. "Jack, I'm here."

He must not have heard her, because he kept walking away, directly toward Hendrick Simmons.

One minute inside the grange hall, and Jack knew he shouldn't have come. He'd spotted Darcy the moment he entered, and it had nearly undone him. She sparkled in her emerald-green gown and rhinestone-studded hairpins. The faraway look and flushed cheeks stole straight to his heart.

Even though she danced with another man, he could see she wasn't interested in him. Too much space. She was too eager to break away. The old attraction raged back full force.

He forced his gaze from her and searched for Simmons. Business only. That's what he'd told himself the entire train ride, though he didn't know a soul who would believe that excuse.

He spotted the kid and walked straight toward him. She followed. He tried to ignore her presence, though it was already clouding his thoughts. Business first.

He cleared his throat. "Mr. Simmons. Might I have a moment of your time?"

The kid looked agitated, but he greeted Jack politely. Jack stuck to his plan. The moment Simmons stood, he launched into the speech he'd rehearsed dozens of times en route to Pearlman.

"I'm the new manager of a flight school in Buffalo. We have twenty trainer aeroplanes and no mechanics. I've seen your work and can think of no one I'd trust more to maintain the fleet. If you're interested, we can discuss details tomorrow, but I wanted to give you the offer tonight so you can think it over." He could feel Darcy behind him, drawing closer like iron to a magnet.

Simmons looked to Darcy. Jack should have known. It had always been Darcy for the kid. Had they connected while he was gone? Had he lost his chance?

"I, uh," Simmons stammered, "...dunno. I like it here. Pearlman's a good place." He said it fiercely, as if protecting his homeland from invaders.

Jack didn't care anymore. He just had to get out of there. "I understand. Take time to think it over. The position doesn't start until spring. If you have any questions, we can talk in the morning. I'm staying at Terchie's." Jack extended his hand.

Simmons limply shook. If Jack hadn't known the kid could

work wonders with motors, he'd have misjudged that lack of firmness in his grip.

"Terchie's. Room six." Jack deliberately turned to his right, away from Darcy, as if he didn't know she was there. Coward. He should say something. He should at least greet her, but he knew that once he began, he'd never be able to stop. He wanted to be with her so badly, but that relationship could never be.

"Is that all?" She followed him to the door and wiggled in front of him.

The hurt in her eyes tore through him. He never wanted to see that look again. Ever.

"You could at least say hello," she said.

No, he couldn't. If he greeted her, it would all be over. He didn't have the strength to walk away. He burst past her onto the stoop and breathed in the icy air.

"Stop pretending I don't exist." She struggled to put on her coat, but she had the arms all mixed up. She finally gave up and wrapped it around her shoulders like a cloak. "Worthless coat."

He took pity. "Allow me." He motioned for her to give him the coat.

"Oh, now you notice me. What is going on, Jack Hunter? You didn't come all this way to ask Hendrick Simmons to be your mechanic." She untangled the coat and shoved her arms into it.

Jack held up his hands in surrender and stepped backward into the street, his breath rising in a light cloud. She was right of course. He couldn't explain away his bad behavior. "I'm sorry. I didn't want to hurt you."

"You did a poor job of it." She fought tears, which only made him feel worse. "I thought we were friends."

Friends. The word didn't begin to address what he felt inside, but it did cover the safe ground he'd sculpted for himself. "We are."

"I want to be in Buffalo. I want to continue lessons. I'm sorry I had to leave. But I can't return yet. N-not now." Her breath caught, like she couldn't bear to say why, and Jack instantly thought of her sister.

He should have asked. Any decent, caring man would have asked. "How is Amelia?"

"Fine." The word came out choked. "Still in confinement. Your sister?"

In confinement. "She's well."

The pleasantries over, they stood in awkward silence, the cold creeping into fingers and toes. "You said you're coming back. When?"

"After the baby is born in April."

"If it's too early to fly, you can tear that motor apart and reassemble it."

She laughed and his heart soared. "I can hardly wait." Just as quickly she turned serious. *Her sister's condition must be graver than she let on.* He wanted to comfort her. He wanted to say everything would work out the way she wanted, but he couldn't. Hold a glass ball too tightly and it shatters.

Snow drifted lazily from the sky, glistening where the light from a window caught it. The sandy brown of the road had started to whiten. He kicked a stone and it skittered ahead ten feet, creating a thin, brown trail across the white.

"I'm headed back to the boardinghouse," he said.

"I'll walk there with you."

"And then I'll have to walk you back. That defeats the purpose, don't you think?"

"I suppose it does." Still, she kept walking beside him. "Tell me everything that's happened since I left. Did my article bring in new students?"

Jack hesitated. "Inquiries."

"How many signed up?"

He hated to disappoint her, but he couldn't lie. "Just one, for the spring."

"Then how are you making do?" Her voice hummed with alarm.

"I pick up jobs here and there." He couldn't tell her the truth, that he was looking to fly exhibitions in Texas for the winter.

"Is that enough to live on?"

"Don't worry about me."

"And of course you live with your sister."

Jack started to correct her but got caught by those deep, dark eyes. They reflected a full moon that peeked out from between the snow-laden clouds. They also reflected him.

A snowflake landed on her lip and melted. Another stuck on her lash. She blinked. Another clung to her brow. Carefully, he brushed it away.

It was dark. Late December. Snowing. He should be cold, but he wasn't. Not a bit.

He combed the snowflakes from a strand of her hair.

"You're beautiful," he said in far too throaty a voice. How he wanted to take her in his arms and hold her forever. How he wanted to protect her from everything bad that could ever happen. How he wanted to kiss her.

Her eyes reflected the same desire. Her lips softened, accepting him. He leaned closer by small degrees, gauging her willingness.

Her lids slowly drifted shut, and he brushed his lips across her cheek. She drew back.

He flinched. What now?

Her attention focused on the street, where a motor car sloshed through the snow. "You're getting covered in snow," she laughed. "Come with me." She grabbed his hand and led him down the street to a park with a little wooden pavilion.

His initial shock subsided into pleasure at her touch. Her

cold fingers could turn cream to ice cream, but the place where their palms met radiated warmth. He raised her hand to his mouth and blew to warm her fingers. She giggled and tugged him toward the pavilion.

"What is this used for?" he asked as they climbed the steps to stand under the roof. It was open on three sides and stacked with rough wooden benches.

"Speeches or rallies or revivals," she said, still holding his hand. "We had a big suffrage rally here last summer, before you dropped out of the sky and graced us with your presence."

She might have said they slaughtered pigs there. It wouldn't have mattered. She had a sparkle and a way of talking that reminded him of a time long ago, before all the pain had begun, a time when he still had parents and his sister could run, a time when he still believed in God and miracles.

She was talking, but Jack didn't hear a word. He reveled in the timbre of her voice, the way her hands constantly swooped open in a gesture of inclusion, and the delicate tendrils of dark hair that fell loose. He wished it would never end.

Darcy Shea was not like any woman he'd ever known. She had courage. She was strong. She inspired him.

And yet she was reckless and vulnerable and so much in need of someone to take care of her.

She paused a moment, and the moonlight revealed her rare beauty. Lips slightly parted. Hair spilling to her shoulders. He wanted to touch her. He wanted to hold her close and kiss her, but that was the worst thing he could do. She wasn't ready.

Somehow he had to stop this attraction. He had to break the thread that connected them. The truth would do it. It had always worked in the past.

"I don't live with my sister, because she's an invalid," he blurted out. "Polio. She's at St. Anne's Hospital. That's why I was there, to visit her."

Jack waited for the usual signs of emotional withdrawal. He'd seen them often enough. The flustered exclamation of sympathy, the darting gaze, the tiny step back as if he was contagious. He waited, but it didn't happen. Yes, she looked surprised, but not horrified.

"Oh, Jack." She clasped his hands, and he just couldn't pull them away. "Is she in pain?"

"No, not at all."

"Thank the Lord," she sighed.

The old anger and resentment started to bubble up. His mother's church friends had said exactly the same thing, but God didn't deserve thanksgiving. He'd abandoned them.

"That doesn't mean she isn't suffering," he snapped. "She can't do what you do. She can't walk around town. She can't fly."

Darcy tilted her head. "Why not?"

"Didn't you hear me? She can't walk."

"That doesn't mean she can't fly. The controls in the trainer are all operated by hand. And even if she can't use her hands, you could fly for her. It's not holding the controls, you know, it's experiencing the wonder, seeing God's world spread out below."

Jack was stunned. He'd never considered taking Sissy in his plane. Too risky. Something might happen, and he could never live with that. "You have the most outrageous ideas."

Instead of being affronted, she laughed. "Like attempting the transatlantic crossing?"

He concentrated on the swirling snow. If he looked at Darcy, he'd be lost. "That's just plain foolish."

"Is it? You own a plane built for distance flight."

"Not for that long a distance."

"And you have the skill. All you need is someone with nerve, connections and organizational ability. It can be done, Jack. Everything is possible if you believe."

He broke away, clawing for solid ground. If he looked into those eyes that so perfectly reflected him, he'd agree. And that would bring disaster. He had to put a stop to her wild ideas. Emphatically.

"It's not going to happen. Ever."

Chapter Eight

"Why not?" Darcy spun around, catching snowflakes on her bare palms. The cold didn't matter. Jack and this flight would rescue her from drudgery. "It's the answer to everything."

The transatlantic flight would set her on the world stage. She would be first. Not second. Not following a man's success. First.

"Whoa, whoa." Jack dragged her to a halt. "It's not that easy. You need the right plane, which I don't have, and then you need backing—lots of it. Then you have to plan every second of the trip. One mistake and you're dead."

"We can do all that."

"Do you happen to have an extra forty thousand dollars, because I'll tell you right now it's going to cost that, and probably more."

Forty thousand dollars? The amount staggered. A person could buy half of Pearlman for forty thousand dollars.

"You're teasing," she said. "Who would go for a fifty thousand dollar prize if it cost forty thousand to do it?"

He crossed his arms. "For what comes afterward: lectures, books, interviews. Publishers will pay big money for the rights to the story. There might even be a film. The lecture circuit alone has funded many an expedition."

Of course. She mentally regurgitated all those expedition narratives she'd read. Books, articles and lectures had been part of them all.

"It's not the payoff that's the problem," Jack said. "It's the upfront money."

"Forty thousand?" Not one expedition had been funded by a sole benefactor. "If it takes that much, then we'll find patrons. Lots of them." She threaded her arm around his. "And I know right where we can start."

"I don't want to be indebted to your family."

Other than Perpetua, Darcy doubted anyone in her family would contribute. "That's not who I had in mind." She tugged him toward the grange hall. "We can start tonight. Everyone's there."

"You're loony."

"Crazy, mad and naïve," she laughed as they skidded through the slick snow, back to the hall. The squalls had stopped, and the moon glimmered off the newly fallen blanket of white.

Guests streamed out the front door of the hall. Motorcars chugged home, while other guests walked in merry little groups, reliving their favorite moment from the wedding.

"Follow me." Darcy eased past the departing guests and found Beatrice just inside the door, thanking each person for coming.

"Darcy, where have you been? O-oh." She'd spotted Jack. "Mr. Hunter. You came." Strangely, she didn't look surprised.

"Beattie? Did you send Jack an invitation?"

Beatrice looked chagrined. "Are you terribly sore?"

"How could I ever be sore with you?" Darcy hugged her friend and whispered, "Thank you."

"I'm so glad." Beattie held her hands and looked like she

wanted to say more, but the Grattans approached, calling her to duty.

"Hunter?" Blake popped out of the crowd. "Good to see you again. What brings you back to Pearlman?"

"A grand adventure," Darcy said.

Jack filled in the details. "Attempting the first nonstop transatlantic flight. We might be looking for subscribers."

"That so?" Blake grasped Jack's hand and nodded for him to follow into the hall. "Let's talk."

Blake drew Jack through the throngs of guests donning coats and mittens, and Darcy began to follow, but Beatrice held her back. "Not this time."

Darcy shook off her friend. "What do you mean? It's my idea."

"Not anymore. Like it or not, men prefer to think they come up with the big ideas. Don't look so disappointed. We know who truly thought of it."

"But I need to be part of this," Darcy insisted. "I'm going to be in that plane."

"Let them have their moment. Your turn will come, I promise. Mr. Shea." Beattie elbowed her.

Papa. She hadn't seen him coming.

"It's time to go, Darcy." He did not sound pleased. "Your mother is waiting."

"I'll be right along." She couldn't leave now, when her whole future was about to be decided.

"It's late, and you have responsibilities. Amelia needs your help."

Amelia. Always what Amelia needed. Never what she needed.

"Please let me stay a bit longer. Jack is going for the transatlantic prize, and I need to help him."

"Jack?" Papa placed undue emphasis on his name. "Jack who?"

She lost nerve. He'd never met Jack, didn't even know he was her flight instructor. She looked to Beatrice for help.

For the first time since childhood, her friend abandoned her. "Speaking of which, I believe my new husband might be getting himself talked into subscribing to Mr. Hunter's project. I had better see what he is agreeing to." She scurried off, leaving Darcy alone with her father.

"Jack Hunter?" Papa's brow furrowed. "The aviator who landed here in September? You are on a first-name basis with a man you've barely met?"

All the air left the room. Perhaps she should have mentioned earlier that Jack was her flight instructor, but it was too late now. She looked around for an escape. The snow had begun again, whirling like a blizzard in the light from the door. Snow. Of course. Papa loved expeditions.

"He's going for the *Daily Mail* prize, Papa. You remember. For the first aviator to cross the Atlantic nonstop. It's better than Peary reaching the North Pole. If we make it, our names will be immortalized."

"We?" He donned his top hat. "How are *we* involved?"

"If we subscribe. Jack, uh, Mr. Hunter, needs sponsors."

Papa's frown deepened. "Sounds to me like throwing perfectly good money away."

"But you've always wanted to be part of an expedition."

"Expeditions are fraught with danger and risk. They are for younger men than I. Come along, Darcy."

Darcy couldn't give up. Not now. She had to make him understand. "But Papa, this is our big chance. We may never have an opportunity like this again. How often does an adventurer come to Pearlman? Never. At least not until now."

"Darcy, the joy of an expedition is not in paying for it; it's in participating, in experiencing the danger and the reward."

"That's what I want."

"You? What role could you possibly play?"

Darcy's heart pounded like a steam engine blasting through a tunnel. "I might fly. Ride as navigator. You see, Jack Hunter is my flight instructor."

Papa went pale. Not a single muscle moved, beyond the twitching of the artery in his neck. "When were you going to tell me this?"

"I—I—" Darcy couldn't find an answer.

The color flooded back into his face. "This is mad, daughter. Do you have any idea of the risk? I can't believe Mr. Hunter would agree to this. I should tell him what I think of his plan."

"No, Papa." She grabbed her father's arm. "Please don't."

He looked at her long and hard. "Mr. Hunter hasn't agreed, has he?"

Tears rose, but she blinked them back. "He will."

"Listen, Darcy. I went along with your flight lessons. I don't understand, but I can accept it. But this flying across the Atlantic Ocean is too much. You have responsibilities to your family. Your mother needs you. Amelia needs you. Those children need you."

"The flight wouldn't take place until spring, after Amelia has delivered."

"That is not the point, daughter. I would never forgive myself if something happened to you."

"But Papa—"

"I hope you understand that your care is my responsibility. I love you and want only the best for you. It might not seem like it now, but trust me, you'll thank me one day."

Darcy couldn't see how. "But I want to be part of this. I want to make history. That's what's best for me."

Papa kissed her forehead. "Then if this foolishness transpires, wish Mr. Hunter well. Tell everyone you know that he was your flight instructor, but I need you to stay close to home and on the ground."

Crushed. Ground to tiny bits and flung out in the snow. That's how Darcy felt. For once, hope failed her.

Things progressed far too quickly as far as Jack was concerned. Blake Kensington had an adventurer's soul and a wealthy man's wallet. What he couldn't provide financially, his father could—for a price. Like everything else in town, the Kensington name would be emblazoned across his plane.

Within minutes, Jack had enough support to begin preparing for the transatlantic attempt. The Kensingtons wanted the preparations done in Pearlman, which meant shipping the plane. It really needed two motors to make the crossing, requiring a lot of reengineering. He had to arrange an airfield in Newfoundland, file the paperwork and pay the fee. He needed to get permission to take off and land on foreign soil. Supplies had to be ordered and tests run on the modified plane.

And then there was Sissy. She'd support him, of course, and the Kensingtons paid enough to cover her hospital bills, but who would care for her if he didn't survive?

"I'm not sure I can commit to this," he told Blake the next day.

He stood in Branford Kensington's mahogany-paneled study while Blake's father shouted into the telephone.

"Turn the bloody shipment around and send it to Pearlman. How difficult can it be?"

Blake seemed to think the whole thing humorous. "You've just got cold feet. Had a bit of that myself before the wedding. Father'll set you right." He jabbed Jack in the ribs and headed out of the room.

The elder Kensington resumed ranting. "I know it's the holiday season, but there are four business days left this week."

Jack edged away from the Cape buffalo head mounted at

eye level. Its huge black eyes and curved horns made him more than uneasy. The blood-red carpet and smell of polish recalled childhood and the parlor he was never allowed to enter. People with houses like this did not accept "no." He could sure use Darcy right now. She had a way of bulling around any obstacle to get her way.

"It's done," Kensington said, hanging up the telephone receiver. "Imbeciles. They don't know their brains from their bums, but rest assured, your aeroplane will be here within the week or they'll pay a hefty price." He clapped Jack on the back. "Care for a drink? Eugenia, have the housekeeper run in some ice."

The sleek Mrs. Kensington, who had appeared from nowhere, pursed perfectly formed red lips. "It's Sunday."

"For heavens sake, can't I offer the man a drink?" Kensington's walrus mustache bristled with irritation.

"Thank you anyway," Jack said quickly. "I have things to do."

"On a Sunday evening?"

"Do stay for supper." Mrs. Kensington touched Jack's arm lightly. "The newlyweds will be joining us."

Reason enough to leave.

"Thank you, ma'am, but I have things to do. Mr. Kensington. Thank you. You've saved me a lot of travel."

"It's my money," the man joked, though Jack didn't find much humor in it. Bad enough he was into these people for thousands. When they realized how much it would really cost, he expected them to back away in a hurry. Blake was young enough to ignore the cost for the thrill of adventure. Blake's father was another matter.

Jack hustled out into the night, glad to leave the sterile house behind. Flurries fell on roofs and porches. Lights glowed through front windows, beacons of warmth lining the streets. In one house an old man danced with his wife, their steps slow and painful, their faces rapt with tender love. It was achingly domestic. In another home a family said grace around the Sunday meal, heads bowed. Jack could almost taste the roast turkey.

How long had it been since he'd sat for a family meal? Before Mom died. Before boarding school and the army and flying. There were meals, sure, and people to share them with, but never a family, never a wife or mother to welcome him home. Never children who laughed and told stories.

For the first time in years, he longed for it—not what was lost, but what could have been. He—Jack Lindsey Hunter—wanted a family. The idea stunned him. He'd never quite imagined himself with a wife and children. He'd never allowed himself that fantasy.

He shook his head. This foolishness had to be brought on by fatigue. He hadn't slept well in days.

That was it.

Yet, as he walked back to the boardinghouse, he looked for Darcy in every parlor window. She must live in this grandest of Pearlman's neighborhoods, where the three-story Victorian and Federal homes towered over the town. He walked past house after house, but none of the windows revealed her.

The snow was coming down harder, sticking to every branch and limb and accumulating on the sidewalks. He trudged through it, collar turned up.

Darcy was right. He had returned to Pearlman to see her. He needed her. Her fire and spirit energized him. She made him believe anything was possible. When he was around her, he actually believed he could cross the Atlantic.

Then he spotted her in a modest two-story house. She stood in the front window, back to him, gesturing the way she did when she was excited. He lingered as the snow piled onto his shoulders and cap.

She was directing a trio of children in a game that

apparently involved jumping on and off the furniture. Little heads bobbed up and down, followed by Darcy's larger, more lovely one.

The ache intensified. He wanted this so badly it hurt.

A large snowflake landed on his jacket. Its minute crystals spread in glorious beauty. He touched a finger to it, and it melted. By trying to hold the snowflake, he'd destroyed it.

Just like with Darcy. Hold on too tightly, and he'd ruin everything that made her wonderful. Protect her, and he'd lose her, but at least her family would have her.

No matter how much she argued and protested, he had to keep her on the ground. For her sake. Unlike him, she had too much to lose.

A church bell tolled the hour and reminded Jack that he didn't belong here amongst the happy memories and loving families. He had to let them go. He had to let Darcy go.

He shook off the snow and walked back to the boarding-house.

Darcy tossed and turned for two nights, torn by her responsibility to her family and her desire to make the transatlantic flight. Or was it her desire for Jack? Every time she closed her eyes, she saw him. Jack. He'd come back to her. The thought filled her with such bliss that she could easily lose her head if she didn't keep reminding herself that flying came first.

If she could ever fly again. She growled in frustration. Surely God had planted the desire to fly within her, so why did she face so much opposition? Wouldn't God ease her path?

She shoved back the heavy quilts and switched on the lamp. After her eyes adjusted, she took her Bible and let it fall open at random, looking for an answer. She eagerly scanned the chapters from Luke and read the familiar passage about a man being unable to serve two masters.

Disappointed, she closed the book. She knew the passage

well. But which master, Lord? Family or aviation? That's the answer she needed.

As night wandered toward icy dawn, no solution came, only a stiff neck and heavy eyes.

Beattie told her that Blake wanted the preparations to take place in Pearlman. Of course. That was the answer. Start small and work her way toward her goal. Papa said he wanted her to stay close to home and on the ground. Well, that's exactly what she'd do.

After washing and dressing, she went downstairs to prepare breakfast. She would have preferred to tell both her parents at once, but her mother had stayed the night at Amelia's house. That left Papa.

She struggled for words as they ate in silence. As usual, Papa perused the newspaper. To her surprise, he spoke first.

"I hope you understand my reasoning last night." He set down the newspaper and took off his spectacles.

Darcy tried not to rush. "I do, Papa, and I should have told you that Mr. Hunter was my instructor. I'm sorry I wasn't more forthcoming."

He nodded. "And I'm sorry I had to be so harsh." He tapped off the top of his soft-boiled egg with his knife.

Darcy took a sip of tea for fortitude. "You said you wanted me to stay close to home and on the ground."

"That's right." He scooped out a spoonful of egg.

"Beatrice said they're putting the plane together right here in Pearlman."

He paused, spoon in midair. "I don't want you involved with that flight."

"I'm not asking to fly, Papa. I'd like to help with the groundwork, putting parts together and that sort of thing. I'm sure half the town will help, and I'd like to do my part."

He didn't answer for a long time. "On the ground?"

"In Baker's barn, I understand. May I, Papa? Please?"

He would give in. He always gave in. Eventually. At least he used to, years ago, before Amelia had Freddie.

He shook out the newspaper. "Your work at your sister's house comes first."

"Yes, Papa."

"As well as anything your mother needs."

"I promise, Papa."

He sighed. "I can't say I'm pleased, but I don't suppose I have any choice, do I?"

"Oh thank you, Papa." She flung her arms around his neck, jostling his spectacles.

"Now, Darcy."

But he was pleased. She could tell. And little by little she'd convince him to let her fly.

Chapter Nine

On the tenth of January, the plane arrived in pieces and was hauled by wagon to Baker's barn for reassembly. Darcy followed it there and discovered Jack had set up a workshop inside, complete with coal oil lanterns and gasoline heaters.

He flat-out refused her help. She suspected Papa had interfered, but when she told Jack that her father had restricted her to groundwork, he relented.

"Groundwork only," he'd echoed.

She was tired of men telling her what she could and couldn't do, but ranting about it wouldn't change their minds. She needed to work slowly, showing them she was more than capable. Since Jack seemed to follow Papa's lead, she'd start there. Surely, within three months she could convince him she belonged in the cockpit.

On schoolday afternoons, Darcy helped Jack assemble the wings while Simmons worked on the motor. After putting the children to bed, she wrote stories for Devlin, who'd relented the minute he heard about the transatlantic attempt. By the end of the month, they began modifying the plane for transatlantic flight. More load capacity, heavier struts and bracing, reengineering for the two motors, building the twin nacelles.

The work went on and on. Darcy helped with the lighter tasks, as well as compiling the supply requisition lists.

She and Jack spoke often over the weeks, but always about the plane, and never with the camaraderie they'd shared in Buffalo. By February Papa relented, agreeing she could renew flight lessons in the spring after Amelia delivered the baby, but Jack wouldn't confirm. Every time she asked, he brushed aside her inquiry. The closeness they'd shared on Beattie's wedding night had vanished.

"He could tell me a little about himself," Darcy complained to Beatrice as she helped her friend unpack the dozens of items she'd purchased on her wedding tour. She'd missed having a confidante the past month. "Even acquaintances chat about friends and family to pass the time. I've babbled on and on about Pearlman, but other than his sister, he's told me nothing. Don't you think that's odd?"

Beattie calmly folded a linen tablecloth. "Men, as a rule, don't care to discuss their family."

Darcy wasn't sure she liked her friend's newfound sense of superiority. The old Beattie would have pondered the problem.

She ripped the paper off a heavy object. "A mechanical monkey bank? Why do you need this?"

"For children," Beatrice said quietly.

"Whose children? Oh," she gasped, realizing what her friend meant. "Beattie. You're not."

"Not yet, but soon. I'm sure of it."

Darcy couldn't picture her friend round like Amelia. Bedridden. "Why rush? There's plenty of time."

Beatrice smiled faintly. "That is why two people get married."

True. That's why she wouldn't marry. At least not until she'd flown across the Atlantic. "You seem so young."

"Minnie Alexander was seventeen when she had her first, and Paulette Grozney just turned eighteen."

"Yes, but don't you feel a bit...inexperienced?"

"If you mean am I scared, yes. Something could go wrong."

Darcy paled.

"Don't worry." Beatrice patted her hand. "The women in my family deliver easily. My little sister was born in only six hours. Doc Stevens didn't arrive in time, and Daddy had to deliver the baby."

Darcy tried to imagine Jack delivering a baby. Impossible.

"My biggest concern," said Beattie, "is being a good mother."

"No worry there. You'll be the best mother ever. Would you like to practice with three lovely children?"

Beatrice burst out laughing. "That's your blessing."

"More like my penance."

"You're doing just fine, from what your mother tells me."

Darcy found that difficult to believe. She ripped the tissue off a porcelain teacup. Yet another pattern. How many had Beattie bought? "It's not what I want to be doing."

"I know," Beatrice sighed compassionately. "Tell me everything that happened while I was gone."

"What's to tell?" Darcy set the cup on the nearest saucer. Never mind that it didn't match. "I take care of Amelia's children morning and night. I work on the plane while they're in school. Jack barely talks, and when he does it's about nothing personal."

"Have you asked about his family?"

"Of course. But he always turns the topic back to aviation."

"Maybe he's afraid."

"Of what? I would never say anything against them." Darcy picked up another cup-sized bundle.

"Maybe that's not what scares him," Beattie said quietly, smoothing her chintz apron.

"Then what?"

Beattie hesitated long enough for Darcy to know she wasn't sure how to pose her reply. "Does he ever ask you questions?"

Darcy shrugged. "Nothing significant. How Amelia is faring, if the bank is doing well, who owns what business in Pearlman, if I like rutabagas. Ordinary chitchat."

"Nothing significant? Why Darcy, that's as significant as a man can get."

"What?" Darcy dropped the teacup she was unwrapping. Thankfully it bounced on the sofa.

"A man in love wants to know about all the little things in a woman's life."

"In love?" The thought was oddly warming. "You must be mistaken. He won't do anything with me other than work on the plane. He won't even go to a church supper."

"You've asked?"

Darcy dug deep into the box. "I've mentioned them."

"And said you were going?"

"Of course." She pulled the paper off an object that turned out to be yet another teacup. "Worse, I never see him at church."

"He could attend another church. We do have three in town."

"I know, but..." Darcy couldn't shake the worry that he attended no church at all. He reacted so negatively whenever she mentioned her faith.

"Don't make trouble where there isn't any. If you're meant to be together, it'll work out."

Darcy didn't share Beattie's confidence. "We're not as close as we were in Buffalo. Something's changed, but he won't tell me what."

Beatrice paused in her unwrapping. "Are you saying you're in love?"

Darcy felt her color rise. "No. Well, maybe. But how can I find out if he won't talk to me?"

Beattie unconsciously tapped a finger on a box. "That is a problem. Perhaps he isn't interested."

Darcy recalled the moment in the snow the night of Beattie's wedding. He would have kissed her if that car hadn't gone by. "I'm pretty sure he is."

"Is there anyone else?"

"Another woman?" That thought had never occurred to Darcy. The idea made her stomach flip-flop in a horrid way.

"He could be involved in a serious relationship."

Darcy felt sick. Suppose it was true. He hadn't attended a single social function. "I d-don't think so." But she wasn't sure.

Beatrice nodded and went back to unwrapping dishes.

"He would have mentioned her," Darcy said, "if there was someone. At least I think he would have."

"There's only one way to know for certain," said Beatrice, setting another dessert plate on the already tall stack.

"Spy on him?"

"Certainly not! Don't even think such a thing. The only sure way is to ask."

Darcy gagged. "Ask? Just go up to him and ask if he's courting anyone? I suppose you'd also like me to say that I'm wild about him?"

"It wouldn't hurt."

"No, no, no."

"Why not?"

"I don't want to give him the wrong impression."

Beatrice laughed. "What wrong impression? You just told me you might love him."

"But I can't think about marriage until I've made my great flight."

"Marriage? That's a bit of a leap. First you spend time together and get to know each other, and then you decide if you're compatible. In time, you consider marriage."

Darcy concentrated on the army of teacups she'd unwrapped. She knew all that. "But what if you already know?"

"Darcy, are you telling me that he's the one?"

"Maybe." Even that felt so final.

"But you said you don't want to consider marriage." Beattie shook her head. "You can't have it both ways. Oh, Darcy, if only I could convince you how wonderful marriage is. Why, it's liberating to have a man take care of you."

Liberating. Indeed! Darcy turned abruptly and knocked over a half-empty box. She fumbled to collect the spilled contents. "That's not the sort of liberation I want," she said, while stuffing tissue and straw and thankfully unbroken china back into the box. "I mean, it's fine for most women, just not me."

"You make it sound like torture. I assure you, it's wonderful. Blake is so considerate, and we work in concert, like a tandem bicycle. Truly, I feel ten times stronger than ever before. With Blake at my side, I can do anything. *We* can do anything. You and Jack both love to fly. You like the same things. Why not work together?"

As reasonable as that sounded, Darcy knew it wouldn't happen. "Because married men don't let their wives fly."

"Jack might be different."

She shook her head. "He's worse than most. He doesn't think *any* women should fly. He would never let his wife fly. Besides," she paused, weighing if she should reveal what

Burrows had told her. "His mechanic said that Jack's not the marrying type."

Beattie laughed.

"That's hardly funny. Hendrick Simmons happens to feel the same way."

That only made Beattie squeal louder.

"What's so funny?"

"Don't you know?" said Beatrice, hand cupped over her mouth to stifle the spasms.

"Know what?"

"That Hendrick Simmons has been in love with you for years?"

"No he hasn't." But Darcy felt a tad uncomfortable. "We're just friends. You know that. We've been friends since childhood. Besides, I haven't done a thing to encourage him."

"Haven't you?"

Darcy stared, confused. "What do you mean?"

"Isn't he helping with the plane?"

"So?"

"He wouldn't give so much of his time unless he hoped to gain something—your admiration, for instance. He deserves to be treated fairly, Darcy."

She felt like a child caught doing something wrong. But she hadn't. Beatrice was the one who was mistaken. "We're just friends. We've always been friends. He knows I'm not interested in anything more. I've practically said so."

"Good," Beatrice said, handing her another tissue-wrapped bundle. "If you can tell Hendrick, you should have no difficulty telling Jack."

"Tell him what?"

Beatrice unwrapped a fat little porcelain cupid and pantomimed shooting an arrow. "You know what."

Darcy blanched. "I could never."

* * *

Jack cut the fuel to the second motor. It wasn't running right yet. Maybe the cold had something to do with it. The gasoline heater didn't raise the temperature in the barn very much. He should have bought a new engine, instead of trying to reclaim army surplus.

"Too much oil," said Simmons. "I'd better pull the head and check the rings."

"We just did that." Jack swung out of the cockpit, frustrated. Mid-February, and only one engine ran. If they couldn't get the second motor running soon, they'd never be done on time. What he wouldn't give to have Burrows here.

"What's wrong?" asked Darcy from her position at the worktable. She'd been jumpy all day, and it was wearing on Jack's nerves.

"Nothing."

She grabbed a book off the top of a stack that had to be a foot and a half high. "I thought maybe you'd hurt yourself."

"I didn't hurt myself," he snapped. "I'm working on this piece of junk engine. What on earth are all those books for?"

She stood bolt upright, as if offended. He waited for the retort, but oddly enough, she clamped her mouth shut and turned back to the books. "I'll have the supply requisition lists for you soon." Her voice sounded peculiar, like she had a sore throat.

"You feeling all right?"

She jutted that little chin out again. "Perfect."

"Great. Good." He rubbed his hands. "Well then, Mr. Simmons, let's dig into this motor."

Everyone worked in silence for a while. Simmons was right. There was too much oil in the cylinders. Piece by piece, they tore it apart until their hands and overalls were coated with black grease.

"Did you meet anyone new in Buffalo after I left?" Darcy suddenly asked.

"Huh?" He'd been concentrating so hard on the motor that he wasn't prepared for conversation.

"Did you meet anyone new? Like new students."

"All the inquiries were written."

"Oh. Is that all?"

"All of what?" Jack held a lamp over the engine so Simmons could see into the deepest recesses of the cylinders.

"All of the people you met."

"What?"

Darcy had stopped working on the supply list. She watched him, arms crossed and pencil tucked behind her ear. "You never seem to go anywhere or do anything other than work. I thought you might have visited Mr. Burrows or—or someone else."

Jack would never understand the way women's minds worked. "I work. I sleep. My life is routine."

"Oh. I thought if you happened to visit Mr. Burrows, you might have heard some news about the other group interested in the transatlantic attempt. You know, the people with the flying boat."

So that's what this was about. "No word yet."

"Oh."

He squinted to make out her expression. "You sound disappointed."

"Not at all. I just figured you might have heard something." She wiped her forehead. "Well, I guess not."

"That's right."

"Too bad." She went back to her books.

"Could you move the lamp a little more this way?" asked Simmons.

Jack obliged, glad to get back to work.

"So," said Darcy, "is your sister married?"

He glared. "She's in the hospital."

"That doesn't mean she's not married. Of course not every woman wants to marry. Me, for instance." She paused dramatically.

Clearly, that point was for his benefit, but it didn't make him any happier. "Is that so?"

"You either, I hear, but I'm sure you've had female friends."

Why was she asking about old girlfriends? And where had she heard that bit about not marrying? It was true, but he didn't generally reveal the fact until necessary. He was certain he'd never told her. "If you're asking whether I consider you a friend, I do."

"Oh. Thank you." She sounded disappointed.

Jack hazarded a glance. Darcy was leaning over the table, writing something down, looking like she didn't care one bit about their conversation. But her coffee cup was still jiggling, betraying the fact that she'd knocked against the table on a quick turnaround. So, she wasn't as disinterested as she claimed. He went back to working on the motor with smug satisfaction.

"Are any of your female friends beautiful?"

So that was it. She was looking for a compliment. "Don't worry. You're perfectly attractive."

Simmons accidentally cracked him on the knuckle with a wrench. "Sor-ry."

Jack rubbed the sore finger on his overalls.

"That's not what I meant," Darcy said. "I was trying to learn what your friends are like."

"My friends."

"Exactly. You can tell a lot about a man by the friends he chooses, but I'm having a difficult time figuring you out."

Even though she didn't look up, he could tell she was nervous by the number of times she shoved her hair behind her ear. That could mean only one thing.

"Good," he said. "I don't want to be figured out."

"Why not?"

"Takes the mystery out of it, don't you think?"

Simmons slipped again with the wrench. Jack shook his aching hand.

"Maybe I don't like mystery," she said in that wonderfully determined way she had. "Maybe I like to know."

"Maybe you don't always get what you want."

"I see." Instead of playing along with the banter, she frowned and went back to her books.

Now what had he done? Jack searched for a compliment.

"I understand you're doing a fine job taking care of your nieces and nephew."

Her head snapped up, fire in her eye. "Thank you, I suppose."

Oh no. He'd hit a tender nerve. "I meant it as a compliment. Children need love and care and someone to teach them what's right. It's an important job."

Her expression only got tenser.

"Someday I hope to have children," he said. "The next generation. Hope for the future."

"Me, too," said Simmons.

That echo didn't extend to Darcy Shea, widening the gulf between them. She didn't want to marry or have children. A future together was impossible. Fine. It had never been likely anyway. At least now he could stop worrying about her.

Jack Hunter had turned out to be like every other man. Darcy hated when men resorted to the old adage that a woman belonged in the home raising children. Childrearing was important; it just wasn't the only vocation.

What's more, he'd never told her if he had a serious

girlfriend or not. All that grief for nothing. Very well. If Jack Hunter wanted strictly professional, she'd be strictly professional—as long as she flew in the transatlantic attempt.

The next morning she marched to the barn to complete the requisition list. Despite a thawing rain, the workspace was freezing. Jack stood alone on the ladder, working on the left motor.

"Where's Hendrick?" Darcy had never worked at the barn without Simmons near. Given her determination to be professional, it shouldn't have made a difference, but the atmosphere definitely felt different.

"At the garage, trying to get a nick out of the ring." He didn't even look at her.

"I'll have the requisition list for you shortly."

"Good." Again, not even a glance.

Despite every attempt to convince herself that his opinion didn't matter, his coolness toward her hurt. Fine, she'd concentrate on flying. "I hope to resume lessons in the spring. Papa said I could. I remember everything you taught me. The elevators, the rudder, and even how the ailerons work."

"Good." He leveraged his weight against a wrench, and the ladder wobbled.

Darcy raced over to steady it. "I'll hold the ladder."

"No need. I got it." He held up a grimy nut.

"The list is finished."

His eyebrows rose. "Already?" He climbed down the ladder and wiped off his hands before taking the clipboard from her.

Darcy rubbed her hands together to get some warmth in her stiff fingers.

"A ladder is too heavy and completely unnecessary." He crossed it off with a stub of pencil.

"Suppose we land on a glacier?"

"This is a transatlantic attempt, not a polar crossing."

"Oh." She had been thinking in terms of a polar expedition. All the supply lists she'd found had come from the expedition narratives in her father's library. "There are icebergs."

"If I hit an iceberg, I'm dead."

"Don't say that." The thought of Jack splattered on the ice sickened her. "All right. No ladder."

He skimmed down the list. "We don't need a hatchet."

Darcy had already given up the ladder. She wouldn't budge on the hatchet. "It's for safety, in case of an emergency. You can use it to make a shelter or chop firewood."

"The idea is not to crash. Besides, there aren't many forests in the ocean."

"It's just a little hatchet," she insisted.

"It weighs three pounds that we don't have."

Darcy stubbornly clung to her point, and in the end Jack agreed to keep the hatchet if she'd drop another item of equal weight.

"The rest looks satisfactory." He handed the list back to her. "Get the best price. Money is running low."

That wasn't good news, with the second motor still not working. In addition to supplies, they'd have to transport the plane and hire crew.

"Who is going to be your navigator?" she blurted out as he climbed back up the ladder. "Me, I hope."

He glanced up from the motor. "Very funny."

She climbed the other ladder. "Why? I could do it."

"You know nothing about navigation, for one."

"I can use a sextant."

He cocked one eyebrow. "You're joking."

"My father taught me when I was young."

He slid down the ladder. "There's more to navigating an aeroplane than using a sextant."

"I know—" she followed him down "—but you could show me."

"Give me one good reason why."

She knew better than to mention the transatlantic attempt. He'd shown no sign of relenting on that point. "Doesn't every pilot need to know navigation? If I'm going to fly someday, I'll have to learn."

The old grin reappeared. "Someday, eh? You have a point. As long as you realize this is just instruction."

"When can we begin?"

"We have some time now." He led her to his personal trunks. "What do you know about aeronautical navigation?"

Darcy did not want to disappoint him. She also didn't want to get it wrong. "The way I figure it, a sighting has to correct for altitude, and you'd need a true horizon. Another difficulty has to be measuring drift. I haven't seen an instrument for that in any of the planes."

"You're right. Those are big challenges in aerial navigation." He ran a finger along the curve of his lips. "It's what makes an experienced navigator such a vital part of the crew."

"Especially over water, where there are so few landmarks, and on a transatlantic crossing, where you must fly in darkness."

His expression darkened, and she instantly regretted mentioning the transatlantic attempt.

"That is," she added hastily, "where your navigator will face the toughest challenge, whoever he is." It hurt to concede the role to someone else, even for a moment.

He nodded, visibly relieved. "That's the problem that needs to be solved before we can have viable commercial aviation."

"That's why the transatlantic attempt is so important."

"It will connect the continents in hours instead of days. Just think, Columbus took months to cross the Atlantic. Now ocean liners can make it in a week. A plane can cross in less than twenty-four hours. It will change the world."

Jack's eyes had taken on that glow. He loved aeroplanes, loved everything about aviation, and she loved hearing him talk about it.

"Teach me what you know," she breathed. "I want to learn."

In seconds he dragged a sextant box from his trunk. As soon as he removed the instrument from its case, Darcy saw the difference between his and the one her father owned.

"The bubble level is used for the horizon?" she asked, and Jack launched into a detailed explanation.

When she didn't understand a point, he carefully explained again. Sometimes he drew the concept on paper. Sometimes he demonstrated by having her peer through the lens while he stood behind, guiding every move.

His touch conveyed strength. The vibration of his voice flowed down the nape of her neck to the small of her back. It embraced her, steady and solid. This was a man who would guard and cherish those he loved.

She settled back on her heels and accidentally brushed against his shoulder. The instant charge made her pull away, embarrassed. "Sorry, I lost my balance."

He lowered the sextant. "I've probably overtaxed you enough for one day. We can continue tomorrow."

"I'm fine. Let's go on."

He moved back into position, and she discovered he had a little nick on his thumb that she'd never noticed before. The skin in the curve between thumb and forefinger stretched pink, and he kept his nails neatly trimmed. A man who took such care with small details would not neglect the large.

This was getting dangerously close to intimacy, and yet she trusted him. Jack Hunter would not take advantage, even when they were alone. He'd had opportunity before and had broken away. He would never hurt her.

"You hold the instrument like this." But his hand trembled,

and he set the sextant on the worktable. "I must be getting tired."

"I'm sorry," she whispered, unwilling to break their closeness.

For a terrible moment, Jack didn't speak. His eyes had softened. The little lines around the corners of his mouth disappeared. His breathing deepened.

He was going to kiss her.

Darcy's pulse quickened. She tilted her face slightly and partially closed her eyes. This time a car couldn't interrupt them.

Instead of a kiss, he dabbed at her face with a rag.

"What are you doing?"

"Stand still. You have some grease on your forehead." His touch was gentle. The folds of rag grazed her nose and lips, and she could smell the solvent. It wasn't romantic, but the spark still arced between them.

"There," Jack said, "it's gone now." He dropped the handkerchief but not his gaze.

He looked at her far longer than respectable. No grin. No smile. Serious. An uncontrollable fluttering started deep inside her.

"Thank you," she whispered.

He ran a thumb down her jaw to her chin. She leaned slightly, letting him tilt it up. Every nerve ending tingled. His touch was gentle, caring. His eyes had turned a darker, deeper blue. He brushed the corner of her mouth.

"A crumb." His voice was raspy.

She closed her eyes, feeling the connection between them tighten, like a stay between two wings. They ran parallel, yet together, equally important. His breath whispered across her lips. She reveled in his touch.

Crash. Metal hit metal.

"Oh!" Darcy shot into the air, bumping Jack's nose.

"Sorry."

He held the rag to his nose, but she didn't see blood. In moments she located the source of the noise. Simmons. A pile of tools at his feet.

"Uh, sorry." Simmons held up his wooden toolbox. "The handle come loose. Just wanted to let you know I got the ring fixed. Oh, and another thing…" He dug into his pocket. "Cora sent over a wire. Said it come in an hour ago."

"A wire?" In a flash Jack grabbed the cable and whipped it open. He read it. Twice.

"What's wrong?" Darcy tried not to worry. "Not bad news, I hope."

Jack scanned the message again. "It's Burrows. The navy is backing the transatlantic project with the NC flying boats."

Her spirits fell the rest of the way. "What does that mean?"

He didn't answer at once. That told her all she needed to know. He was going to leave Pearlman and join Burrows.

He ran his hand through his hair. "If I read it right, even though the navy is attempting the crossing, they've sworn off the prize."

Darcy could hardly believe her luck.

Jack tucked the cable in his pocket. "I need to place a long-distance telephone call."

"But why, if they're not going for the prize?"

He didn't answer.

Her panic grew. "You are still going for the prize, right?"

Jack extinguished the heater. "Let's call it a day. We'll tackle the motor tomorrow."

"But—" He hadn't answered her question. Were they still making the transatlantic attempt?

"No buts."

She could tell by the set of Jack's jaw that he wasn't going to answer her. That meant just one thing. He was leaving. He intended to join Burrows in New York. That's why he had to place the call.

"I—I," she stammered, but she had no power to stop him.

Escape when I am still leaving . . . and it was Yvonne's
Darcy had said, just a while ago, that J . . . Shea, why . . . he'd
made the call."

". . . it's coming . . ." she felt, and he pulled it straight. . .

Chapter Ten

She wasn't proud of it, but Darcy followed Jack. He went directly to the post office, where he attempted to place a call and ended up sending a wire.

"Where did he send it?" she asked Cora after the office had emptied.

"Humph." The postmistress and telephone operator continued to sort letters into the little wooden cubbyholes that corresponded to each Pearlman family and business. "That's confidential."

"That's never stopped you before."

"Well I never." Cora tossed her short ringlets. "Take that back, Darcy Shea."

Darcy wouldn't take it back, because it was true. Unfortunately, her words had ruined any chance of getting information from Cora.

She gnawed her lip. How could she find out if he was leaving? A train whistle sounded the afternoon departure. Of course. Dennis Allington, the train depot manager, would know if Jack had purchased a ticket.

The walk across town took twenty minutes. She had to detour around muddy puddles and avoid the dwindling snow banks that had softened so much in the rain that her feet would have sunk clear to the bottom.

No one lingered at the train depot, and Allington had nothing to offer. "Nope. Haven't seen 'im since the last shipment come in Tuesday."

Darcy prayed that meant he was staying, but she wouldn't know for sure until morning. The ringing of the school bell brought an end to her free time. She spent the rest of the day cooking and cleaning and putting her nieces and nephew to bed.

After a dreadful night's sleep and a painfully slow morning getting the children to school, Darcy raced to the barn. Had he gone? Would she find the barn empty? She threw open the door and stepped into the dim light. Simmons stood on a ladder propped beside the troublesome motor, and Jack hung on another.

"Jack. You're here," she gushed.

"Shea. You're late."

She laughed from pure relief. "You didn't leave."

"Where'd you expect me to go?"

"The telephone call you were going to make yesterday." She pulled off her gloves. "I thought maybe you were going to New York."

"Not at present." Jack refocused on Simmons. "What do you think? Shall we give it a try?"

"What do you mean, 'at present'?" Darcy demanded, but he either didn't hear her or didn't want to answer.

When Simmons agreed that they should try the motor, Jack swung into the cockpit. The engine started, revved, decelerated and ran smoothly for several minutes before Jack shut it off.

"Is it fixed?" Darcy asked as the propeller slowed.

A grin crept across Jack's face, and then he nodded and whooped. "Open the doors, I'm taking her up."

Darcy grabbed her goggles from the worktable.

"Whoa. Not this time," said Jack. "Let me test her out, make sure everything is running properly."

"But don't you need someone up front for weight?"

He winked. "This girl's not tender. Did you get those calculations done yesterday? I'll check them when I get back."

Her disappointment ebbed with the roar of the engines. Jack had stayed to fix the motor. That meant he was still attempting the transatlantic crossing. Soon she'd be in the air again. Then she could make history.

Darcy covered her ears as Jack coasted down Baker's field. The wheels bounced on the half-frozen turf. The plane rose gently: five feet; ten feet; and then it curved upward. Oh, he could fly: tight spirals and huge arcs across the blue sky, but Darcy's favorite was the slow, simple turn, curving elegantly like a hawk on an updraft.

How she longed to be at the controls or even riding in the other cockpit. Instead, she finished the navigation calculations. He would need a navigator, and she intended to fill that position.

Jack brought the plane down fifteen minutes later, after an effortless flight. Darcy met him at planeside, calculations in hand. "Now that the plane is running, can we resume lessons?"

"Not yet." He headed straight for Simmons. "I thought I smelled a little extra oil in the exhaust."

Darcy waited until Simmons crawled up to check the motor.

"I thought it ran brilliantly," she said as Jack wiped lubricating oil off his face. "You did some terrific maneuvers."

"Pretty good." He tossed the rag aside. "Let's look over those calculations now."

Darcy waited an eternity while he verified her mathematics.

He pointed to the paper. "This figure is off by one degree."

"It's just one."

"One degree at the beginning of a long-distance flight translates to miles off target at the end. You could start out aiming for France and end up over water and out of fuel. Do it again and don't rush this time."

The blunt criticism stung, but Darcy bit back her temper. "Once I get it correct, may I have a flight lesson?"

"That will depend on the plane."

That, or any of a dozen other excuses.

Over the following weeks, Jack used them all. Weather, engine, wind, field conditions. Some problem always kept her grounded and perfecting her navigation skills on paper.

Still, when Jack guided Darcy's hand on the sextant, her heart beat a little harder. When he directed her gaze to the proper star, she barely breathed. Her frustrations vanished under his touch.

"This morning looks good," he said early in March, after most of the snow had melted and the nighttime frost had firmed the ground.

"Good for what?"

"Flying, what else?"

The rush of excitement made her miss part of his instructions.

"...that means we need to go through the controls first. This plane uses a wheel to control both the elevator and ailerons."

Darcy concentrated as he showed her how the controls worked in tandem. Once again their hands worked side-by-side as he demonstrated the movement of the rudder and ailerons. She thrilled to feel him moving the wheel, jumped when the rudder bar shifted, and longed for the side-by-side cockpit they'd shared in Buffalo.

"If you make a wrong move I can correct it," he said, "but the engines are too loud for us to talk. You must follow my preflight instructions exactly. No deviation. I only want you doing turns. No elevator. That means no moving the wheel forward or back, understand?"

She shook off a twinge of irritation. She could do more. She'd already done ascents and descents, but now was not the time to point that out. Patience. "Yes, of course."

"It's easy to promise on the ground, but everything changes when you're in the air. Wind currents can grab a plane and throw it up or down. I'll handle any sudden shifts. I need you to trust me. Do not attempt to make corrections yourself."

"Of course. I wouldn't dream of it," she said, but the man was being ridiculously overcautious. "Nothing is going to happen."

"You don't know that. I've seen students clutch onto the wheel like a life preserver or lose their nerve. I've seen them send the plane into a spin or sideslip. Some have gotten badly injured or died. If you need to catch your balance, grab the sides of the cockpit, not the wheel."

"Yes, sir." She saluted him.

"This is serious, Darcy."

She tried to be serious, but she wanted to giggle. He was acting just like her father. "I know. I promise." She reached for her goggles.

He cleared his throat and crossed his arms.

"What is it?"

"You're forgetting something." He waited until she figured it out.

"The preflight check? I thought maybe you'd already done it."

"Never get in a plane you haven't personally checked," he said. "Make it part of your routine, like washing your face in the morning."

"Or saying grace before meals."

He scowled. "Right."

How she wished Jack didn't put up that wall every time she mentioned God or church. It created a sore spot that refused to heal.

After checking the plane thoroughly, they took off. Darcy had no time to revel in the flow of air over her face or the scene below. She followed Jack's instructions to the letter. One wrong move, and he'd stop the lessons. It took tremendous mental effort not to touch the wheel during the ascent. For the descent, she sat on her hands. No air currents buffeted the aeroplane, and they landed smoothly.

She swiveled to face him the moment he cut the engines. "How did I do?"

"Good turns," he said. "Next time we'll increase the degree of your banks."

Next time. She had done well enough to fly again. "This afternoon?"

The skies were clear and the winds light.

"We'll see."

His vague reply raised the old alarm. The last time he refused to fly in perfect weather, he'd gone to the hospital. Though she knew his reasons for that, she still scanned his face for signs of fatigue or illness. He looked the same as always, though perhaps a bit more worried.

"Is everything all right?" She recalled the wire he'd sent and wondered if this had anything to do with that. "You can confide in me. I won't tell a soul."

"I'm fine." The gruff answer was all she'd get. Jack Hunter kept the deepest part of himself quite private.

Darcy progressed through the lessons with remarkable speed. Jack had to admit she exhibited the same ability as his better students, except for her landings. She still came in too fast and too steep. If he had time, he'd spend hours with her in practice, but he had to get started on the load and fuel tests.

The tests. Jack groaned and fingered the cable in his pocket. He'd been wondering when Pohlman would show, but he hadn't expected this. What was the man thinking? Time was short, and the competition was further along. Jack had to come up with a new plan soon.

By the time he arrived at the barn, Darcy and the kid were already at work. While Simmons checked the engines, Jack spread out the Chicago newspaper on the worktable.

Darcy looked over his shoulder. "Where did you get a Chicago paper?"

"Reporters," he said without looking up.

"Chicago reporters here? Whatever for?"

"Why do you think? Uh-oh." A small headline grabbed his attention.

"What is it?"

"Hawker's bringing the *Atlantic*."

"You knew there'd be competition," she said in a sympathetic tone.

Jack was in no mood for female empathy. He had a flight to prepare and a huge problem to overcome. "That makes a solid handful. St. John's will be crowded."

"St. John's is the departure point?"

He nodded.

"Why Newfoundland and not New York?"

Hadn't she heard a thing he'd been saying the past two

months? "Everyone leaves from Newfoundland." He pointed to the map he'd tacked to the wall. "Here's Newfoundland and here's England. See how much less distance it is than flying from New York? Of course the North Atlantic course brings its own hazards. Fog, icing, storms. And there's nothing in between except ice-cold water. Ditching means almost certain death."

"From the cold?"

"And the fact you're flying outside the shipping lanes." Jack emphasized the dangers. Maybe he could frighten Darcy out of her crazy ideas. "Go down, and no one will find you until you're frozen stiff."

Darcy paled. "Like the *Titanic*."

"Trust me, the *Titanic* had a hundred-fold better chance of making it safely across."

"But the plane won't go down."

She sounded a little worried, so he piled on the risks. "It very well could. This flight has a less-than-ten-percent chance of success. Odds are I'll have to ditch before reaching land."

She gasped. "But why would so many try it if it's that dangerous?"

"Fame. Money. Aside from the prize, the winner will make tens of thousands, maybe hundreds of thousands, on speaking engagements."

"Is that why you're doing it?"

Jack hadn't anticipated that question. It cut too personal for him to answer. "*You* want to do it. What's *your* reason?"

"To prove a woman can do anything a man can do." She jutted that cute little chin out again, and he was tempted to tweak it.

Instead he asked, "Is that worth dying for?"

"Of course." Bold, confident and without hesitation. That was Darcy.

Such conviction and drive came from deep within, from a cause even she might not recognize, something so important she'd give up the best of life to gain it. "Don't you want more? A family, a home?"

She hesitated just long enough for Jack to know he'd struck truth. "That can come later."

"Unless there is no later."

She pressed her lips into a tight little smile. After two months working together, he knew that look. She thought she held the upper hand. "I don't plan to die."

He laughed, glad of her answer. It would make telling her she wasn't going much easier. "Good, because neither do I. If you haven't put a raft and flares on the requisition list, do so." Of course he might not be able to take them due to the already burgeoning weight.

"I'll order them tomorrow."

"Good girl." He chucked her under her chin. "I can always count on you."

Pop! The bright flash made him blink. Three reporters circled round, notepads in hand.

"Jack Hunter?" said the reporter in the gray wool duster, flipping open his pad. "This the plane you're taking on the transatlantic crossing? Kind of small, isn't it?"

Jack bristled. "*The Kensington Express* has twin motors, two hundred horsepower each, one more than Hawker's *Atlantic*."

They all scratched away on their pads. The mustached reporter asked, "Does Hawker have an insurmountable jump on you?"

"No such thing as insurmountable." Jack chuckled. He was beginning to sound like Darcy.

"She your girlfriend?" The first reporter nodded to Darcy with a snicker.

Jack's gut twisted. He did not want Darcy's picture spread

across the newspapers. He could imagine what the articles would say. They'd point out the impropriety, comment on her wearing overalls instead of a skirt, and insinuate she was somehow less than moral. Darcy Shea was the most moral and honest woman Jack had ever met.

"Miss Shea has been instrumental in getting this flight underway." He stepped in front of her to prevent additional photographs. "Without her assistance, I wouldn't be making this attempt."

"Will she be flying with you?"

"Of course," said Darcy, popping out from behind him.

"No," Jack said at nearly the same time. He stepped back in front of her. "Dwight Pohlman will fly as navigator. Miss Shea's not certified. *The Daily Mail* requires all entrants to have an IAF certificate." He heard her gasp. He had not wanted her to learn about Pohlman this way. "Miss Shea has supported this effort through her groundwork. It's impossible to list all her contributions."

"She's an investor then," the reporter prodded.

Darcy practically quivered with rage, yet she kept her voice steady. "I'm a partner and journalist, whose stories are on exclusive to *The Pearlman Prognosticator.*"

Jack had never been prouder of her. She could stand up to anyone.

"You can't have an exclusive on news," sneered the reporter.

"If the lady says she has an exclusive, she has an exclusive," Jack said fiercely. "If you take issue, I suggest you contact the paper's editor, Mr. Devlin."

Her anger dissolved into the most dazzling smile, and Jack nearly forgot what he was doing.

"Mr. Hunter, how long do you expect the attempt to take?" From the look on the reporter's face, he'd asked the question more than once.

Jack answered their questions, but as the interview progressed, Darcy drifted off, the hurt back in her eyes. She acted as though he'd betrayed her, but he'd never agreed to let her fly. Yes, he should have told her Pohlman was going to be navigator, but he'd been afraid of losing her.

"I had to hire someone with experience," he said to Darcy after the reporters left.

She stood silent, lip quivering, and that shook him even more. What had he done?

He struggled to right the situation. "Pohlman is certified."

"I could get my certification." She angrily wiped away a tear. "If you'd just give me more flight time."

Jack inwardly groaned. He didn't want her to cry. He hated tears.

"I'm sorry, but Dwight Pohlman is better qualified."

She started to protest, but he cut her off.

"He has ten years' experience. He's taught as many students as I have, and he's an expert in navigation."

She choked back a retort, but he could tell she wasn't pleased. At least she wasn't crying.

"I'm sorry, but I have to go with experience. You do want me to return alive, right?"

She stood dead still for a full minute before barely nodding.

"I'm glad you care if I live or not."

His joke fell flat. She wouldn't look him in the eyes. She wouldn't even turn her head toward him. Her hurt was palpable, and Jack couldn't stand it. He had to lift her spirits somehow.

The test flights. Dare he? Those flights were still risky. Many a test pilot had died in a faulty machine. Still, no one knew this plane better than he. No one was more cautious or careful. He could practically ensure her safety by eliminating weather and mechanical variables. It would put him behind, but it could be done.

He took a deep breath and plunged in. "I need your help with the test flights."

She whipped around. "You do?"

"Pohlman can't make it here until April. Before then, we need to run the load and fuel tests. If the weather stays fair, we also need to get in a distance test. This is important, Darcy. Without these tests, the flight will not succeed. Believe me, you're one hundred percent a part of this."

With a quick little sob, she flung her arms around him, sending his heart into a tailspin.

"Thank you," she whispered against his shoulder. It was better than nothing. It kept her in the cockpit, and anything could happen before April. She didn't wish Mr. Pohlman ill, but a travel delay would be fine. She might make that flight yet.

He smoothed a stray strand of her hair, sending a jolt through her. She'd never understand that man. Hot and cold.

"Plane's ready, Mr. Hunter," said Simmons.

Hendrick. He'd been there the whole time.

Darcy jerked away and straightened her coat.

Jack grinned, like he'd made some conquest. "Ready?"

"Now?"

"You do want to help with the test flights, right?"

"Yes. Absolutely. I'll be right there." She scrambled to get her goggles while Jack took the plane out of the barn.

The man both frustrated and excited her, one minute saying no and the next changing his mind in the most unexpected way. She was still angry he hadn't told her about Pohlman, but she had a few weeks to prove herself the better navigator, get her certification, and convince Jack to let her fly the transatlantic attempt.

She waited beside the barn until Jack stopped the plane. The coldness of the ground seeped through the soles of her boots. Spring showed no sign of arriving early. The dead, brown grass poked its spindly stalks to the bright sky.

"Sorry," said Simmons, walking over to stand beside her.

"For what?"

He shuffled his feet. "It won't work."

"Sure it will. The plane's running great."

"Not the plane," he said. "With him."

Darcy felt a twinge of discomfort. Could Beattie have been right? No, not possible. She and Hendrick were chums. They'd always been chums. He couldn't possibly think she felt something more. Yet he was acting jealous of Jack.

Simmons poked at the ground with his boot. "He's not the only one. I—I would...you know."

The words ripped through her. Poor Hendrick. How much had it cost him to tell her how he felt? She should have seen it. She should have listened to Beattie and set things straight months ago. She had been unfair to him. "I'm sorry, Hendrick."

"Don't say it," he said. "Some things a man don't want to hear, even if he already knows. Just, well, if things ever change, I'm not going nowhere."

Darcy couldn't look at him. She'd known Hendrick Simmons all her life. They'd played together as kids, gone to school together. She never meant to hurt him. "I'm sorry."

He cleared his throat. "Yep, well, I should get back to the garage." Without another word, he got on his motorbike and left.

Darcy walked to the plane, her feelings a jumble. Poor Hendrick had seen her hug Jack. He probably hoped for a split, but she couldn't help how she felt. She loved Jack.

Concentrate. She had to forget her feelings and operate

objectively. Flying was serious stuff, especially test flights. She couldn't risk a mistake.

The motors sounded smooth, and she didn't smell the heavy, burnt-oil exhaust anymore. The skies stretched wide above, painted with wispy high clouds that cut down the glare. The field was still a bit sloppy, but Darcy had seen Jack bring the plane down in worse. Everything lined up for a perfect flight, if she could keep her head.

"We're flying empty so we can measure fuel consumption at light load," Jack said as he helped her into the forward cockpit. "I want you to note any unexpected weather conditions and track the altitude and speed every sixty seconds. Got your watch?"

She nodded and belted in before attaching her watch to the clipboard. Every minute. "Including the ascent and descent?" she asked as Jack settled in behind her.

But the motors were too loud for him to hear. She'd take the readings. More couldn't hurt.

Within moments, the plane leapt ahead and they bounced down the field. The takeoff went as smoothly as was possible from the muddy field. Darcy watched the instruments and the time, making sixty-second notations on the log sheet. Once the plane gained an altitude of three thousand feet, Jack flew straight and level for ten minutes, turned and flew back.

The flight had gone so quickly.

Darcy watched as they circled round and lined up for the landing. Funny, the pine boughs were waving. A breeze must have come up. She made a note on the log.

She watched the wheel move and tried to anticipate what Jack would do next. He hadn't been pleased with her landings, and now she saw why. He eased into them at a lower altitude and much slower speed. She had come in too fast.

They neared the treetops then dropped a bit lower, just clearing the branches. She wouldn't have cut the descent that close. Suppose they clipped a limb? Julia Clark, "the Daring Bird Girl," had died when her plane hit a tree. First American woman to die in a plane crash. Darcy held her breath until they'd safely passed the trees.

They skimmed the field, passing a few snow patches and last year's tangled weeds. Soon they'd touch down and bounce through the ruts to the barn. If she had her way, they'd grade the field come spring.

Suddenly the plane shot up and rolled wildly to the right.

Her stomach jumped into her throat. She grabbed the wheel. Her feet hit the rudder bar. The trees. The plane was heading straight for a stand of aspen.

She braced against the wheel.

Jack turned sharply left.

Her feet flew off the rudder bar.

The right wing slanted forty degrees up. The left wing dipped. He wasn't going to pull out in time. The barn. The silos. The trees. Everything was coming at them too quickly.

Thud. The left wing hit the ground. With a horrible rending sound, the wing's bracing crumpled and the fabric tore. In seconds the machine came to a crashing halt and twisted forward, throwing Darcy against the seat belt and whipping her head toward the leading edge of the cockpit.

Chapter Eleven

Jack sat stunned for a full minute as the plane shuddered in its upended position and then dropped back to its wheels. The remnants of the left wing hung to the fuselage by wires. The left motor, still in its nacelle, had broken off the wing and lay on the ground.

He must be all right. Nothing hurt. No sharp pains. No blood anywhere.

"Darcy?"

What had happened? An updraft—but he'd handled those before. This time the wheel had jammed. He'd barely been able to move it, then it broke loose and he overcorrected.

"Darcy?" She was still slumped forward. Still hadn't moved. A cry tore out of him as he jumped forward, only to be yanked back by the seat belt. He fumbled, desperate to get it off. "Darcy, can you hear me?"

She didn't move.

He threw off the belt and scrambled forward. "Darcy?" He shook her by the shoulder.

"Jack." She sounded groggy.

The sharp tang of gasoline hit his nostrils. No time. He had to get her out now.

He pushed aside the splintered frame of the upper wing

and stood on the precariously slanted lower wing. He brushed the hair from her forehead. Still warm, thank God.

"Can you move? I need to get you out of here."

She mumbled something incoherent.

No time to think. He had to act. He undid her safety belt and her head lolled to the side. Blood ran down her forehead. He pressed his handkerchief against it to slow the flow. "Can you move your legs?"

"Yes."

Thank God. "Can you lift yourself up?"

"Mmm-hmm." But she didn't move.

Gasoline dripped just outside the cockpit. The fumes could ignite at any moment. No time to waste. He had to get her out now.

Jack wiggled forward to get the best leverage, and lifted. She was surprisingly light, a sprig of a girl for all her toughness. He held her close, inhaled the violet scent. Her head curled against his shoulder.

"Jack, Jack," she murmured, eyes closed.

"I'm here. I have you. You're safe."

He skidded down the wing to the ground, holding her tightly.

"I can walk," she protested.

"No." No time. He ran. Had to get help. Had to find a doctor.

"Jack," she said a little more clearly. "Stop running."

People streamed across the field, on foot and in motorcars. One car halted beside him, the doors flew open and three people hopped out.

Jack kept running.

Someone blocked him to a halt. Blake. "Hold on, sport."

"Doctor," Jack gasped, winded.

"We've got one right here."

"Let me look at her," said a panting, doughy-faced man.

Jack recognized him as the man who'd danced with Darcy at her friend's wedding.

"I need a doctor." Jack pushed past the man. Darcy's head banged against his chest, and she gripped his shirt tightly. She clung to him, yet he was the one who'd done this to her. He should never have let her fly. He should never have taken her up in the plane. He should have forced her to stay on the ground.

"Jack." A woman's voice. "We're here to help."

"Beattie," said Darcy.

Jack spun, the people's faces unfamiliar masks.

"Doctor," he muttered. "Need a doctor."

"We have a doctor." Blake Kensington routed him to the rear door of his motorcar. "Set her on the seat."

"No here, on the ground," commanded the doughy man with surprising authority. "The light's better. I'm a doctor. Please let me help."

Jack dropped to his knees and set Darcy on the coat someone spread on the damp earth.

She hung onto him. "Don't go."

"It's all right. I won't leave." He removed her arms from around his neck but held tight to her hand.

Beatrice covered her with a blanket. The doctor knelt on the other side.

"I'm all right," said Darcy, but she didn't sound all right.

"I need some cloth to stanch the blood," the doctor said.

Somewhere, he'd lost the handkerchief. Jack dropped Darcy's hand to rip off his shirt.

"Jack." She reached for him.

"I'm right here."

"Clean cloth, if possible," added the doctor when he saw Jack peeling off his shirt.

Someone shoved a wad of white cloth into the doctor's hand.

"Beatrice, will you hold this firmly to her head? We'll want to slow the bleeding and then get her home."

Home. Not to any place he could take her, but to her parents' house. Though Jack held her hand, he could not heal her. He couldn't even give her a piece of clean cloth to stop the bleeding.

They lifted her into the motorcar, and he had to let go.

She called to him, but there was no room in the car. "I'll follow."

"Meet you at the Sheas' house," said Blake, hopping into the driver's seat. "Know where that is?"

Before Jack could answer, the car drove away, leaving him standing in the field. Darcy had to be all right. She had to be. He looked to the cold, infinite heavens, and for a moment considered praying, but only for a moment. God hadn't heard him then; He wouldn't now. Jack shivered and began the long walk to her father's house.

Jack. Where had he gone? One moment he held her hand. The next he'd vanished. Events muddled in Darcy's head, which throbbed. She tried to open her eyes, but the pain made her close them at once.

"Don't move, dear." Mum. Soft and comforting.

"You're going to be fine." That was Beatrice.

"Where is he?" She smelled and felt the familiar sheets and quilt of home, but how did she get in her bed? The last thing she remembered was letting go of Jack's hand.

"Just rest," Beatrice said. "You've had a bad spill."

Why wouldn't they answer her? "Is he hurt?"

Darcy felt her hand being squeezed.

"You took a nasty blow to the head," Mum said, "but Dr. Carrman says you'll be fine."

"George is here?" Why? She forced her eyes open despite the pain and tried to sit up.

"No, no, dear, lie still." Mum gently pressed her back against the pillows.

"Do you want something to drink?" Beatrice asked.

Darcy's mouth did feel dry, but what she'd really like was something to stop the pain. "A powder," she croaked.

"I'll ask George." Beattie glided out of the room.

Since when did she have to ask George's permission? And why did Mum look so worried?

"Is he...dead?" The word stuck to her tongue.

Mum dabbed at her eyes with a handkerchief. "I'm just so grateful you weren't killed by that horrible machine."

The plane. She relived each moment in seconds: soaring high in the sky, swooping down on the field, and then the lurch. The wild turn right and then left. The trees. She'd held on tight. To the wheel. Oh no, just what Jack told her not to do. What if? Impossible. She'd let go.

"How bad is it?" she asked tentatively.

"You'll recover," said Mum.

That wasn't what she wanted to know. "The plane."

Mum placed a cool cloth on her forehead. "Mr. Hunter got you out of the wreck."

Then he must be all right. Relief brought tears. Jack was alive. But the plane. And the transatlantic attempt. "Can it be fixed?"

"I wouldn't know, but I must say Mr. Hunter was quite the hero the way he rescued you." A little smile danced across Mum's face. "Blake said the plane might have caught fire."

Darcy gasped. "It burned?"

"No, no dear, but it might have. Mr. Hunter disregarded his life to save yours. Perhaps I misjudged him."

Mum's turnabout didn't make Darcy feel any better. If the plane was badly wrecked, the transatlantic flight might be over.

"Where is he?" Darcy asked. Best to get this over now,

when the pain in her head might drown out the pain in her heart.

"Mr. Hunter? Downstairs, I believe. Did you wish to see him?"

Darcy nodded and closed her eyes. Perhaps he wouldn't condemn an injured woman.

"I'll try to drag him away from those pesky reporters."

Darcy groaned. They'd not only failed, they'd done so in front of the Chicago press. It would be all over the newspapers. Jack would never let her fly again.

"How are you feeling?" said a masculine voice. George Carrman, not Jack.

Darcy swallowed her disappointment. "My head hurts. I'd like a powder."

George held some fingers in front of her face. "How many do you see?"

"Four."

"And who is President of the United States?"

"Stop this," she snapped. "I'm fine, other than a headache."

"Then you can answer the question."

"Woodrow Wilson, though if women had the vote it might have turned out differently."

George chuckled and turned to Mum. "She needs to rest, but otherwise sounds fine. You may give her aspirin, but I'd avoid laudanum."

Mum handed Darcy the powder she'd requested. She poured the bitter grains into her parched mouth and reached for the glass of water.

"Darcy?" Jack stood in the doorway, cap in hand. His hair stuck out at odd angles, and his trousers were covered in mud. He looked nothing like the dashing hero who'd captured her heart the first time she saw him, but somehow she loved this Jack even more.

Darcy let the aspirin melt on her tongue.

So many times she'd wished to see him in her house, but not this way, not after a catastrophe.

"We can fix it," she croaked, tears forming. "There's still time. Don't lose hope."

His jaw tensed. "Just get well. Rest. That's more important." He replaced his cap. "Good night, Darcy."

Why did it sound more like goodbye?

Jack followed Carrman downstairs. The doctor had stood guard at Darcy's bedside, preventing Jack from telling her that he was sorry and would never hurt her again.

Darcy's father waited in the parlor. He glared at Jack before addressing Carrman. "How is she?"

"It will take time."

Jack needed his news straight up, not in couched language meant to soothe. "She'll recover fully?"

"Most likely." Carrman spoke to Darcy's father, not Jack.

Apparently everyone blamed him. Rightly.

"She appears to have suffered no serious effects," Carrman continued, "but a blow to the head is tricky. In rare instances there's a hemorrhage in the brain that cannot be detected. The next few days will tell. To be safe, keep her in bed and alert as much as possible. I've already given your wife instructions for her care." He shook Mr. Shea's hand. "I'm optimistic she will be herself within the week."

Darcy's father heaved a relieved sigh. "Thank God. May I see her?"

"Yes, of course." Carrman packed his medical bag.

Mr. Shea leveled his attention on Jack. "Mr. Hunter, tell me why my daughter was in your plane."

Jack stared. She hadn't told him? But she said her father had given her permission. "She said—" He couldn't betray her. "That is, I asked her to take readings. It was a short flight, and the weather was good. There shouldn't have been a problem, but a sudden updraft caught the wings too close to the ground."

Shea's stony expression didn't ease.

"It's my fault, sir."

Shea nodded curtly. "It won't happen again."

No, it wouldn't, but not because of anything her father might say. Darcy had nearly died. Never again. Jack Hunter would never again teach a woman to fly.

After two days of doctor-ordered bed rest, Darcy welcomed company. She didn't welcome Beattie's news.

"He's gone?" Darcy stared at her friend, mouth agape. "Are you sure?"

Beattie nodded. "I'm afraid so. Blake said he went home to arrange shipment of the plane. They towed it into the barn, and then he left."

Darcy threw off the quilt. "But why? He could have waited. He could have seen me, talked to me. Why did he sneak off? It's only March. We have time. We can fix the plane and still make the attempt." Beatrice tried to pull the covers back over Darcy, but she was having none of it. "Has anyone surveyed the plane? We need to order supplies."

"Didn't you hear me? Jack called off the flight. He's going to have the plane shipped to Buffalo."

"Did Blake agree to this?" The project was funded with Kensington money, after all.

"With no pilot, he didn't have much choice. Jack said he'd repay our investment."

"How?" As far as she knew, Jack lacked money.

Beattie's brow puckered. "He said something about exhibiting."

"Flying exhibitions?" That meant Jack would go south, perhaps to Texas. Darcy hopped out of bed and threw on her robe. "Then we need to hurry. We'll fix the plane before Jack comes back. First, we need to order the materials. There's not much time." She rummaged in her desk for paper and a pencil. "We'll need wood, preferably spruce, enough good, strong linen cloth to cover the wings. Doping compound, paint, wire, screws, of course. Do you know if the metal nacelle mount was damaged?"

Beattie stared. "Darcy?"

"Never mind. I'll check. We need to place the order right away." She pressed the flat end of the pencil against her chin. "It could take a week to get everything."

"Darcy." Beattie scolded, hands folded atop her lilac satin bag like she was sitting in church. "Slow down. You don't know if Jack will come back."

Darcy locked eyes with her friend. "Of course he will, if I have to go to Buffalo and drag him back by the ears."

"Darcy! You can't force a man to do something he doesn't want to do."

"I'm not forcing him. This is his dream. He told me so."

Beattie slowly shook her head. "If you're right, then something made him walk away. Something upset him enough to give up his dream. Maybe the crash?"

Darcy almost countered that Jack couldn't be upset by a little accident, but then she recalled his boast that he'd never crashed a plane before. Was that enough to shake him? If so, she had to bring that confidence back.

"It doesn't matter," Darcy said. "Now is the time to support him. Now is the time to press forward. Obstacles are mere detours on the path to success. No great explorer has ever succeeded without overcoming setbacks. When Jack comes back to fetch his plane, he'll find it good as new. He'll find us ready, and he'll know that we stand behind him."

Beattie threw up her hands in surrender. "You *are* a dreamer."

"Maybe," Darcy seized her friend's hands, "but don't you see? This attempt isn't just for Jack and me, it's for Pearlman. Hendrick can work on the motor. We can get Mrs. Baumgartner, at the upholstery shop, to sew the wing coverings. Lyle Hammond could shape the wood at his shop."

One by one, Darcy ticked off how the townspeople could help. "All we need to do is organize them. It can be done, Beattie, and think how Jack will feel when he sees his plane back in one piece. We can do it."

It took no time at all to convince Pearlman's craftsmen to help out. Blake and Beattie canvassed the town, and by the end of the following day had lined up enough materials and workers to get the repairs underway.

The following morning, Darcy surveyed the plane with Blake and Hendrick's assistance. They took measurements from the good wing and located unbroken pieces from the wrecked wing to use as forms for the new pieces. The carpenter, the upholsterer and the welder took the measurements and pieces back to their shops. Simmons began to fix the motor and Darcy worked with the rest of the crew to disassemble the broken wing.

Darcy returned home at dusk to find both Mum and Papa home. Mum seldom ate supper with them anymore, so something must be wrong.

"Who is with Amelia?" Darcy asked as she took off her coat.

"Her sister-in-law, Grace, stopped by." Mum nudged Darcy toward the parlor. "We'd like to talk with you, dear."

Now what? She hadn't done anything wrong. "Doc Stevens said I could get out of bed today."

"Out of bed, yes."

"But?" Darcy sensed a lecture.

"Sit down, Darcy." Papa set aside the newspaper and folded

his spectacles. His grim expression sent her high spirits plummeting.

"Yes, Papa?" Darcy balanced on the edge of the sofa, her chest squeezing tighter every moment. Mum held her hand.

Papa frowned. "I understand you've instigated work on that aeroplane."

The pressure tightened. "Yes."

"Do you think that wise?"

The invisible corset squeezed tighter, but she wouldn't back down. "Of course. The faster we repair it, the quicker we'll be back in the air."

His eyebrows rose. "We? Do you think you should be flying after your accident?"

"George said I'm fine." That assertion did not bring the desired results. "Oh, you want me to help out at Amelia's house. Of course. I'll be there tomorrow morning. I'll put in extra time if you need me."

"I'm not talking about your time. I'm talking about your safety."

She'd heard that argument on the night of Beattie's wedding. She'd won him over then. She could do it again. Only this time, she had a crash to overcome. "I'm perfectly safe. That bad landing was a fluke." She didn't want to mention that she'd held onto the wheel while Jack tried to steer. "Jack said he'd never had an incident before. I'm sure it won't happen again."

Papa's frown deepened. "You can't predict that."

"No one can predict the future, and no one can be totally safe. Why, any one of us could have died from the Spanish influenza. Flying is where I belong, Papa. As soon as I get enough flight time, I'm taking the license test."

He tapped his fingers on the end table. "Do I understand correctly that you were in that plane of your own volition?"

She slipped her hand from Mum's. "You said I could resume lessons."

"After Amelia delivered."

Darcy's cheeks burned. "Why do I have to wait for Amelia? Why is it always what Amelia wants? Why can't I have this one little thing? I still help out at her house. I've never neglected my chores. Taking lessons doesn't affect a thing."

"Until you were injured. That changes everything. No more flying. Do I make myself clear?"

In that instant, Darcy knew why Jack had left. "You told Jack to leave, didn't you?" Angry tears nipped her eyelids. "You made him quit. How could you? That was *his* project, *his* dream."

"Darcy, you're being unfair," Mum said gently.

"I'm unfair? I'm not the one trying to control other people's lives."

Papa's face had turned dark red. "The man made his own decision."

But she knew better. Papa had said something to him. Jack wouldn't have left otherwise. Every muscle vibrated. "All I wanted was my own grand adventure. You had yours when you shot the grizzly. Why can't I have mine? Is that too much?"

"Darcy, we love you and only want what's best for you."

"Then why take away my dream? Why deny Jack his?" She hiccupped, the tears close. "Even if you deny me, you can't take away Jack's dream."

"Deny you?" Papa gripped the arms of the chair so tightly his knuckles turned white. "How can I deny you? You're grown now, and it's apparent you do precisely what you want, with no consideration for others."

No consideration? He was the one who showed no consideration. All she wanted to do was fly. Well, he was right about one thing. She would do what she wanted. She would fly.

"You're dismissed," he said. "Go to your room, child, and ponder where your loyalties lie."

She didn't have to ponder. She knew. Papa was the one who didn't understand. Trembling, she ran from the room.

Chapter Twelve

The snow was still piled high in Buffalo. It drove a chill deep into Jack's bones, a chill that St. Anne's Hospital certainly didn't thaw.

Sissy looked up from her book the minute he walked in. "What happened?"

"I should know I can't hide anything from you." He pulled the chair close to her bed and sat, elbows on thighs, twirling his cap.

"That bad?"

Jack set his cap on the bedside table. No way around it. "The transatlantic attempt is off."

"Oh, Jackie. I'm so sorry. That was your dream. What happened?"

"Plane crash." Even the words hurt.

"Thank God you're not injured. That's the most important thing. What will you do?"

He shrugged. "Reopen the flight school, I guess." He stared at the linoleum flooring. Yellow with flecks of gray. Ugly. He wondered how Sissy stood it. "Finances will be tight for a while."

She nodded solemnly. "I will move to the ward."

That's not what he wanted. Why should Sissy suffer for his

error? Yet, that's what happened to the women he loved. In the end, they were the ones that bore the cost of his mistakes. "It won't be for long." His voice clotted. "I'm so sorry."

"Jackie." Her light touch was meant to console, but it only reminded him of what he'd lost. Darcy. If she died... A tremor shook him.

Her eyes flew open. "You are hurt."

"No, I was just thinking about..." He couldn't even speak her name.

Sissy pursed her lips, deep in thought. "You weren't alone in that plane, were you? Someone else flew with you. It was her, wasn't it?"

Jack had no idea how Sissy read his mind. He tried to bury his guilt behind an impassive mask, but he was failing badly.

"Was she hurt?" she asked.

Jack couldn't sit anymore. He walked to the window. "The doctor says she'll recover."

"Thank God." She heaved a sigh. "Oh, Jackie, you must have been terrified."

She didn't know the truth of it. She couldn't. Even now, his stomach tightened at the memory of Darcy's limp form.

"She'll recover," he repeated. At least he hoped she would. A brain hemorrhage. He didn't know what he'd do if she died.

"Shame on you."

"What?" Jack snapped to attention.

Sissy sat with arms crossed, glaring at him. "Why are you here, when she needs you?"

Her condemnation scorched his brittle soul. "She doesn't need me. She has a good family. They're taking care of her."

"But she loves you."

Jack tried to stomach that idea. She did hang on his every

word, but that could be because she wanted to fly. "I don't think she does."

"Oh." Her sharp intake of breath meant she was back on his side. "Unrequited love. Oh, Jackie, how sad."

This whole conversation was unsettling. He didn't want to think about Darcy. He certainly didn't want to talk about her. "Would you like to take a walk?"

She nodded. "I saw a robin yesterday."

Jack glanced at the window, frosty at the edges. The sunshine offered little warmth. "Maybe that wasn't such a good idea. It's cold out."

"That's why we have coats. Not to mention mittens and hats and scarves."

The next several minutes involved the necessities of dressing for the cold. Jack lifted her into the wheelchair and tucked a blanket around her legs.

"I don't need a blanket," she protested. "My legs can't feel cold."

That stubbornness reminded him of Darcy, but he could be stubborn, too. "That's exactly why you need it. I won't go outside unless you cover your legs with a blanket."

"It makes me look like an invalid."

Though she grimaced and called him a tyrant, she finally acquiesced. Once outdoors, Sissy directed him to the little courtyard garden she loved. Its sheltered southern exposure melted the snow. Here, the sun warmed. Hyacinths poked their fragrant purple heads through last summer's rubble. A chickadee hopped from branch to branch, tilting its head inquisitively.

Sissy pulled off a mitten, reached into her pocket and pulled out a handful of sunflower seeds. "Tweet, tweet," she mimicked, drawing the bird close.

"You've done this before."

"Hush." She persisted until the bird ate from her hand, plucking a seed then nervously hopping back to the branch.

Jack watched the small miracle, his heart breaking. How could she be happy in such a place? How could she delight in the tiniest pleasure that came her way? How many hundred chickadees had he ignored, always striving for the big goal, the grand gesture. And now he couldn't even do that. He took a ragged breath.

The chickadee flitted away.

"That's it," said Sissy, flinging the rest of the seed on the ground for the sparrows. "Now tell me exactly what happened."

Jack dug into the softened earth with the heel of his boot. "There's nothing to tell. We were making a test flight. An updraft caught the wing during descent, and the plane crashed. There's not enough time to salvage the transatlantic attempt. It's over."

Sissy listened carefully. "What's her name?"

"Kensington Express."

"Not the plane, silly, your girl."

His girl. Jack had never had a girl before. "Darcy."

"That's a pretty name. Different."

"Irish, I think."

Sissy's eyes twinkled. "Ah, the Irish have spunk. That's a good match for you."

"Are you saying I don't have spunk?"

She laughed. "I'm saying the woman who loves you *needs* spunk. What's she like?"

"About your size. Brown eyes. Dark brown hair."

"That's not what I meant. What's she *like?* What are her passions, her interests? Does she have brothers and sisters? What does her father do? What are her dreams?"

Jack stopped listening when he heard the word *father.* That was the whole problem. Darcy's father would never accept him, and even if Darcy went against her father's wishes, *he* couldn't. She had the most important thing in the world: a family. He couldn't let her throw it away.

"Her father's a banker," he said.

"So she's severe and unsmiling."

"No!" Darcy was anything but. "She's bright and sure of herself, even when she's wrong."

"That's a good quality. Is she pretty, Jackie? Tell me she's pretty."

He remembered Darcy from the day she told him her dream of flying: the shining eyes, the excitement, the dots of color in her cheeks. "She's beautiful."

"I'm so glad." She clasped her hands to her breast. "And she likes to fly."

The pleasant memory crashed. "That's over."

"Why?"

"Didn't you hear me? The plane is wrecked. The transatlantic attempt is off."

"There are other reasons to fly."

He hated when she got rational. "No good ones."

She didn't reply at once. Judging by her expression, she was considering whether or not to speak. Naturally, she did. "Stop playing God."

"What?" He didn't even believe in an intervening God. He sure wasn't playing Him.

"Stop playing God."

"I'm not."

"Aren't you?" He heard the wheelchair creak as she moved, felt her grasp his hand. "You're deciding for her, telling her she can't fly. Well it's not your decision. It's hers."

"But she'll get hurt."

"You don't know that. No one does. None of us can know the future. We can only enjoy the present. Love her. Enjoy your time together, and then you will have no regrets. And when you're afraid, turn to God. He's the only true protector."

"This doesn't have anything to do with God." Jack shook off her grasp. He didn't want to explain how God had let them both down, how *he* hadn't answered Jack's most desperate plea.

She sighed. "You can't escape the risk, not if you want the prize."

Jack knew she meant marriage, not flying, but he couldn't face that topic. "I know flying is risky."

"I'm not talking about flying, and you know it. I'm talking about love. You're willing to risk your life for that transatlantic prize, and it's only money. Love is so much more."

Sissy knew nothing about love. How could she, when she was confined to an institution?

Yet she smiled at him, urging, "Go ahead. Take the risk."

Jack frowned. She didn't understand. She was safe here, protected, surrounded by nurses and doctors. Real life wasn't like that. Real life was filled with danger and heartbreak and loss.

"It's worth it Jack." Sissy squeezed his hand.

"You don't understand," he said, pulling away again. "I won't be responsible for another person getting..." He stopped before he said the fateful words.

"Getting what?"

He turned away so she wouldn't see his face.

"Answer me, Jackie. Getting what? Sick? You can't help illness."

"Not illness," he said angrily, whirling around to see the wheelchair and her withered limbs.

It should have been him. He shouldn't have agreed to go to the river. He shouldn't have suggested they build a mud dam. He knew better. He could still hear his father's rebuke.

"How many times have I told you never to go to that germ-infested place? Mud carries disease. This is your fault. You're responsible." He'd shaken his finger in Jack's face, had stuck it in his chest.

Then Sissy never came home from the hospital, Mom died and he was sent away to school, never to return home.

"I'm not talking about illness," he said, fighting past the memories. "I'm talking about injury. I don't want to see anyone get injured or die."

"Like Darcy? Oh, Jack, no matter how hard you try, you can't protect those you love. Illness, injury and death happen. That's why we need God so desperately. He grants us the strength to go on."

He turned away to hide his bitterness. "How can you talk about God, when He took away your life?"

For a long time Sissy didn't speak. He'd finally gone too far. Even the squirrels scolded him. He began to apologize, but she spoke first, and with a quiet assurance that stunned him.

"I have my life. This is where I'm meant to be. I'm surrounded by people, many of them dear friends, and yes, I have a purpose here. I've spent long days and nights with the inconsolable. I've prayed with families at bedsides. I do my best with what God has given me, and He has rewarded me richly."

Jack struggled with her words of faith. He could understand it. He could admire it. But he couldn't summon it in himself. "I don't know how."

"Go to her. Go to Darcy. God put her in your life for a reason. See where that path leads. And trust, Jack. Trust."

Jack trudged across town from the Pearlman train depot, shoulders hunched against the wind. The last of the snowbanks had melted, and the sun shone, but it wasn't warm by any definition of the word.

"Hello there, Mr. Hunter," someone said in passing.

"Same." Jack glanced up to see the newspaperman, Devlin, coatless and in shirtsleeves. Clearly, the people here were made of tough stuff.

So was Jack Hunter.

It was time to assess the damage to his plane and figure out what, if anything, could be salvaged. He owed a fortune to the Kensingtons. If the plane could be repaired, he could fly exhibitions. It'd take years to pay off his debt, but he'd do it.

He'd also have to face Darcy. She wouldn't be happy with his decision. She'd try to talk him out of flying exhibitions, or even beg to go along, but he'd made up his mind. Despite Sissy's arguments, he was flying solo now.

He bitterly kicked a stone along the dirt road. He'd need to convert the plane to single engine. It would take time, but it could be done.

The breeze chapped his cheeks. Jack huddled deeper into his jacket and headed across the field to the barn. Strange. Half a dozen motorcars were parked between the barn and the house. Baker must have guests. Odd for a Monday.

When he drew near, he noticed the barn door stood ajar. What on earth would guests be doing inside the barn? In a flash he put it all together: Kensington was salvaging Jack's plane and selling off the pieces to the highest bidder.

Jack barged through the door. "What do you think—?" The sight made him freeze. A dozen people worked on, around, and alongside his plane. Some he recognized, like Blake Kensington and the Simmons kid, but most he didn't. Moreover, they weren't disassembling the plane, they were rebuilding it.

The people of Pearlman had stepped up to help *him,* Jack

Hunter, a man who had given them nothing. He rubbed his eyes. He must be dreaming.

"Jack! It's about time."

Darcy. His gut turned over.

"Everybody, it's Jack," she called out. "He's here."

The work crew all stopped and looked at him. Some nodded or waved. Everyone smiled.

"Uh, hello." He waved awkwardly. "Thank you." He struggled against emotion. "I'm, uh, overwhelmed." He sounded like a fool. Why were they doing this?

He searched for Darcy. The dark-haired beauty, dressed in greasy overalls, stood in the rear cockpit. He went to her.

"You're not shipping this plane to Buffalo," she said as he drew near. She had a pencil shoved behind her ear and a dab of grease on her nose. She'd never looked so beautiful.

"Excuse me?"

She cocked her head in that wonderful way. "Considering the cost of repairs and all the time we've put into it, the citizens of Pearlman have decided that the plane is ours."

Jack could find no rational response.

"Meet your new partners. Blake and Beattie and Simmons you know." She then proceeded to introduce him to everyone there. Each smiled and nodded at him.

What was he supposed to do now? "I..." His voice trailed off as he surveyed his machine. He could barely tell it had been damaged. The twisted left wing had been replaced with a brand new one, gleaming with fresh paint and pungent from doping compound. He ran his hand along the smooth leading edge.

Simmons was reattaching the engine. Scraps of wood, old canvas and wire sat in a pile to one side, along with sawhorses, saws, nails, screws and tools.

"What did you do?" he said, unable to comprehend what was happening. Why would they help him? These good people had taken time from their work and families to help him on a desperate venture certain to end unsuccessfully. "Darcy, what? Why?"

"We'll have it ready in no time," said that most exquisite object of loveliness as she shimmied down from the cockpit.

She showed no ill effects from the crash, other than a yellowish bruise and scab on her forehead. Somehow, even that made her more attractive.

"Aren't you pleased?" She circled in front of him, hands clapped on her hips.

When she did that, her figure showed just a little. He tried not to look. "Yes. Of course."

"Good." She squeezed his elbow. "Come up to the cockpit and survey the work."

He followed in a stupor. "Why did you do this?"

"To get ready for the transatlantic attempt, silly." She said it so matter-of-factly that he almost believed.

"But there's not enough time. By now, Raynham and Hawker will be on their way to Newfoundland."

She shrugged. "Who cares about Raynham and Hawker? I only care about Jack Hunter."

The ice that had encased Jack's heart for so long cracked and started to slip away, like icebergs calving from a glacier. The soul beneath ached, raw and tender and unaccustomed to the air. And it was all because of her.

She climbed back into the plane, and the hem of each pant leg rose slightly when she bent her knee. Jack couldn't take his eyes off her. Why hadn't he ever noticed how her hair tumbled over her shoulder? When had it grown so long? Had it always been that shiny?

He climbed willingly into her net. Her plan wouldn't work of course. Not enough time. But he couldn't disappoint her. Not today.

She was attaching a bracing wire to the upper wing.

He settled into the forward cockpit and leaned over the back of the seat to watch her work. She was gorgeous, abloom with the scent of violets. "What's that you're wearing?"

She gave him a scathing look. "Overalls."

"No. Your perfume."

Her smile could have thawed Antarctica. "I'm not sure what scent it is. My aunt—the one in Buffalo—gave it to me."

"Smells like violets."

"Violets. Hmm, maybe you're right. Or perhaps it's the added aroma of engine oil that does it."

"I happen to love the smell of motor oil."

She laughed. "I'll bet you do."

She drove the screw with all her strength. Such determination. Such certainty.

"I'm sorry." He didn't know where that had come from, but he knew without a doubt that it had to be said. "I shouldn't have left."

She turned those deep, dark eyes on him. "Don't you ever leave me again, Jack Hunter."

The force of her statement stunned him.

"Here I was, trying to recover, and I found you had left town without so much as a note. I thought we were working together on this."

Jack gulped. "It was wrong of me."

"Yes it was." Her lip quivered slightly, and the sight tore through him.

He'd hurt her terribly, and not just in the plane crash. He hadn't considered her feelings. He'd been too possessed by his own selfish guilt. Maybe Sissy was right.

"I'm sorry," he said once more. It was inadequate, but he didn't know what else to say.

"Well, don't ever do it again."

He nodded. He owed her that.

* * *

As the afternoon waned and daylight dimmed, the barn gradually emptied of workers. Jack personally thanked each one. Blake waited at the worktable, perusing the acquisition lists and navigation notes. It made Jack nervous. The man clearly wanted to tell him something that couldn't be said in front of others. It had to be about the money.

As Jack shook the last hand, Blake walked toward him. With his pulse pumping, Jack extended a hand. "Thank you for organizing the repairs."

"You'd better thank Darcy. She's the one who did it all."

The warmth returned, tugging at Jack's heart. After he'd mishandled the landing and caused her injury, she'd done this for him.

"If you ask me, she didn't do it just to get ready for the shot at the record." Blake gave him a wink and a nudge.

The revelation that Darcy might have engineered the repairs because she cared for him distracted Jack for a moment from the rest of Blake's statement.

"So, when can we ship?"

Jack wiped his mouth. "You still want to take a shot at the transatlantic crossing?"

Blake stared blankly, and then broke into a hearty laugh. "You fooled me for a minute, sport. Not go for the transatlantic record? Why do you think I'm pouring so much cash into this plane?"

Jack forced a chuckle. Darcy was right. This wasn't his plane anymore. He calculated how long the test flights would take. Pohlman should arrive in a week. Add a couple weeks for the tests.

"Three weeks, maybe four if the weather doesn't cooperate."

"Great." Blake clapped him on the shoulder. "See you tomorrow."

Jack scrubbed his head. What if Pohlman canceled again?

He walked to the worktable where Darcy had left the requisition lists in perfect order, each item numbered. Each number had then been written on a crate or box stacked along the barn wall. Everything had arrived. He was ready to make the transatlantic attempt, except for the test flights.

"You can't stop her, you know." Simmons's voice startled Jack. He hadn't realized anyone else was still there.

"What do you mean?"

The mechanic squared off before Jack. "Darcy's got a mind of her own, and she's gonna do what she wants, no matter what you or anyone says."

"I've discovered that."

Simmons didn't look convinced. "This flying is what she's wanted for a long time, and she ain't gonna give it up. If you won't teach her, then she'll find someone else."

The man was dead right, but he didn't have to deal with her father. Jack stood in an impossible place. She would demand to fly, and her father had made him responsible for ensuring she didn't. He should have stayed in Buffalo.

Darcy preferred any amount of work to staying home. Papa barely spoke to her. They studiously avoided any talk of the plane or flying, though Papa must have known Jack was back.

Mum surprisingly took her side, even offering to get the children ready for school so Darcy could work more on the plane. "Give your father time. He's a bit set in his ways, but he'll come around."

Darcy wasn't so sure, but she wouldn't let Papa stop her. The plane was nearly ready. Soon they'd be back in the air, resuming the test flights.

When morning dawned bright and clear, without a breath of wind, she hurried to the barn. This might be the day.

She found Jack on a ladder checking the left motor. "Is it working?"

He looked up, startled. "Didn't hear you."

"Sorry. Did Hendrick get the motor running?"

"First thing this morning." He scurried down the ladder. "Started and ran a good twenty minutes. I was just checking the spark plugs."

"And?"

"And they're still clean." The old lopsided grin flashed across his face for a moment.

Her heartbeat escalated. "Then it runs."

He wiped his hands clean, leaning against the wing strut the very way he had the day she met him. "I thought I just said that."

"Can we take it up? On a test flight?"

He shook his head. "I want to do these with Pohlman."

She clenched her fists. He didn't even look at her when he said that. "If we start now—"

"Too late."

"What do you mean, 'too late'? You're waiting for Pohlman."

He wiped the wrench for the tenth time. "There's no need to rush, because we're already too far behind. Hawker and all the others are weeks ahead of us."

"So? That's no reason to give up."

"I'm not giving up," he said curtly. "I'm facing reality."

"Reality is an excuse for pessimists."

"I appreciate your enthusiasm, Miss Optimism. It's one of your more endearing qualities. But the fact is, I have at least five test flights before we can ship the plane. By then the prize could be claimed."

"Perhaps." Darcy gathered speed. She could convince him.

She knew how. "But what if it's not? What if none of the teams succeeds, and we didn't even try? This isn't about only you, Jack Hunter. This attempt is for much more. It's for Pearlman. It's for the little guy, the unheralded, the unknown. It's for every person who volunteered his time to repair your plane. It's for every person who believes in miracles. It's for all of us. No matter who you have in that cockpit with you—and yes, I accept that you want Pohlman—we'll all be there, cheering you on. Don't give up on us, Jack."

His expression never changed. Grim determination. He looked over the plane, wing tip to wing tip. "What does your father say?"

So that was it. Jack feared her father. Not her. Trials had forged her tough. "My father knows I am going to fly. Whether or not it's with you is your call."

He rubbed his forehead as if he had a headache.

"I am a grown woman, and perfectly capable of making my own decisions."

He jerked and stared at her. Then at the plane. Then back to her. "So—if I understand correctly, you're saying it's a perfect day for a test flight."

After all that hesitation, she wasn't ready for this response. "A what?"

The grin exploded across his face. "Are you ready?"

"Of course I am." She bounded to get her goggles.

"I'll pilot. You handle navigation. I want exact figures, speed, altitude, noted every thirty seconds." He launched into the full explanation while she jotted it down on the clipboard.

It felt good to have him bark orders at her again.

It felt even better to be in the air. She attached the watch to the clipboard and marked the required readings he wanted. The flight lasted an hour, the most she'd ever been aloft. As they approached Baker's field, she couldn't help tensing, but this time Jack touched down perfectly, with only a few jolts and bumps from the rough terrain.

"What does this test tell us?" she asked as they climbed down.

"Fuel consumption for a light load. By the time we reach England, we'll be empty."

"We?"

"Don't get any ideas." But he said it with a grin, and her spirits soared even higher.

"Darcy?" Papa's voice startled her. He stood stiffly in the barn door, dressed for work in his charcoal gray suit and waistcoat. His black derby sat firmly on his head. What was he doing here? Papa never came to the barn.

"I, uh," she stammered, checking the watch. "The children are still in school."

His expression was grim. "Your sister went into labor last night."

"Already?" Amelia wasn't due for two more weeks. Icy numbness seeped into her hands and feet. Papa wouldn't be here unless there was a problem. "How is she?"

"It's not going well."

Only then did Darcy notice his ashen complexion. It must be very bad. "Doctor Stevens?"

"He's with her. Come. She asked for you."

Darcy's legs nearly gave way. "She asked for me? Why?" They weren't close. In fact they fought. A terrible dread filled her. She looked to Jack.

"Go," he said softly, nudging her toward the door.

"The motorcar is outside," said Papa.

The motorcar? Papa rarely drove it, not even to Chicago to visit his family.

Darcy wiped her hands clean and followed Papa. Amelia. A wave of guilt washed over her. Every resentment. Every bitter word. Always blaming Amelia. Dear Lord, she'd been so selfish.

Papa's hand trembled as he opened the passenger door.

No. No. Please God, don't let anything happen to Amelia. Papa couldn't take it. Not after all the quarreling. He must be so disappointed.

She should have considered his feelings. She should have spent more time talking to him, rather than demanding.

"Papa?" She put her hand over his. "She'll be all right."

He started shaking.

No.

"I'm sorry, Papa." She could barely fit the words through her constricted throat. "I'm so sorry."

He pulled her close and hugged her as if afraid she would slip away. That was it. He was afraid of losing her, of losing them both. He shook with stifled sobs.

"I'll always love you, Papa."

"Me, too, Darcy. Me, too."

She wept, and she didn't care who saw her.

Chapter Thirteen

Amelia's shuddering cries made Darcy wish she'd never climbed up the stairs. The bedroom door stood ajar, and Darcy could see a pile of damp, blood-tinged bed linens on the hardwood floor. The corner of an oilcloth hung from the bed. To protect the mattress from blood. Blood. Her stomach churned.

She pressed against the wall, taking deep breaths.

"Darcy. Thank God." Mum pulled her into the room where death crouched in the shadows.

Doc Stevens, his shirtsleeves rolled up to the elbow, nodded at her. "Call if the baby starts to come," he said as he left to wash his hands.

Amelia panted, her color even more ashen than normal, her usually perfect hair a matted flaxen mess. A sheet covered her round belly, but the struggle of hard labor showed.

"Darcy." Amelia turned a haggard face to her. "I'm so glad." She winced and panted again, short little breaths, as if the pain was too much to even breathe normally.

Mum guided Darcy to the bedside chair.

She shook. This was why she wouldn't marry. "How are you?" What a foolish thing to say. "Sorry." She knit her fingers around her knees, feeling out of place in her greasy overalls. "I don't smell too good."

Amelia smiled wanly. "I wanted to talk—oh." Another pain began, contorting her face and sending a spasm through her entire body.

"Hold on, dearest." Mum put a knotted rope in Amelia's hand and pressed a cool compress to her forehead.

A rope? Whatever for? Darcy followed it to the foot of the bed, over the end and underneath where it was tied to the bed's leg.

Amelia yanked. Hard. The rope strained. Amelia's eyes bulged and perspiration poured off her face. "Aaahhhgggh." The cry tore out of her, but the baby did not.

After the spasm ended, Amelia lay panting again, exhausted. Mum handed Darcy the compress. "I'll be just outside. Don't fret, Amelia. The baby will come soon." Though Mum smiled when she gazed at Amelia, her confidence vanished the moment she turned away. Mum was worried.

What if Amelia didn't survive? Women still died in childbirth. Not as often, but it still happened. Every spat and jealousy between them meant nothing now. How foolish she'd been. How trivial her complaints. Flying didn't take half the courage of childbirth.

"I'm sorry," she whispered, grasping Amelia's cold hand. "I'm sorry for not understanding, for everything."

Amelia squeezed tightly, and Darcy feared another contraction was on the way. What if the baby came while Mum and Doc Stevens were gone? She looked around for her mother.

"I'm as much to blame," Amelia said. "Sometimes I provoked you."

"I know. I shouldn't have let it bother me." She laughed a little. "I probably deserved it."

"Sisters," Amelia sighed.

"Sisters." Somehow that said everything that needed to be said. Darcy hugged her tight.

Amelia gasped and her eyes widened. Not another contraction.

"Mum?" Her mother didn't appear, so Darcy handed Amelia the rope, applied the compress and waited until the spasm passed.

Amelia coughed and gasped, her eyes feverish. "I need to ask you."

Darcy reached for another compress, but Amelia stilled her hand.

"If I die," her sister said, clutching at her with bony fingers, "take care of my babies. Un-until Charles remarries."

The room began to spin, Darcy's ears buzzed, and her vision grew foggy. No. Impossible. "I…you won't die. You can't."

Sweat beaded on Amelia's face. "Promise me. Please. Mum will help, but Freddie and Lizzie and Helen need you. They love you."

"They do?" Her nieces and nephew had never shown any extraordinary affection.

Amelia nodded. "Please?" Her grip tightened.

This couldn't happen. *Dear Lord, please spare Amelia.* If not? What if *His* will was to take her to heaven? Then the children would need her. She couldn't turn her back. "I promise."

Amelia's grip eased, and with a sigh she settled back, eyes closed. She looked peaceful, though wan and exhausted.

Mum stepped in just as the pain returned. "Doc Stevens is washing up to turn the baby, dearest. Hang on. It will be over soon."

"Turn the baby?" Darcy asked. "How?"

"By hand of course."

"You mean…inside?"

Mum nodded and Darcy ran from the room, queasy. She stood in the hall, trying to compose herself. She couldn't go downstairs like this. The men would think the worst.

Mum came out when Doc Stevens returned. "Thank you, dearest. I know how difficult that was, but it set Amelia's mind at ease."

"W-will she live?" Darcy steeled herself for the cries of pain that were sure to come when Dr. Stevens turned the baby.

"Only God knows." Mum squeezed her arm. "Pray without ceasing."

But Darcy couldn't seem to pull her scattered mind together. Take care of three or four children, one a newborn? Charles would probably remarry. Most men did. But what if his new wife didn't want to take the children? What if Darcy had to raise them for the next eighteen years?

She took deep breaths. This speculation was doing no good, and standing here didn't help. She needed to clean or cook. Cook. She'd get supper ready. The children must be home by now. That's what she'd do.

The parlor looked much the same as when she left. Papa sat by the grandfather clock. Charles paced. Unlike before, the three children sat on the sofa, quieter than Darcy had ever seen them.

"How is she?" Charles asked.

What to say? "Tired but well." She forced a smile.

"I should go to her." Charles looked upstairs with trepidation.

Papa defused the idea at once. "Let Doc Stevens handle it." He leafed through a farm tool catalog with the vigor ordinarily saved for heart-stopping adventure novels.

Charles paced.

At that moment, an anguished cry came from upstairs.

"Mama," Helen sobbed, tucking a thumb into her mouth.

Charles dashed to the staircase, his naturally somber face even more drawn. "It's been so long."

"Not that long," Darcy said. "Some births can take days."

"Days?" Charles swallowed, his Adam's apple bobbing. "I didn't know. My mother died in childbirth."

"Darcy, this isn't helpful," said Papa. "Is there something you could do with the children?"

Supper. But not with the children underfoot. "Outdoors you go." She corralled them through the kitchen, drawing Freddie aside. "Will you please keep them busy with games?"

Freddie absorbed the responsibility, his expression grimly serious. "Is Mama going to be all right?"

"Of course." Darcy smiled and patted him on the shoulder. "The doctor is here."

"Would it help if I threw away my treasures? Mama wants me to get rid of them."

Darcy's heart broke. The poor boy. "That's brave of you, but I don't think that will help. Why don't you clean them up and give them to her after your baby brother or sister is born? For now, could you keep your sisters busy?"

Freddie nodded solemnly. "We'll play hide-and-seek."

"That sounds wonderful."

Darcy took sanctuary in the kitchen, preparing supper. Every anguished cry from upstairs shook her. She had to lean against the worktable to steady herself. She'd been so wrong about Amelia. She squeezed her eyes tight to hold back the tears. Perhaps she should have invested more time in family and less in flying.

Long minutes passed before she gathered enough strength to resume the simple task of getting supper ready. She opened the door to the warming oven and found two meat pies. She sniffed. Beef.

A rap on the kitchen door drew her attention. She could still hear the children shrieking in the yard, so it wasn't them. She hoped it wasn't Cora or any of the other town gossips. They did not need visitors in the midst of crisis. She set down the hot pie, snitched a bit of crust, and cracked open the door.

"It's us," said Beatrice. "How is she?"

"Nothing yet." Darcy fell into her friend's embrace. "I'm so glad you're here."

"Don't worry. It can take time." But she looked worried. "In the meantime, we're here to help."

"We?"

Beatrice stepped inside and revealed Jack standing on the bottom step.

Darcy blinked. "What are you doing here?"

"That's a fine welcome." He tugged off his cap. "Just wanted to see how you're holding up."

"Me? I'm not the one in labor." Darcy returned to the worktable and cut into the pies. The rich brown gravy bubbled up through slits in the crust. She knew she'd snapped at Jack, but she didn't want him to see her so frazzled. She needed to talk with Beattie. Alone.

Beatrice located plates and forks. "I'll send over some sweet buns a little later."

"Thank you," Darcy said softly. "I need to round up the children for supper."

"I'll help." Jack popped out the door.

"He's a good man," said Beattie after the door closed. "And he likes you very much."

"I'm not so sure." Every time she got a little closer to Jack, he pulled away. Sure, he let her fly the test flights, but that was it. Real closeness required sharing what was deep inside, his hopes and desires, his pains and sorrow.

"Is that why you snapped at him?"

Darcy jabbed into the second pie. "I'm not snapping at anyone."

Beatrice set down the utensils and hugged her. "It's all right. Amelia will be fine."

Darcy struggled for words. "She asked me...to take the children, i-if she dies. Until Charles remarries. What would I do? She can't die. She can't."

Beattie hugged her closer. "Let's pray." They folded their hands together into one, the way they did when they were children. "Dear heavenly Father, we ask your blessing on Amelia tonight. Guide her baby safely into this world and preserve that dear child's mother—"

The door flew open.

"I hope you're ready for the troops," said Jack.

Darcy broke from prayer, hoping God understood. She quickly dried her face on her sleeve, but a bit of gasoline stung her eyes. She rapidly blinked to hold back the tears.

"March, one, two, three." The children pushed behind Jack. "Youngest first, hands out for inspection. Palm up."

One by one, the children paraded into the kitchen and showed their hands to Darcy. She swallowed her emotion and played along for their sake. After each passed inspection, the child marched into the dining room. Beatrice then followed with the first of the plates.

"How did you manage?" Darcy asked Jack as she handed him two full plates. "Take these into the dining room."

Instead of obeying her directive, he set the plates on the worktable. "Military school. Do you know you're lovely when you give orders?" He took her hands.

"Which you are disobeying." But her voice faltered, and she had to look away. No man liked to see a woman cry.

"It will be all right." He wiped her tears and took her in his arms. Strong and safe. He gently rocked her, and she let her head rest on his shoulder. The familiar scent of shaving soap. She lingered as he stroked her hair. Then he kissed her forehead and then kissed away the tears. His lips found hers, and she melted into the embrace. So this was love, feeling so much a part of another that she'd do anything for him. Anything. She remembered Amelia. Love put her sister close to death.

She pushed away. "Stop, stop." She fought to free herself.

"What's wrong?" Jack looked confused.

How could she explain? He'd never understand.

Waaaah. An infant's cry pierced the air.

Jack's lips slowly curved upward.

Seconds later, Charles burst into the room. "It's a baby. She had a baby." He dashed into the dining room to tell his children.

This time Darcy let the tears fall. "A baby," she burbled, "Amelia had her baby." But the joy was tempered with fear. Had her sister survived? She accepted Jack's outstretched arms and sobbed on his shoulder.

"Isn't it wonderful?" said Beattie, bursting into the kitchen. "Oh."

Darcy pulled away from Jack and dried her eyes. "It's not what you think."

"What do I think?" Beatrice smiled coyly as Papa pushed open the kitchen door.

"It's a boy," he said.

Thankfully, he hadn't seen her in Jack's arms. "How is Amelia?"

"Tired but well."

"Thank God." A hundredfold.

The moment of domestic joy disappeared as quickly as it had come. The children. Darcy. A real home. None of it belonged to Jack, but for precious minutes it had felt real. Then she'd pulled away.

Alone in his room at the boardinghouse, Jack took off his grandmother's ring, the one he wore on a chain around his neck, the one his mother had given him before she died. He'd never intended to give it to anyone, but that evening, watching Darcy rejoice with her family, he'd considered it.

He pressed the ring into his palm, where it left a hard imprint, slightly jagged from the three sapphires. Darcy had stated flat out that she didn't want to marry. He had a trans-atlantic flight to make. What was he thinking? Maybe after the crossing. If he made enough to buy Sissy a real home. If Darcy gave up flying.

The next day, Jack returned to the cold barn and the first of what turned out to be many obstacles. Pohlman pushed back his arrival by two more weeks. Winds and rain kept delaying the test flights. They managed a medium-load flight in early April, and then the rains returned. A tumbling crate crushed the flares, and they had to be reordered. The engines required constant adjustment. This project was taking years off his life.

On yet another rainy day, he and Darcy loaded the plane for the full-load test. This flight would measure fuel usage at the heaviest load. After that, he would be able to calculate how much fuel and oil he'd need for the crossing.

All of the test flights until then had been important, but this one was critical. This one determined if they could take off successfully at St. John's. It was also the most danger-ous, with all that fuel onboard. He hoped Pohlman showed, because he did not want to take Darcy. Forget about it being her decision. He was the pilot.

He had made a point of inquiring about her family each day. "How's your sister?" he asked during a rest between hefting fuel cans into the plane.

She beamed, the same as she did every time he asked.

"Back to normal, and the baby is so beautiful. You must go see him."

Jack wasn't ready to see babies. He climbed up to the cockpit. "Hand me the next can."

Darcy hefted it up the ladder, panting a bit from the exertion. "How many more test flights?"

"This full-load test and one distance flight." He surveyed the nearly full plane and considered holding back a couple of hundred pounds to ensure they'd clear the trees. In Newfoundland, he'd take off from the cliffs, allowing for an initial drop and using the updraft to advantage. But here he had to rise a hundred feet in a relatively short distance.

"If only the rain would stop." Then she abruptly changed subjects. "What's your sister's name again?"

"Cecelia Marie." Jack slid the last fuel can into the space behind his cockpit. "Everything's secured. What's the total load?"

She picked up the clipboard. "Twenty-seven pounds over."

"How can that be? Let me see." Jack took the clipboard and reviewed her calculations. No error. They were overloaded. He tossed out the raft. He needed five more pounds. He crouched and reached along the inside wall of the fuselage toward the tail of the plane.

"Do you have a middle name?"

"Lindsey." His fingers brushed the hatchet. Totally unnecessary, but she wanted it.

"Mine's Opal."

"Like the stone?" His hand landed on the radio transmitter and dry cells. They wouldn't need it for the full load test, just the distance test. He'd pull the equipment now and put it back after this flight.

"The stone? Of course the stone. Do you know another meaning for opal?" She laughed, clear and pure. "Darcy Opal

Shea. Darcy O. Shea." She laughed again, like it was somehow the funniest thing she'd ever heard. "Aunt Perpetua said Mum chose the name just because it started with an O. You see, Papa's last name used to be O'Shea, but he thought it sounded too Irish, so he dropped the O. Mum put it right back."

A wave of jealousy swept over him. How wonderful if the most embarrassing thing was a name that sounded too ethnic. Darcy didn't realize how blessed she was to have a father and a mother and a sister and a whole family that all loved each other.

"What does *your* father do?" She hovered at his shoulder.

"Nothing." He shuddered to think what her family would say if they knew the truth.

"How can a man do nothing?"

"Believe me, it's possible. Enough chatter. We have more important things to do." He cleared his throat. "Did you check the weather forecast this morning?"

"High pressure, clear skies, light southwest winds. Perfect."

Promising. He couldn't afford any more delays. He'd have to go, Pohlman or no Pohlman. He'd just lighten the load with Darcy. "If the weather holds tomorrow, we'll make the test run. Be here at eight."

"Yes, sir." She offered a mock salute and laughed.

How he loved to see her happy, and nothing pleased her more than flying. Sissy and Simmons were right. He couldn't stop her, even though he wanted to. She loved flying more than anything or anyone. Including him.

She stood so close, yet utterly beyond reach—like an expensive jewel on the other side of a shop window. He wanted to take her in his arms. He wanted to hold and protect her forever, but that would crush the very spirit he loved.

"You look worried," she said.

"Twin motors have never been tried on this model."

"We've made three successful flights."

"One less than successful." Her dark eyes nearly made him forget what he was saying. That's why they couldn't make the transatlantic flight together. That's why he wished he didn't have to fly with her. He pulled away.

A flicker of disappointment crossed her face. "But the last two went beautifully."

"I still I wish I had the opinion of a good aviation mechanic."

"Would an aviation engineer do?" said a very familiar voice.

Jack whirled around. "Burrows." He couldn't help grinning at the sight of his old friend. All his problems were solved. Burrows could check the calculations and tell him in an instant where to shave pounds. He could also navigate the last two test flights.

Darcy felt the chill the moment Jack turned away from her. Their connection had been so solid. They were working out the problem together, full partners in the venture. True, he hadn't revealed much about his family, but she'd broken through a little. Before long they'd be telling each other everything.

Now Burrows claimed Jack's full attention. She stood to the side, forgotten.

Jack grasped Burrows's hand in a firm shake. "What brings you to this outpost of civilization? Hopefully it's to drag Pohlman here."

Darcy stiffened. She'd hoped Jack had ruled out the tardy navigator.

"Don't know about Pohlman," Burrows said. "After I found out about the crash, I had to come. See what was really going on here."

"Where did you hear about that?" Jack actually looked affronted.

"How are you, Miss Shea?" Burrows shot a smile her way. "Just as lovely as I remember."

Darcy knew flirting when she saw it.

"How's *your* girl doing?" Jack said a little too pointedly.

"My girl?" Burrows screwed up his face. "Oh, you must mean Beulah. That was never serious." He smiled again at Darcy. "There are fun women and then there are serious women. I can tell Miss Shea is the serious type."

Darcy rolled her eyes. This was ridiculous. "Serious enough to know you're nothing but trouble."

Jack grinned broadly at her response. His cornflower-blue eyes fixed on her, and she felt that wonderful glow deep inside.

Burrows cleared his throat. "Shall we get back to business? Is it true that you're considering the transatlantic attempt in this old crate?"

Jack's attention went back to the plane. "Can't see why I should be talking to the competition."

"No competition here, sport. The navy isn't going for the prize. Besides, they're still finishing the NC-4." He leaned against the worktable. "I can bring you up to speed on the competition, though." He pulled a newspaper from his inside jacket pocket and spread it out on the table. "Look at this."

Jack bent over the paper.

Darcy could sense Jack's growing anxiety. He glanced at Burrows. "I'm figuring Hawker, with the Sopwith group, has the best shot."

"Don't count out the Martinsyde fliers. They're already there, Jack. Both groups."

"In St. John's?"

Burrows nodded. "According to this, Hawker and Grieve planned to take off on the twelfth, the day after Raynham and Morgan arrived with their Martinsyde."

Darcy sucked in her breath. This was terrible news.

"They're already gone?" Jack looked panicky. "By now Hawker and Grieve will be sipping Champagne in England."

Burrows shook his head. "Called it off due to bad weather, but they're ready."

Jack looked sick.

Darcy felt for him. "Maybe they won't make it. Anything could happen." Again she was ignored.

"I gather you're not ready to go," Burrows said.

Jack silently reread the article.

Darcy had to save him. He couldn't give up now. "We will be. Just a couple more test flights, and we'll be there."

Jack raked a hand through his hair. "Then we need to ship the plane, get a decent place for takeoff." He groaned. "I'd like to have an expert on my team to check the engines—here and in Newfoundland."

"I can take a look here," Burrows obliged, "but not in Newfoundland. You know I'm tied to the NC project."

"And if they take off from the same field, what's a little assistance here or there? You said the navy wasn't going for the prize money."

"Just like you to show up without a mechanic and hope someone will donate time. First things first. How soon will you be ready to ship?"

Jack ran through the remaining steps before departure. "If the weather holds," he finished up, "I should be able to ship around the twenty-third. Get there in a couple days. Reassemble, test and be ready to fly around the end of the month."

Too late. Even Darcy knew it. "You could save time if you flew to Newfoundland. Just send the supplies ahead by train, so they're there when you arrive. That eliminates the reassembly time."

Jack scoffed. "No one flies his plane to a major record attempt."

"Why not?"

Burrows supported her. "Actually, it's not a bad plan. That's what we're going to do with the NCs."

"See? It'll work."

Jack resisted. "The NCs are flying boats and can land on water if they have a problem. I'd have to fly over Canada and some pretty remote terrain."

"Then follow the St. Lawrence." Months of staring at the map had taught her something about geography.

"I suppose you'd have me make a landing on Niagara Falls?"

Darcy refused to give in. "You're being silly. I agree with Mr. Burrows. It'll trim days off our plan. Let's do it."

"Just like that."

"Why not?"

Burrows laughed. "Two against one. You lose, Jack."

Darcy wished Jack didn't look as though he'd lost the transatlantic prize. "We can do it. I know we can."

Jack folded the newspaper and handed it back to Burrows. "Could you fly the last two test flights?" He didn't even look at her when he asked him.

Burrows? He asked *Burrows? How could he?* He'd only been there ten minutes. She wanted to pound her fists against Jack's thick head, but it wouldn't do any good. Once Jack set his mind, he didn't retreat. She had no choice. She watched as Jack Hunter threw away her dream.

Jack hated to hurt Darcy that way, but Burrows was the answer to all his problems. "Stay the week," he begged his friend after they retired to the boardinghouse.

"Sorry, we're getting close to launching the NC-4. She has four Liberty motors, Jack, *four.* Sixteen hundred horsepower."

Jack could see the sparkle in Burrows's eyes, but he couldn't resist comparing, even though his paltry two engines and four hundred horsepower could never top the NC. "My girl's a Curtiss, too."

Burrows laughed. "Your girl's a Shea."

Jack squared his shoulders. "I meant the plane."

"Just like you to keep your eyes on the machine and not the woman."

"Women only bring trouble," Jack pointed out as he unlocked the door to his room. If Burrows didn't know that, with his string of failed relationships, no one would.

"Ah, but what sublime trouble it is. The French sing of it. The Italians romance it."

"And Dick Burrows jumps in with both feet."

"Watch that tongue of yours," Burrows said, laughing.

"Got a minute?" Jack nodded toward his room. "I'd like to talk."

"Me, too. If you've given up Miss Shea, is she fair game?"

"Who said I've given her up?"

Burrows whistled. "Jack Hunter is snared."

The words made Jack flinch. "Let's get serious. I meant what I said back at the barn. I could use your help for the last two flight tests."

"I thought Darcy was flying navigator?"

"She's not experienced."

"Sounds to me like she is."

"This isn't a little hop across farm fields. This is deadly serious—emphasis on deadly—which she doesn't understand. To her it's a lark. She thinks she'll be just like her heroine, Harriet Quimby, but we all know what happened to her. Darcy doesn't realize the risk."

"You like her, don't you?"

"This has nothing to do with what you're thinking."

"What am I thinking?" But Burrows was grinning too broadly for Jack to think he didn't understand.

"You know."

"I don't suppose this little reluctance has anything to do with the fact she's a woman?" Burrows suggested.

"Of course not," Jack snapped. "You know how dangerous this attempt is. I don't want her hurt or…" He couldn't bring himself to say the last word. *Dead.* Jack couldn't live if Darcy died.

"Is that so?" said Burrows. "Or is the danger just an excuse? Darcy's not your wife, she's your student. I doubt you cried over the army pilots you sent to Europe."

"That's different."

"Is it? Yet you trained her, despite insisting women shouldn't fly."

Jack shifted uncomfortably. "I didn't have a choice."

"Suckered you into it, eh? Well, well. Don't feel bad. Happens to the best of us. Besides, if there ever was an even playing field for the sexes, aviation is it."

"I don't want to debate." Jack had to drag this conversation away from Darcy and back to the problem at hand. "My point is she's inexperienced. Whether male or female, a transatlantic attempt takes enormous experience. These last two test flights are the riskiest. Either one could go wrong in a hurry. I need experience in the other cockpit."

"Didn't you read in the *Times* that Grieve only has four hours dual flight experience?"

"I'll bet he didn't crash a plane on his first attempt."

Burrows hooted. "Like Jack Hunter did?"

Jack, red-faced, protested, "I didn't wreck the plane."

"Semantics. Tell the truth, old sport, that's what you love about her. She's got the chutzpah to succeed. Mark my words. She'll be great someday, maybe in a few weeks."

This was not going the way Jack wanted. He'd counted on Burrows to support him. "Then you won't step in?"

"You don't need me. I wouldn't, even if I could, but you know I can't. I'll look over your engines tomorrow. That's it. I need to get back to Rockaway Beach for the launch. Then we head north."

"You're flying?" Jack couldn't keep the envy from his voice.

"Ground support. The necessary and unheralded part of any successful journey. See you in St. John's." He reached out a hand.

Jack reluctantly shook. He'd pinned his hopes on Burrows, feeble though they were. "Maybe."

"Miss Shea's not a maybe kind of woman."

"Miss Shea doesn't understand the danger. She doesn't know how far we are from going and how close the others are to success."

"Then you'd better get busy. First thing in the morning, unless you want to work tonight." Burrows patted his jacket pockets. "Almost forgot. Saw Cecelia on my way here. She wanted me to give you her best." He pulled out an envelope.

"You saw my sister?" Jack was stunned.

"We've corresponded for years. She's a real peach."

Jack did not like the idea of Burrows anywhere near Sissy. "Don't get any ideas."

"Trust me, that's the last thing you have to worry about. She's too smart to fall for a lout like me. In the morning?"

Jack nodded. Though he should go over the engines tonight, he had to read that letter. He had to know what his sister and best friend had been talking about all these years. And why hadn't either one of them happened to mention it?

After Burrows left, Jack ripped open the envelope. The single sheet said much the usual: how she missed him, what had happened with such and such a nurse, and absolutely nothing about Burrows. But that was all forgotten when he reached the last paragraph.

"Jackie," she wrote, "I hope you'll be happy for me. I've met a wonderful man here, a doctor. He sees me everyday, and we talk and talk. He's such a good friend. He listens to me babble on and never once mentions my useless legs. I'm mad with happiness, and I so want you to meet him."

It went on from there, but Jack didn't need to read more. He crumpled the letter and tossed it in the wastebasket.

Sissy was in love, but she'd only get hurt. No man would marry her. No man would make a life with a cripple.

Jack wanted to drop everything and get on the train to Buffalo, but of course he couldn't. He had a flight to make, win or die.

Chapter Fourteen

Darcy stomped to the barn the next morning. The ground crunched under her feet. Jack Hunter could not displace her on a whim. Knowing Pohlman could arrive at any moment was one thing, but giving the cockpit to Burrows was quite another.

Well, he would not get away with it. She'd get back in that cockpit.

To her surprise, the plane was already out of the barn. Jack and Simmons watched from the ground while Burrows crawled along the wings and around the engines, measuring, noting the results and calculating with his slide rule.

As Darcy drew near, Burrows hopped to the ground.

"This girl should get into the air with no problem." Burrows handed his notes to Jack. "You did a great job."

"I had nothing to do with it. Mr. Simmons here did the engineering."

Burrows shook Simmons's hand. "I'd like to have you at Curtiss Engineering."

If only Darcy would get such an offer. Simmons, of course, shook his head. He wouldn't try anything new.

"And the wing repairs are Darcy's doing," Jack added.

The icy knot of fury inside her melted. He'd acknowledged

her contribution, though she hadn't done the repairs herself. "I only organized everyone."

"She's too modest. Sure you can't stay?"

Burrows shook his head. "Gotta run, old sport. The NC-4's waiting, and I still need to pack."

Darcy took in the turn of events in disbelief. All night she'd stewed for no reason. Burrows wasn't staying. He wouldn't fly today.

Jack didn't give up. "You could always take tomorrow's train."

"You've got all the help you need." Burrows nodded to her. "Just use the takeoff pattern I suggested, lose a little weight, and you'll do fine."

After a few more pleasantries, he set off for town, leaving Darcy alone with Jack and Simmons. She still didn't believe what she'd heard.

"We're doing the full-load test?" She followed Jack into the barn. "And I can go?"

"Yes." Judging by his expression, he wasn't pleased.

"I can do it. You don't need to worry about me."

"Of course I worry about you." His jaw had tensed so much that the muscles stood out. He cared enough to worry. Only Mum and Papa had ever worried about her.

"I can do it."

He swallowed hard. "You don't realize how dangerous this flight is."

Though a nervous flutter teased her stomach, she kept up the confident front. "Burrows said it would go fine."

"In theory. Practice is another matter. We're carrying hundreds of gallons of fuel. The weight might be too much for us to lift off. One mistake, one updraft like the one that wrecked us in February, and we'll go up in a ball of fire."

Fire. Her flesh prickled as if seared. "I know the risk." No adventurer let fear stop her. She took precautions, yes, but she plowed ahead. Darcy reached for her goggles, but Jack stopped her with a touch to the arm. The old electricity still arced.

"If anything happens…" He didn't finish the sentence, but the meaning was all too clear.

"Nothing will." She gently removed his hand. Strong, slightly callused yet warm, and capable of such gentleness. He would hold her for all of time if she let him. But if she let love get in the way, she'd never get off the ground. "This transatlantic flight is what I want. It's what I've always wanted. Living without ever having tried isn't living at all."

Instead of the encouraging response she expected, his expression hardened. "Then let's get going."

What cost? A large part of her cried out, preferring love to adventure, but she'd set her sights on the horizon years ago, and she wouldn't be dissuaded by an overly cautious man.

They climbed into their respective cockpits and within minutes were taxiing to the far end of the field at slow speed. Darcy swiveled around to glare at him. What was he thinking? They needed a lot more speed to lift off.

As Jack turned the plane, Darcy realized he'd chosen to take off in the opposite direction. She also saw why. A longer runway stretched south, away from the barn and toward a gap between clumps of poplar. With the heavy load, they needed the extra distance.

The pounding in her ears intensified as the plane gathered speed. What if it didn't lift off? Would Jack be able to pull out in time? Her earthbound bravado vanished. She clutched the clipboard as the bushes and trees whizzed past.

They weren't rising yet, and the treeline was getting closer. They'd nearly reached the end of the open runway and still no elevation. She stared ahead, willing the plane to rise. She bounced in her seat, trying to be lighter.

Go. Go. Up.

The motors howled on either side of her. At last the plane left the ground. A little. The bumping stopped, but they weren't rising quickly enough. The trees loomed. They were going to hit them. She shut her eyes.

A thwack made them fly open. They'd hit a tree. No, they were still in the air and buzzing higher. She glanced to the left and saw a twig caught in the undercarriage. They'd made it. Barely.

"Wheee." She reveled in the victory and the sense of freedom that only flying gave her. The wind rushing over her skin, the air so clean it left her breathless, the drone that proclaimed to the whole world that Darcy Shea could fly. *Fly!*

A tap on the shoulder ended her celebration. Jack pointed to her clipboard. Back to work.

She noted the time and altitude. Again when they reached cruising altitude, she noted the time, weather conditions and speed. Then Jack took the plane due west, away from the sun.

In thirty minutes, they reached the Lake Michigan shoreline. A necklace of white sand rimmed the sparkling sapphire-blue waters. From three thousand feet, she couldn't distinguish the mounding dunes that formed the shore.

Years ago, just after Amelia married, Papa and Mum had taken her there for a picnic. They'd strolled the beach, collecting pink granite and taffy-colored jasper. They ate roast chicken and chocolate cake with quite a bit of sand mixed in. They waded in the lake and laughed when a wave wet their skirts and Papa's trousers. It had been a blissful time.

Just like today. She could have flown on forever, but Jack turned the plane back east, jerking her to the present. Time, altitude, revolutions per minute. All went onto the clipboard.

They landed too soon, dropping heavily into the whip-like

grass. After the plane rolled to a stop in the barn, she cast off the seat belt and threw her arms around him. "We made it."

Just like the very first time, he resisted. "Darcy," he cautioned as he unwrapped her arms. "We have work to do."

Couldn't the man celebrate? "Aren't you excited? It was a success. Exactly what you wanted."

He jumped to the ground, his face grim. "Not exactly."

"What do you mean? We got in the air. We have all the data we need." She shimmied down and shoved the clipboard at him.

He took it but didn't even look at her figures. "We're still too heavy. We need to lose eighty to a hundred pounds."

But that wasn't it. Jack didn't fret about easy adjustments like reducing weight. He just made the cuts and went on.

She set her goggles on the worktable. "There's something you're not telling me."

"No there's not." He leaned against the table, pretending to study her figures, brow furrowed.

She eased alongside him, placing her hand beside his on the table. "You can talk to me. I won't tell a soul, not even Beattie."

He continued to pour over the figures, his jaw working through the problem. "I suppose I could. You are a woman."

"And what does that have to do with anything?"

"You might know what my sister is thinking."

Though tempted to point out his lack of tact, Darcy sensed pain beneath the mindless comments, so she waited until he gathered the nerve to spill his worries.

"She's found someone," he said. "A doctor. She thinks she's in love."

"How wonderful."

He scowled. "Not wonderful. She has polio. She can't have

children. That's not something a prospective husband wants in a wife."

"If he loves her…"

"How could he love her?" Jack exploded. "She thinks she's in love because he talks to her." He tugged at his hair, a gesture she noticed he did when worried. "But it will end up in disaster. How can I break it to her before she gets hurt? What do I say?"

"You don't say a thing." Darcy could not believe the man's audacity. "Your sister is how old?"

"Twenty-seven."

"She's a grown woman and perfectly capable of making her own decisions."

His scowl deepened. "But she'll be hurt."

Darcy was touched by his desire to shield his sister from pain, misplaced as it was. "We're all hurt at times in our lives. Besides, you're condemning the relationship before you know anything about it. Who is he?"

Jack shrugged and again pretended to review the times she'd recorded during the flight. "A doctor."

"I happen to know that doctors can be compassionate. George Carrman certainly is."

"How compassionate is he?"

She ignored that flash of jealousy. "He helped me when I was hurt."

Jack did not look appeased. He handed the figures back to her. "Calculate fuel usage per hour."

She couldn't tell if he was angry or not, but he clearly didn't want to talk about his sister any longer. Time to stick to business. "When do we make the distance test?"

A fine white line outlined his upper lip. "I'm sorry. I reached Dwight Pohlman by telephone last night. He'll be here Friday."

Shock slashed through her with the force of a windstorm.

After so many delays, she'd begun to believe Pohlman would never show. She thought she'd be the navigator. She thought she'd won Jack's respect.

She was right. On Friday morning, Pohlman wired that he would meet them in Newfoundland. Darcy rejoiced. Jack fumed. She suspected he was secretly happy that the weather had turned foul.

"You're afraid to let me fly this test," she pointed out.

He glared. "I'm not afraid, I'm cautious. No one flies in bad weather."

"Suppose the weather turns bad underway?"

"You find a place to land and wait it out."

"So that's what we'll do."

He growled, "We'll be over water."

Darcy didn't want to admit she hadn't thought of that, so she went to the telegraph office to pick up the weather forecast. Rain and wind. Naturally.

The flight had to be put off over a week, but on the twenty-sixth, when Darcy picked up the forecast, she knew the wait was over. Three days of fair skies and steady high pressure, bringing low wind.

"I want you here an hour before sunrise for preflight," instructed Jack. "Bring coffee, chocolate, sandwiches. It's going to be a long day." He listed a dozen things for her to do.

There was just one problem.

"Tomorrow?" She bit her lip, hesitant. "But it's Sunday."

He looked up from his notes. "What does that have to do with our flight?"

"We never work on Sunday."

He went back to the notes. "That's a luxury we no longer have."

"But—" Darcy hesitated, torn by the call to fly and the duty to her soul. "The forecast calls for three days of fair weather. Can't we wait until Monday?"

"The forecast changes, especially this time of year. If we wait we may lose the transatlantic attempt entirely. The chief competitors are already there."

"Then let's skip the distance test and go straight to Newfoundland."

Jack scowled. "We can't skip the distance test. Haven't you been listening? That test will tell us if this plane can make the distance. Without it, we're flying into certain death. No skipping steps, understand?"

"Yes, but the weather."

"Is awful right now in Newfoundland. Remember, they have our weather from two days ago. Rain and wind. Maybe even snow at that latitude. No one's flying. See you in the morning."

Darcy could not quell the flutter of foreboding in her stomach. Was she wrong about Jack, or didn't he realize the implications? She gently said, "But, we shouldn't fly on the Sabbath."

"This is no time to get superstitious." He climbed into the cockpit.

He didn't believe. Darcy had told herself he must belong to another denomination, but she'd never checked with the other churches. She'd never asked. She was afraid of what she might find out. He couldn't be a nonbeliever. She couldn't fall in love with a nonbeliever. The tiny pit of emptiness inside swelled and swelled until she ached all over. She could never seriously consider a man who didn't believe in God. But she loved Jack.

She made a final attempt to convince him. "Harriet Quimby wouldn't fly on Sundays."

He glared down from the cockpit. "I don't care what she

or anyone else did or doesn't do. We need to go tomorrow, so do whatever you have to do to make peace, and be ready at dawn."

Darcy felt sick. She had never missed Sunday worship, except for illness. It was a special time, a sacred time. It wasn't superstition. If Jack didn't understand that, how could they ever be together?

"You do believe in God, don't you?" She held her breath, hoping and willing the right answer.

Jack rummaged in the space behind his seat where they stored the extra fuel and oil.

"Did you hear my question?" she called up.

"I heard you, but you don't want to know my answer."

"Yes I do," she insisted.

Jack looked pained, but he didn't hold back. "Why should I believe in God when God doesn't believe in me?"

The rancor made her gasp. "You can't mean that."

"Yes, I do. No matter what ministers say, I know for a fact that God doesn't answer prayers."

"But he does," she cried. "He hears all prayers."

"Not everyone's."

She wanted to know what unanswered prayer had turned him from God. She wanted to plead for his soul, but his tensed jaw told her to say no more.

"Be here an hour before dawn," he said. "If you won't go, tell me now. The transatlantic attempt is on the line." The blue of his eyes had turned to ice.

She couldn't bring herself to say no.

Darcy tossed and turned that night, unable to reconcile her desire with what was right. She wanted to make the transatlantic attempt. She believed God had given her the opportunity. Then why this test? Why bring Jack into her life? And why was he an unrepentant unbeliever?

She could no longer deny that she felt something for him. Beattie might call it love, but to Darcy it was the most horrible pain imaginable. She couldn't imagine not being with Jack, yet she could have no future with a man who refused to acknowledge God. He both encouraged and held her back. He delighted children, yet angered her father. He could be tender or cruel. If this was love, why did anyone want it?

She tried to pray, but his denial, crackling with hurt and anger, rang in her ears. He acted as if he'd been personally injured. What had he said? That he had proof? Something had happened to shake his faith. If only it could be regained. She had to pray it could. The Lord said He would go after every lost sheep. *Lord, please help Jack. Please bring him home.*

She felt a little better after that simple prayer, but the choice still remained: deny her faith or give up her dream and lose Jack. The dilemma churned in her stomach. She threw the covers off one minute and yanked them back up the next. What to do? What to do? Try as she might, she couldn't find a solution that allowed her to choose both. Either way she lost.

Darcy didn't think she'd fallen asleep until the alarm rang at five. Groggy and numb, she splashed her face with cold water. She could put off the decision no longer. Pushing aside the thick sweaters, jacket and riding breeches she'd set out the night before, she took her navy gabardine dress from the closet.

After dressing, she pulled up her hair. Her eyes looked puffy and her complexion wan, but her family and her church would still accept her.

She located her father's tissue-wrapped bear claw in her dresser drawer. She should have given it to Freddie when Papa first asked, but she'd had this foolish idea that giving up the claw would somehow mean giving up her dream. Well, claw or no claw, her dream was shattered.

She breathed deep for courage and went downstairs.

"Darcy?" Mum stood in the kitchen doorway. "I'm surprised to see you up so early."

"I couldn't sleep."

Mum looked her over, doubtlessly noting the dress. "Does that have anything to do with a rumor I heard that Mr. Hunter intends to fly today?"

She nodded.

"I thought perhaps you would be with him," Mum added softly.

"I'm going to the barn now to tell him I can't go on the flight."

"I see. What changed your mind?"

Darcy bowed her head. "It's Sunday. I can't fly." As she said the words, she realized they condemned Jack. "I'm praying for him."

Tears glistened in Mum's eyes. "Me, too."

Darcy's throat squeezed shut, and tears threatened to fall.

Mum hugged her close. "You're doing the right thing, dearest. You will never regret putting God first. You could give no greater example to Jack."

"I don't know. I just don't know."

Mum gazed at her with calm assurance. "Trust in the Lord, and He will guide your steps. He is a mighty God, capable of changing the hardest heart. Believe it, dearest, with all your heart and all your soul."

"And it will become true?" Darcy wiped away a tear.

"If you only have faith the size of a mustard seed."

"It's so hard," Darcy choked out, blinking back the tears.

"I know this flight means the world to you," Mum said, "but there will be other flights and other days."

No there won't. Darcy's lip quivered. She didn't want to think of what she was losing.

She handed the tissue-wrapped claw to Mum. "Give this to Papa, please."

"What is it?"

"The bear claw. Tell Papa to give it to Freddie."

Mum nodded. "I'll do that. Thank you, Darcy. And remember to trust. All will turn out well in the end. You'll see."

Darcy pulled on her black coat and slowly walked to the barn. Even from a distance, she could see the coal oil lanterns burning inside. Jack was already there. Her heart beat miserably, banging a death dirge with each step.

If this was right, why did it hurt so much? She dreaded speaking the words, seeing Jack's face, hearing his fury. He'd asked her to tell him yesterday if she wasn't going, but she hadn't. No matter what she did, she let someone down. It tore her to pieces that this time it was Jack.

She stepped softly into the barn, hoping he wouldn't notice her right away, but he looked up at once. He stood at the worktable, pencil in hand, cap off. His hair stuck out a bit, like a boy just out of bed. In all her days, she would never forget the way he looked at that moment.

His smile faded as he noted her dress. "You're not going."

She nodded, her throat too constricted to speak.

He returned to the paperwork without a word. He looked pale, his lips were thinned and his face was somehow older in the lantern light. She'd devastated his plans, but he didn't lash out at her. He just stood at the worktable, scratching away at his checklist.

Darcy waited for what seemed forever, and when he made no move to speak, she backed toward the door. "I'm sorry."

He didn't reply. He didn't look at her. He just worked. Disappointment coiled around her heart, squeezing it lifeless. She'd ruined everything. Everything.

She stumbled out of the barn into the dark predawn, barely able to see through the tears.

Chapter Fifteen

Rain spit from the skies before Darcy reached home, and she thanked God for the reprieve. At church she kept glancing to the doors, hoping Jack would come to worship. If he understood how much this meant to her, he would. But he didn't, and the flicker of hope she'd cherished for a future together blew out.

By midafternoon the rain stopped. During Sunday dinner the sun came out. She listened for the aeroplane motors. Jack wouldn't fly, would he? It would be dark before he reached the Upper Peninsula.

Still, she checked the sky every few minutes for the rest of the afternoon, until finally Papa set aside his magazine with a sigh.

"Go," he said.

"Go where? I have nowhere to go."

He shook his head. "I don't consider it wise or safe, but you showed today that your heart is in the right place. Go on that flight. It obviously means a lot to you."

Darcy could not believe her ears. "You're giving your blessing?"

"I wouldn't go that far." He reopened the magazine.

Despite Papa's reluctant approval, it was no use going to the barn that afternoon. Even if she could face Jack, he wouldn't be there. He'd be...where? Surely not at the boardinghouse. A man desired entertainment. Her heart sank. Not at Mrs. Lawrence's saloon? Since state prohibition had been repealed in February, the saloon had reopened publicly in its old location. Never once had Darcy seen signs Jack went there, but after their fight, he might. She sent a fervent prayer he'd stay away.

The next day she awoke well before dawn. Unable to sleep, she donned her riding breeches, two thick sweaters and a canvas coat. Might as well act as if yesterday's disagreement had never occurred. She packed a lunch and walked to the barn. The skies were clear, the wind light. Perfect.

The barn stood dark, as did Terchie's. No sign of Jack. Had he given up, or was he suffering after a night of drink? She flexed her fingers in the chill air. Her pulse pounded as she rehearsed what she would say to him. Something about the good weather. After that, she wasn't sure.

She retrieved the key from the nook in the tree where Jack kept it and unlocked the barn door. Near as she could tell, the plane was still there. She located a coal oil lamp and lit it. Yes. Still there.

Darcy began the preflight check. She stowed her vacuum bottle of coffee and sandwiches in the forward cockpit, and lit the lanterns and gasoline heater to warm the engines. She then began the tedious process of checking every screw and wire.

She had almost finished the left wing when Jack arrived. He didn't smile or greet her, but he did carry a lunch and vacuum bottle. He walked directly to the worktable.

"A-are we on?" Her shaking voice betrayed her nerves.

He set down the bottle and removed his gloves. Still no recognition she was there.

"The sky's clear, the wind's light," she said hopefully.

He rummaged in the toolbox. The clanking made her nervous. Is this the way it would be? Perform the task at hand without even a word? She couldn't work that way.

"I'm sorry," she said again, though she had no idea why she should apologize.

"No need," he said stiffly, not angrily as she expected, more like he was afraid of what he might say. "How far are you?"

Darcy had never been so glad to hear his voice. "Almost done with the left wing."

"I'll start on the right one." He climbed onto the wing.

"You don't want to check my work?"

"I'm sure it's fine." He moved closer to the fuselage, working quickly.

"But I thought…" She was confused. "You said…"

"That a pilot should always check the plane himself?" He finally glanced at her, but she couldn't read his expression.

"You did say that." If he didn't smile, she was going to be sick.

"Yes, I did. But after five months, I know you're thorough. You're also going to be on this flight, so if you miss something, it's your life on the line, too."

The mixed praise and caution made her stomach flip-flop. All Jack's warnings rushed back: icy cold water, no place to land, risky. It had seemed overprotective when she wouldn't be making the flight, but now she understood.

"I'm sorry," she whispered. Her hand shook so badly she had to set down the screwdriver. She held onto the edge of the rear cockpit, trying to regain control.

He looked up from the other side of the fuselage. They crouched opposite each other, with the cockpit between.

"Don't be. Those are your beliefs, and I respect them."

He did? She was a little relieved. "That's not what I meant, though. You were right. I could use more experience before attempting a transatlantic crossing."

His eyes met hers. "You said I was being overprotective."

"I—I might have been wrong."

A corner of his mouth eased up. "Darcy Shea wrong? Impossible."

Tears welled. Goodness, she was a mess if she couldn't take a little teasing. She'd always enjoyed it before.

He lifted a strand of hair from her brow. "You weren't wrong. I was."

Oh, no. Now she really was going to cry. She blinked rapidly. "No, *you* were right."

He laughed. "Are we going to argue over who was more wrong?" He slipped the strand of hair behind her ear.

She could only shake her head no. Her throat was too constricted. She'd expected anger and received mercy. She'd feared reprisal and received understanding.

"You aren't going to cry on me, are you?" he asked.

Again she shook her head, but this time he cupped her chin and drew her eyes upward until she looked into his. There she saw tenderness. And love.

He drew closer, leaning over the cockpit, still holding her face in his hand. She felt his breath on her forehead then her cheek.

Her knees turned to oatmeal. "I—I…"

"Shh." He pressed a fingertip to her lips. "Don't talk."

She caught her breath, which suddenly seemed like a terribly difficult thing to do. The icy cold barn roasted. The light grew fuzzy and the air became thick as pudding. He was going to kiss her. Not maybe or almost but really kiss her. She closed her eyes.

His lips were soft, barely more than the feather-light caress of a handkerchief, but oh so much more alive. He tasted a little salty. She breathed in the scent that was only Jack—soap and leather and gasoline. He paused, lips still close, but she wanted more.

"Is something wrong?"

"No." He brushed a hair from her cheek. "You're perfect in every way."

Then he truly kissed her, telling her without words that he would always be there for her, melting away every fear and excuse. Darcy could barely keep her balance. The earth might have shook and the buildings around her tumbled down. She wouldn't have noticed. There was only Jack.

He held her so close, so tenderly, as though she was the most precious thing in the world. He gazed at her the way Beattie looked at Blake, the way Papa held Mum when he thought they were alone. The world had righted, and Jack stood square in the center.

She reached for him, and her knee let loose. She nearly slid off the wing, but Jack caught her. He scrambled across the cockpit faster than she thought possible. Safe in his embrace, she gazed into those blue eyes, wide as the sky. There was room for her in that limitless future.

He grinned. "I guess I didn't choose the best location."

"No, it's perfect." She sighed like a silly schoolgirl, but she didn't care.

He scooped her in his arms and carried her to the ground, where he set her on her feet. She hated to let go, but he gently removed her arms. "Why don't you top off the oilcans?" He handed her the filter. "Let me know when you're done, and I'll heft them into the plane."

Oh, yes—the flight.

Darcy set the filter on the table and carried the cans to the large oil drum. While she filled each to the top, she marveled at what had happened. Minutes ago she thought Jack hated her, but not now. After that kiss, she had no doubt.

She watched him pull open the barn doors. His stride was

firm, his purpose set. He loved her enough to forgive. He was perfect in every way but one. She bit her lip. He'd accepted that faith was important to her, but hadn't trusted God for himself.

The sky had lightened. It was time.

"Finished?" he asked. "We need to get underway. It'll be a long day."

She had to trust that God would complete the work He'd begun. "I'm ready."

Jack's energy soared. She had responded, really responded. Darcy Shea had feelings for him. It probably wasn't the best time to find that out, but she'd looked so beautiful insisting she was wrong. What man could have resisted?

Thankfully, Blake Kensington, the Simmons kid and half the town turned out moments later to push the plane out of the barn and see them off. Romance got shoved aside and business took over. He had to make sure Darcy was ready. Once in the air, they wouldn't be able to talk over the drone of the engines.

He handed her some cotton. She looked at it like she had no idea what to do with it.

"For your ears." He indicated she should insert some in each ear.

She blushed, and the attraction rushed back. He clapped his hands in the cold morning air. He had to get their attention back on the flight. "Any instructions go on the slate, understand?" He ran through all the signals and made her repeat them.

Her eyes still looked a bit glassy, every emotion visible on her face. Darcy couldn't hide a thing. Her joys and anger and sorrow were right there for the world to see.

He had to look away before he found himself in worse

trouble than he already was. The flight would be long. He didn't need to spend it thinking about her. One of them had to stay calm and rational.

They were airborne within the hour. The haze began to burn off, revealing clear blue sky. Light wind from the southwest wouldn't cause much drift.

He headed for the lake.

The nearly three hundred miles they'd fly over Lake Michigan would provide the perfect opportunity to test over-water conditions. Within minutes they'd be out of sight of either shore, then he'd turn north. Darcy was to take sightings every half hour, plot their position, write the results on a slate and show him. Then he could make course corrections. Crude, but hopefully effective.

After two hours of flight, the motors droned at full revolution. No loss of speed. He'd dumped two cans of fuel into the tank, and the lighter weight was already making them quicker. The deep blue waters sped by below, the waves mere ripples at three thousand feet.

He'd have to add more fuel after the next reading. While he handled that necessary though risky procedure, Darcy took the controls. One sudden move would throw him over the side to his death. He usually hated putting his life in another person's hands, yet with her he felt safe. He'd seen something in her eyes. Love?

After settling back in the cockpit, he noted a low cloud-bank looming ahead. It didn't extend all the way to the water like fog. Probably trailing clouds from yesterday's weather. It would be a good test of machine and pilot.

They flew into the cloud at the three-and-a-half-hour mark. Condensation almost immediately formed on his goggles. He had to wipe them constantly. Impossible to see. He took the plane lower, searching for the cloud's bottom edge, and came out at two hundred feet above the water.

"What now?" Darcy wrote on the slate.

"Under or around," he yelled, but he couldn't tell if she heard him.

Fortunately, the cloud ended minutes later, and he took the plane up to three thousand feet again. They soared past land that jutted out to their right. Must be one of the peninsulas near Traverse City. Given their time in the air and direction, that should be it, but just to be certain, he tapped Darcy on the shoulder and indicated she should take another sighting.

He had to admit she'd been a quick study on the sextant. Navigating in an open cockpit was a constant challenge, with the cold and the blasting wind. If the fingers weren't too stiff to work the sextant and take notes, the map and tables threatened to blow away. To get an accurate reading, she had to take multiple rapid sightings and then average them.

He hoped she was as accurate in the air as on the land.

She held up the slate. He pointed down, indicating he wanted to see the map. She carefully held it up, their flight line penned onto the light blue of the lake. He'd been correct.

Soon they'd cross the last of Lake Michigan and go over the Upper Peninsula, which could still be snow-covered. He hoped that would prepare them for the north Atlantic ice fields.

The land turned out to be speckled with snow and evergreens. He'd forgotten about the trees. That changed the heat of the land and gave them clear flying until Lake Superior.

Three miles over that vast body of water, fog rose. His gut clenched. Fog was every aviator's nightmare. In a light fog with a strong sun, sightings could still be made, but if it thickened navigation got tough. It also brought weight gain from the condensation. Flying east might take them out of it, but that wouldn't test their skills. Chances were, he'd encounter fog over the Atlantic. If he could conquer it here, he could make it there.

Darcy had given him a position less than ten minutes before entering the fogbank. On the present course, they'd come out of the fog in no more than two hours when they reached Ontario.

Once again, he had to constantly wipe his goggles. Between the thick air and the condensation, he struggled to see his gauges. He had to hold his watch close to read it. Finally he gave up and ripped the goggles off. The rushing air made his eyes water, but by squinting he could see better than with the steamed-up goggles.

Daylight waned without a sign the fog would thin. Jack gnawed his lip. It shouldn't be getting this dark at four o'clock. Either the fog was thickening or a storm was building. Neither boded well for their flight. He considered turning back, but they had almost covered the full distance. Just a little farther, and they'd be over land and the fog would clear. It couldn't happen soon enough. He would head east on the return, staying over land. He'd had enough fog for this trip.

Fifteen minutes passed. A half hour. According to the compass, they were on course, but the fog hadn't cleared yet. They should be over land. In the absence of wind, there could be little drift, and with the prevailing westerlies, they'd have drifted toward land, not away from it. Either Darcy's sightings had been wrong, putting them out over Superior's open waters, or the fog extended far inland.

He was about to take the plane east when the left engine coughed. Like with the scout plane, it cranked back up to speed a moment later. Jack glanced over, worried. He'd dumped another can of fuel into the tank before the fogbank. They shouldn't be running low.

Then a droplet hit his cheek. And another.

Rain?

He checked the wings. The slowly winding rope that had been knotting in his stomach balled tight.

Condensation covered the wings, and it wasn't running off. It was freezing.

With the dimming daylight, the air temperatures must be dropping. The *Kensington Express* would soon be coated in ice. Too much, and they'd drop like a stone. He figured he had less than fifteen minutes. He headed the plane to a lower altitude, hoping the temperatures were warmer.

Darcy's head whipped around and then back. She scribbled on the slate and showed him. "Altitude?"

He pointed to the wings and then down. He didn't know if she understood. He'd never explained the problem with freezing temperatures.

Then the left engine choked. It raced to life again for a moment and then died. That knot in his stomach jumped to his throat. Keeping the plane under control with one engine took all his skill. He tried to restart the engine. Nothing. Again. It cranked but wouldn't start.

He slammed a fist against the fuselage. Fog. Dead engine. No visibility. Ice. He needed to land, but how? He struggled to control the yawing.

Then the right motor died.

The silence was terrifying. Darcy gripped the sides of the cockpit, even after Jack leveled the plane. She wanted to take the controls. Everything told her to take the controls, but Jack was at the wheel, and he'd done this before. On the very first ride he'd brought the engine back to life.

But this time he had two engines to resuscitate, and somehow, in the pit of her stomach, she knew he wouldn't be able to do it.

"Take the controls," he said.

It was strange to suddenly hear him after hours of ceaseless droning. She grabbed hold of the wheel.

"What do you want me to do?"

"Keep as much altitude as you can," he said, the worry not at all hidden.

"How?"

"Not up," he shouted. "Keep the nose level. Hold her steady. I'm going to check the fuel lines."

The fuel lines. Darcy's head raced with her heart. They'd strained all the fuel the day before. Like always, they ran it through a triple layer of cheesecloth to catch the sediment. Mentally, she checked off each of the cans. Yes, they'd done them all. They'd been very careful.

Jack crawled out on the wing and checked the fuel line to the right motor. She held so tightly to the wheel that her hands ached. Keep it level. No turns. Don't make any sudden moves.

She squinted against the onrushing air, her eyes painfully dry.

Come back Jack. Come back. What was taking so long?

An eternity later, he inched into the rear cockpit, and she breathed again.

"That's not the problem," he said once he was seated. "Plenty of fuel in the line."

"Tell me you're not going out on the right wing."

"Not enough time. I'll take the controls now."

Darcy's mouth went dry. She remembered how it felt when they'd crashed on Baker's field, the sound of fabric ripping, of wood snapping and wire twanging. The propeller digging into the ground, spraying dirt and grass and weeds everywhere.

"Your seat belt on?" Jack asked.

That meant they were going down.

"It might be a bit of a rough landing," he said. He'd begun to glide noiselessly, taking the machine down gradually without engines. He made large, swooping turns. "Hopefully, we'll spot a clearing when we come out of the fog."

Hopefully, they were over land.

Darcy didn't know if Jack realized just how cold Lake Superior was. They'd freeze to death in minutes.

She heard him try to start an engine. One, then the other. Neither worked.

"If it's not the fuel, then what?" he growled.

The oil. Darcy knew it in an instant, and dread flooded over her in waves. She'd forgotten. She'd been so flustered after the kiss that she forgot to strain the oil. She could see the filter right where she left it on the table. Sediments in the oil had clogged the oil screens, just like the scout plane.

She was to blame. If they died, it was her fault.

Darcy turned to tell him, but he yelled, "Put your head down. You don't want it snapped off."

She turned around and peered into the foggy gloom.

He was trying to find a clearing, hoping the fog had lifted enough that they could get below it, but the gray mist continued unbroken. It must go clear to the ground.

She ducked her head, praying to God, who'd surely forsaken them. "Forgive me," she prayed silently. "Take me, but not Jack. It's not his fault. It's my fault. All mine."

"Aha," Jack suddenly cried, and she raised her head.

They'd come out of the fog barely above the treetops.

Then she saw it. A clearing. Small and far away. Could they make it that far?

"Head down," he yelled.

She ducked. Almost at once the branches ripped through the fabric. The plane elevated for a moment, and then collapsed around her. She shrieked and covered her head as she was flung forward.

Chapter Sixteen

The plane splintered around Jack in an oddly arrested sequence, like a film shown at too-slow a speed. The wings collapsed first, buckled by the trees. Branches scraped past, tearing cloth and skin alike. The lower right wing catapulted over the upper. The motor whirled past their heads. He instinctively shielded Darcy, though if the engine had fallen, they would both have been crushed.

The fuselage shot forward like a missile, and he yelled for her to get her head down.

She turned at the sound of his voice. A branch clipped his cheekbone, opening a gash, but he could think only of Darcy.

"Head down." His words sent her into a crouch, just as the cockpit framing crumpled and the whole thing smashed to a stop.

Jack's pulse still raced after the noise died away and the plane settled. He was alive. Aches and a sore shoulder, but he was still alive.

He surveyed the damage. The forward cockpit took the brunt of the impact, imploding to a third its size. Snapped wood. Ripped fabric. Tangled branches.

Darcy. She was somewhere in that mess. He couldn't see her.

He pawed wildly at the debris. He couldn't find her.

Thwang. A bracing wire snapped.

He dug faster, searching in the semidarkness for her canvas coat or the soft wool of her sweater.

Zzzt. Linen tore, and the plane lurched. They hadn't reached the ground. He saw only framing and branches, not the forest floor.

Then he smelled gasoline. Just like the crash in Pearlman. Only this time he carried ten times the fuel. At any second the whole plane could explode.

He needed to get Darcy out.

He called for her.

No response.

He hoisted himself up, gingerly balancing on the front edge of his cockpit, and pulled aside branch after branch until he got to her. She lay curled in a ball to the left side of the cockpit. What remained of it. A gaping hole breached the right side. The front amounted to a mangled pile of broken wood and canvas.

The wreck shifted, and he grabbed onto a branch to steady himself. They could crash to the ground at any moment. He had to get her out.

"Darcy?" He shook her gently.

She muttered something unintelligible.

Relief rushed in, then abruptly out. Was that a spark? He held his breath while they teetered precariously. Another blue flash. Definitely a spark. No time. No time.

He pushed on the branches above her. A four-inch-diameter limb crossed the cockpit, pinning her beneath it. He yanked. He pulled. The plane shifted with an eerie creak. He had no idea how far up they were. A twenty-foot freefall could flip the wreck, crushing them. If they miraculously fell free, the impact could knock them out, and the ensuing fire would incinerate them.

He stood dead still, wondering how on earth he was going to get Darcy out without unbalancing the wreck.

Another spark. No time to be delicate. He climbed onto a hefty branch that had speared through the fuselage. Balancing like a tightrope artist, he pushed up on the limb pinning Darcy, while reaching under her with the other arm. The plane shifted a couple of inches. He dropped the limb and hung on until, with an ominous groan, the wreckage settled.

He held his breath and began again. This time, when he pulled, the wreck stayed in place. So did Darcy. No matter what he did, she wouldn't budge.

"Darcy, wake up," he barked, lightly slapping her cheeks.

She murmured unintelligibly.

"Wake up," he demanded, hoping the tone would rouse her.

"Where?" Her voice was thick, groggy.

"Can you move?"

Her hands flailed, finding only air. "Belt."

He had no idea what she meant. "I need you to move toward me. Let me know if any part of you is stuck."

"Belt," she repeated with greater agitation. "Can't."

Jack snapped with frustration. "You need to help me." The gasoline smell had increased. One spark, one flash of metal on stone, would send the plane up in a fireball.

"Be-elt," she wailed, and he finally understood.

What an idiot he'd been. The seat belt.

He leaned as far as he could, searching through the rubble for the belt. At last. He undid it and then lifted her.

"Ow!" she yelped. "My leg."

"Is it stuck?" He hoped she'd say no.

"I—I don't know."

"Listen carefully. We need to get you out of here before the plane catches fire."

"I can do it," she said, though with a groggy edge. "I should have done it."

He heard a sob. No, not tears. They didn't have time for tears.

He put her arm around his neck. "Hold on. I'm going to lift."

She held on only a moment. He'd have to do this himself. He lifted, and this time when she screamed he ignored her pain and pulled with all his strength.

"Stop, stop," she yelled much more lucidly. "Let me go. You'll kill me."

"Better me than a fire." He yanked. He tugged. He pulled.

Between her screams and the hum in his ears, he didn't hear her come free of the wreckage, but he felt it. The sudden release sent him backwards.

He caught his balance, crashing awkwardly against the fuselage. His lower back hit the edge of the cockpit, sending a jolt of pain up his spine. But he didn't let go of Darcy. He choked back the pain and got to his knees. *Do this. Get her to safety.* Mustering his remaining strength, he rose to his feet, Darcy in his arms.

The whole wreck began to tilt. It was going down. He didn't think. He skittered downward through the tangle of limbs and branches. The twigs scratched and clawed at them. He seemed to step on air half the time. Then with a crack, the plane pitched forward a few feet, and Jack slammed into the ground with Darcy beneath him. Pain shivered up his arms to the elbows. A twinge shot through his shoulder. Darcy stifled a yelp.

"You all right?" But he couldn't wait for an answer. The

plane had only shifted. He had to get her away from the wreck before it fell the rest of the way.

He picked her up and carried her through gloom and trees and snow and mud until, far enough from the plane for safety, they reached a patch of open ground. Gasping, shaking and exhausted, he dropped to his knees, Darcy still cradled in his arms. The damp earth soaked through to the bone. Icy mist prickled his skin.

No. Not rain. They did not need rain. Darcy would take a chill and get feverish. He had to get her to shelter.

He spied a thick evergreen with dense branches that drooped to the ground. She'd be safe under there. Once again he lifted.

"Stop," she said. "What are you doing?"

"Getting you to cover."

"I can walk."

He ignored her protests and carried her to the tree, where he set her on the carpet of soft needles. The ground felt dry and would likely stay that way unless the rain picked up intensity. He pulled off his jacket and laid it over her.

"Forgot," she slurred.

"Stay here," he commanded, hoping for once she'd obey. "I'm going to retrieve some supplies from the plane." He needed to find at least one of the vacuum bottles and something to keep Darcy warm.

"I'll help." Her voice sounded clear. Odd how the lucidity went in and out.

"No. It's too dangerous. Leave this to me."

"Too dangerous for you."

"I'll be careful," he said, touched that she thought of him.

"You'd better be."

Jack kissed her forehead and sprinted a few steps toward the plane. If he could find the radio transmitter he could get help. Then he remembered where it was, safely tucked in his watertight trunk in the barn.

"No," he yelled to the silent forest. They were stranded in the wilderness without food, shelter or communications. How could he have been so stupid?

He stumbled toward the wreck. It had grown so dark that he could barely see five feet ahead. He spun in a circle, realizing he didn't know where the plane was located. He looked to the sky and got an eyeful of rain.

"Don't leave me," Darcy said, sounding groggy again.

The words tugged him back. In the darkness of the forest, he saw again the dark streets of Pearlman and Darcy in her family's parlor, children all around. Everything he ever wanted. Right there. So why was he here?

He knelt and touched Darcy's forehead. Cool, thank God. "I'm here," he whispered.

She sighed softly, a sound that warmed Jack to the depths of his soul. It reminded him of childhood, of how he felt when his mother tucked him into bed and listened to him say his prayers. It reminded him of the last time he'd really trusted anyone.

He fought back a rush of emotion. Darcy trusted him with her life. Somehow—he didn't know how—he had to save her. He could not let her down.

Pain. It pulsed through Darcy's dreams and summoned her back to the living. She couldn't tell exactly what hurt. It felt more like everything had been pulled apart and then sewn back the wrong way.

Mixed with the throbbing came the sharp smell of pine. Was it Christmas? But then why did she ache? And why was she lying on the parlor floor? She cracked her eyelids. Odd lights flickered in and out. Christmas.

She tried to turn her head. *Ouch.* It hurt. Her arms hurt. Her legs hurt. Everything hurt. She gave up the effort.

A branch snapped. That sound she remembered. The crackle of branches snapping around her, the rush of air, the solidity of ground. She'd crashed. They'd crashed. The plane. Jack.

With a groan, she forced open her eyes, and the sudden light knifed through her head. She squinted against the pain, tried to make out the scene. Smoke. Fire.

Fire.

She gasped. Jack had warned about fire. If the gasoline caught fire, the woods would burn. They'd burn.

"Fire," she rasped, not loud enough to alert a baby, least of all Jack. But nothing in her body seemed to work right. "Fire," she tried again with all her might. Not much better.

She rolled to her side, though it took enormous energy. From that position, she saw that the fire wasn't a raging inferno but a simple campfire, not six feet away. Jack must have built it. A twig popped. That was the snapping sound.

What a relief. She rolled back with a sigh, but a terrible memory wormed into her mind.

She'd caused the crash.

She'd forgotten to strain the oil. The sediment had clogged the screens and made the motors stall. *No!*

No, no, no.

She'd forgotten because she'd been swept out of her mind by their kiss. Jack loved her. But he hadn't said it, had he? She tried to remember but couldn't. She started shivering.

Jack. Where was he? In a panic, she called his name.

"Darcy, thank God." His worried face appeared in the firelight. "You're all right."

She wasn't so certain. "You?"

"Just bumps and bruises."

At least she hadn't killed him. A tiny bit of the guilt ebbed away. "How long have I been asleep?" she rasped.

"A couple of hours. Here, drink this." He shoved a cup into her hand.

She managed to dribble half the coffee down her chin. "Where are we?"

"I was hoping you'd know."

"That's not funny."

"You had the map," he pointed out.

She groaned and tried to remember. In the plane. Cold. Fog. Couldn't see. The sound of branches scraping, splintering. The map. She'd marked it as best she could, but navigating in the fog had been difficult. "Canada?"

Jack drew in his breath sharply.

Oh, no. She'd guessed wrong.

"Yes, Canada, but where exactly?" he said. "We're probably going to have to hike out. It would sure help to know approximately where we are."

Darcy searched her memory, but her thoughts kept getting muddled. "I'm sorry." She started to cry.

"Don't worry." He pulled the blanket under her chin. "We'll search for the map and compass in the morning. It's too dark to look now." He backed from under the tree and added a branch to the fire.

His words comforted her, taking the worry away. The heat of the fire was making her sleepy. Her lids drooped.

"Here." Jack shoved a lump of something into her hand.

She struggled to wake. "What is it?" Only the words came out murky.

Somehow Jack understood. "Chocolate. Sorry, it's a little bit melted from being in my pocket all day."

She couldn't take his food. "We'll share."

"I already ate my half. Go ahead."

She let the rich confection melt on her tongue. It reminded

her of home just a little. Mum. Papa. How much they loved her. How Papa had agreed to let her pursue her dream, and Mum had accepted Jack. How deep their love must be. How much she loved Jack.

"I'm sorry, Darcy." His ragged voice cut through the pleasant memories. "I should never have brought you on this flight. It was too dangerous. Please forgive me."

She had to tell him it wasn't his fault. "No."

His head bowed, dejected.

Oh, dear. He thought she wouldn't forgive him. "No, not what I meant." Her tongue had thickened, and the words came with greater difficulty, but she had to tell him. She couldn't let him take the blame. "Jack?" Her voice sounded far away. Like she was walking down a dark tunnel of pines, their boughs heavy with snow.

"Stay with me, Darcy. Hold on."

She moaned. The pain was overcoming her thoughts. She had to say it now before she forgot.

"I have to tell you," she mumbled.

"That can wait. First, I'm going to check you for injuries. Where does it hurt?"

"Everywhere." She could barely say the word, but that wasn't what she needed to tell him. She had to let him know she'd caused the crash.

His hand ran over her head. "Bit of a bump here, but it's not bleeding. I'm going to check your arms now."

She felt him run a hand down each arm.

"Your right leg," he said. "Can you move it?"

She tried, but the pain brought tears to her eyes.

"May I check to see if any bones are broken? I promise not to touch above your knee."

She nodded, and he proceeded to check her shin and the movement of her limb.

"Twisted knee, if we're lucky." He replaced the blanket. "Get some rest."

"Jack." She had to tell him. She couldn't let him go to sleep thinking he was at fault.

"It can wait until morning. You need to rest."

"No." She grabbed his shirtsleeve, the urgency giving her clarity.

He removed her hand. "Sleep."

"My fault," she blurted out. "I forgot. I forgot." She couldn't get the words out in any order. "The oil. I forgot." A sob seized her entire body, but with it came the pain, wracking her so hard she could only gasp. "I forgot…to strain…it."

He sat back on his heels with an *oomph.*

He hated her. She'd ruined his dream with one silly error, and this time it couldn't be fixed. No transatlantic attempt. No prize. No record. Everything he wanted was gone because of her. All the money. All the effort. All the hope. Gone. She'd been so focused on what she wanted that she neglected his dream. If she truly loved him, she would have put him first. And that conviction hurt worst of all.

His jaw worked as he stared past her into the darkness.

She closed her eyes, unable to watch his pain, fighting the darkness that threatened to engulf her. The last thing she heard before dropping off was his footsteps.

He'd left her.

Chapter Seventeen

The next time Darcy awoke, a dim, gray light filtered through the trees. Morning. The stillness of the forest was broken by the twitter of an occasional bird and the faint rustle of squirrels and chipmunks in the undergrowth. At home, those would be comforting sounds, but here they reinforced the cruel fact that she and Jack were stranded far from civilization.

Her knee still hurt, but her head had cleared enough to remember it all: the crash, telling Jack her error and his walking away. That ached worse than the knee.

Had he left her to fend for herself? He wasn't under the hemlock. She pushed to a sitting position, and Jack's leather jacket slid off. That's what he'd laid over her, not a blanket. He'd given up his jacket for her. The ache grew worse.

"Jack?" She crawled from under the branches into a small clearing circled by pines.

He lay curled beside the smoldering fire with only a sweater to keep him warm. He would have been warmer under the hemlock, but he'd endured the elements to give her privacy and respect. Tears rose to her eyes. She thought he'd walked off in anger, but instead he'd offered love. Undeserved love.

She crawled on three limbs, dragging the useless right leg, and laid his jacket over him. Then she added her canvas coat.

"Sleep," she whispered.

He murmured but didn't wake.

"I'll find help." It would be tough, but she could do it.

First she needed a crutch. A nearby stick proved solid enough and the right length. Next she needed the map and compass. Through the trees, she saw the extent of the crash. The wings had folded back, one stuck high in a tree, the other smashed to bits on the ground. The front of the fuselage had caved in. Amazing she'd survived. One of the motors lay in pieces on the ground. Bits of wreckage and supplies were scattered over the area: fuel cans, oil cans, wood framing, half a sandwich, a vacuum bottle, the match canister.

The map had shown a mining settlement on the Lake Superior coast. She recalled thinking they'd passed over it in the fog. That meant they should be due north. Not that far. No more than a few miles. The map would tell her. She redoubled her search and finally located her clipboard, including the map, wedged under the teetering remnants of the left wing.

She couldn't pull the clipboard free, but by gently tugging and working at it, she got the map out, mostly in one piece. Next she needed the compass, but she couldn't find that anywhere.

Darcy's head ached, and her riding breeches were soaked through. Though winter's snow had melted in most places, the ground was still damp and terribly cold. She shivered, and her stomach growled.

She picked up the sandwich, which had come out of its paper wrapping and was covered with dirt and needles. No matter how unappetizing, it was food. She brushed off as much debris as she could and took a bite. Gritty and soggy, and it tasted like fuel.

She spat it out and looked for something to drink. The vacuum bottle's contents swished when she shook it, but the stopper was jammed. She resorted to snow. The spring melt had turned winter's flakes to granular ice, loose and easy to scoop up. She shoved a handful in her mouth and let it melt down her parched throat.

Her last mark on the map showed them just past the shoreline. When had she taken that reading? How much time between that and the engines dying? Fifteen minutes? It couldn't have been more. The way Jack took the plane down in s-turns, they might be within a mile of the mine. Even with a gimpy leg, she could walk that far.

"I'm bringing help, Jack," she whispered. "By the time you wake, we'll be safe."

The daylight seemed dimmer than it ought to be. The pines and hemlocks blocked a lot of light, but the sky also looked thick with clouds.

If she could find the sun, no matter how weak, she could fix her direction. She scanned the sky until she saw a faintly lighter spot through the trees. That was east. Now she needed to determine north from south. The trees would tell her. She checked for moss and lichens, which grew more thickly on the north side.

Now certain of her direction, she set off due south. A wall of white pines blocked the way. She went around them and resumed course on the other side. She limped forward on her crutch, picking her way over the uneven terrain. Every step hurt, but knowing she would earn Jack's respect eased the pain.

Soon she reached a narrow creek. On any other day, she'd merely hop across, but her knee couldn't stand the impact. The map proved useless. Its scale didn't show minor features like creeks. To the left, the creek burbled over small rock steps. To the right, an ancient pine shaded the stream. One thick limb had split off and lay across the stream, forming a bridge. She tested it. Solid. But less than a foot's length wide. If she fell, her injury would get worse, and she'd be soaked in icy water.

But she had to get across. She edged over sideways, bit by bit, until she reached the other side.

Her triumph was short-lived. Something cold and damp hit her face. Then another and another and another. Rain. No, snow. The fat white flakes came quicker and quicker until the air filled with them.

She'd have to hurry. The mining settlement must be close. She'd been walking for ages. A wooded hill ranged before her as far as she could see in both directions. No way around it. She had to go over. Maybe from the top she could see the mine.

She struggled up the hill, panting and wincing with pain. It turned out to be a narrow ridge, as deeply forested on the far side as the near. Beyond stood yet another hill. Disappointed, she started down the other side, but on the third step her crutch snapped. She fell, sliding at first and then tumbling as she gathered speed. The map flew from her hand. Saplings whipped her. She caromed off a slender birch. Cold, wet, sharp, scraping. Over and over she rolled, sliding and crashing through the underbrush.

Oomph. She came to a stop at the bottom. The pain knocked her flat. She lay prone for the longest time. Courage. If Amelia could endure twenty-two hours of hard labor, she could manage a few twists and bruises.

She sat. Her injured knee had lodged between two young trees. She tried to remove it, and the pain shot bright spots across her vision. She clenched her teeth and tried again, only to repeat the mind-numbing agony. It was no use. She was stuck, helpless.

Panic struck with deadly aim. Jack had no idea where she'd gone. He didn't even know she'd left. The snow fell thickly now, covering any tracks. He'd never find her. She would die.

The thudding in her ears drowned out the sound of the

forest. Was this death? Was this what Robert Scott had felt in the Antarctic, what the *Titanic*'s passengers had endured? Did Papa worry about her? Did he stand at Baker's field, watching for their plane? Dear Mum, who only wanted her happiness. Darcy had never quite listened.

And Jack. Wonderful, forgiving Jack. She could smell the warm leather, see him in Devlin's Model T, assisting Beatrice but watching her. She should have known then that he was the one. She shouldn't have wasted so much time and effort on foolishness, for what good was a great flight with no one to share the excitement? So many times God had shown her the path to Jack's heart, but she'd been oblivious, too busy concentrating on her own plans.

Accolades were hollow. What really mattered were the people around her, those God had entrusted her to love.

Tears coursed down her temples into the snow. *Jack, Jack. I love you, Jack.* Too late. Why hadn't she told him like Beattie suggested? How much could it have hurt?

She brushed the heavy, wet flakes from her face and hair, but others soon replaced them. She would die here without the chance to tell Mum and Papa and Amelia and Beatrice and Freddie and Helen and Lizzie and Jack that she loved them.

Trust in the Lord. The words seemed to come from nowhere. *Trust in the Lord and He will guide your steps.* Mum had told her that, the morning she chose worship over flying.

She was right. Trust the Lord. That's what Darcy should have done all along. That's where she'd erred. God had answered her dream a hundred times over, and she'd never realized it. It didn't take a grand gesture to impact others' lives. It took love.

Humbly, she opened her heart to God. *Please, Lord, forgive my stubborn willfulness. Instead of relying on You, I thought I could solve everything myself. I was wrong. I'm helpless and need You so. Take my will, my body, even my desire to fly.*

None of it means anything without You. She rested a moment, eyes closed, then added, *Please spare Jack*.

Incredible peace came over her. Somehow—and she couldn't say how—she knew all would be well.

Even if she perished.

Jack awoke with a start. Something cold and wet had hit his face, and for a moment he thought he was back at school and his bunkmate had thrown water at him. His aching bones told him otherwise.

With a groan, he rolled over. The dim light revealed the same bone-chilling scenario he'd faced earlier: endless forest, cold dampness and a wrecked plane. Moreover, the fire had gone out, meaning he'd slept longer than intended.

"Darcy?" he called, rubbing the sleep out of his eyes. They'd need to find the map and make plans before dark. By his estimation, it was afternoon, late afternoon. He glanced at his watch. Broken. He knew that. In disgust, he tossed it away.

His stomach growled, reminding him they lacked food. Darcy needed to eat if they were going to hike out of there—provided she could hike. The gnawing in his stomach intensified. She might not be able to walk that far. In that case, they'd need the food for survival. And they'd have to hope someone came looking for them. If only he'd put the transmitter back into the plane.

Another drop of rain hit him. No time for self-recrimination. He had work to do before nightfall.

"Darcy?"

He checked under the hemlock. She wasn't there. She'd probably gotten some fool idea to go out on her own to relieve herself. She must have taken his jacket with her. His jacket. He whipped around to be certain he wasn't mistaken. It lay by the dead fire. It had been draped over him. And so had hers. That meant she was walking around without any protection.

He called her name repeatedly, but the thick hemlocks, cedars and spruce muffled his words.

He clapped his arms for warmth and put on the old leather jacket. It cut the wind but didn't do much against bitter cold. He kept calling out Darcy's name, but he might as well have yelled into an empty well. There was no response.

A light snow began to dust the deathly still forest.

"Hey, Dar—" He broke off when he saw the partially eaten sandwich.

He hadn't touched it. A wolf or fox or bear would have taken the whole thing. Wolves. Bears. Darcy couldn't fight off an attack. He looked more closely at the sandwich. The shape of the bite looked human. She must have eaten it.

Then where had she gone?

He tromped through the woods to the wreck site. Not there.

He returned to their camp, easily following his footsteps. She must have left before the snow, because only his tracks were visible. He had to act quickly, or any evidence of her path would be covered under a blanket of white.

Again he called her name, his hands to his lips like a megaphone.

Nothing but the twitter of sparrows.

"Where in creation did you go, Shea?" he grumbled. *And why?*

The latter didn't take very long to surmise. Once he determined she wasn't near their camp, he knew the answer. She'd gone on and on last night about forgetting to strain the oil. That wasn't what had stalled the engines, but she'd been asleep by the time he figured it out.

A sick feeling settled in the pit of his stomach. Darcy Shea wasn't the typical woman. She didn't fuss or pout. She took things into her own hands, the way she'd bulled her way into flying lessons. She went after the goal, no matter the cost. She was just stubborn enough to think she could get help on her own.

Fool woman. When he found her he'd strangle her.

If he found her.

That thought twisted his stomach. As irritating as she could be at times, he couldn't imagine Darcy dying. She was too stubborn.

But this land could swallow a man whole. A woman? He shuddered. The land didn't care that she had grand plans and the talent to make them real. It didn't understand her boundless optimism. This land would leave her blue and cold beneath a drift of snow.

He should never have let her come on such a dangerous flight. He shouldn't have taught her to fly. If he admitted the truth, he hadn't done it because Pohlman took her money. He taught her to fly because he wanted to be with her. He knew better than to mix romance with flying. It was selfish and stupid. Never again.

If he found her.

Daylight was slipping away. Jack hunted for one of the portable flashlights they'd stowed in the plane. Their provisions had been scattered over the ground for a hundred yards. He picked through the rubble but couldn't find the map, the compass, or the flashlights.

He rummaged in her shattered cockpit. Luck—or maybe providence, or even God—was on his side. One of the flashlights had jammed between the side of the seat and the fuselage. With a little tugging and pushing, Jack was able to pry it free. He put it in his jacket pocket.

Then he saw the compass and sextant. For a second he rejoiced, until he realized that meant Darcy had set off without any navigational aids. She could have gone in any direction.

"Stupid, impulsive," he muttered as he climbed off the plane. *Too wonderful to die.*

What had she been thinking?

Jack tried to focus. To find Darcy, he'd have to determine her frame of mind. Which direction would she take? If she'd had the compass, she would have headed to the closest habitation, a mining camp located, by his reckoning, some twelve to fifteen miles south.

Since she lacked navigational instruments, finding her would take a little detective work. Jack surveyed the area. The hatchet—Darcy's hatchet—lay on the ground. Impulsively, he picked it up. Maybe it would be of some use.

Aside from the sandwich, he found scratch marks in the snow on the north side of the clearing. That direction led all the way to the pole. Of course, she might have eaten the snow to quench her thirst. He both hoped she had and hadn't. She needed water to survive, but not snow. Snow would lower her body temperature, doubly dangerous because she was injured.

The injury would slow her down. She couldn't have gotten far. Jack circled the clearing, looking for broken branches or scuffed ground, anything to tell him which way she went.

To the southeast he found an odd set of holes, an inch in diameter. At first he thought they were snake holes, but then he noticed they were evenly spaced and headed toward a stand of white pine.

She was using a walking stick or crutch. Of course.

He followed the trail to the pines, where it veered to the right. The snow was coming down more rapidly now, filling the holes. He had to hurry. He checked the direction on the compass and snapped off a few branches so he could find his way back.

On the other side of the pines, the trail seemed to vanish. He almost thought he'd deduced incorrectly, when he spotted a foot-tall sapling mashed to the ground. Something had stepped on it. It had to be her.

"Darcy," he called out.

Nothing.

Her path meandered around rotting stumps and fallen trees. It avoided hollows and low mounds. A creek crossed the route. He scoured each bank until he located the holes on the other side. Sometimes there were no holes. Other places the holes punctured the earth in tight circles.

Then they stopped.

Jack broke a branch as a marker and glanced back at where he'd come. He might have made a wrong decision, taken the wrong path. His throat was hoarse from calling her name, but he did so again. The snow was falling steadily now, sifting through the branches overhead, and he could barely see his tracks. He saw none of hers.

He had failed. He couldn't find her. And if he didn't she'd die. What else could he do? He turned in a circle, looking for some clue.

Nothing.

His empty gut ached so bad he had to lean over, but the pain didn't come from hunger. It came from fear. He couldn't lose Darcy. He couldn't. He loved her. Not *liked* or *cared about*. *Loved*.

He had to find her. A rush of wind sent snow cascading down on him. The heavy blobs hit the ground. Wet snow. It would soak through her sweaters and chill her faster. Not much better than dropping into the North Atlantic. Cold and blue, eyebrows frosted white, eyes lifeless.

"Help," he screamed to the silent trees.

Not even the birds answered. He had nowhere to turn, nowhere but... What had she said? That God hears everyone's prayers? He'd once thought that, had believed it with every ounce of his ten-year-old soul, but when those prayers went unanswered he swore he'd never pray again.

He thought he could solve everything himself, but now he knew he couldn't. To save Darcy, he needed bigger help. He needed God.

Jack dropped to his knees. The words came awkwardly, little better than his boyhood plea. "God, if You're listening like Darcy says, she needs You. I guess even I need You. But her mostly. I don't deserve Your help after the way I've been, but she believes in You. You have to save her. Please."

He powered ahead against the welling emotion. "I prayed to You once, long ago, but You didn't answer. I don't blame You. You were probably too busy to listen to a little boy. I'm sorry I was angry with You. I'm sorry for everything. You can hold it against me, but please don't hold it against Darcy. Please let her live."

The words tore out of him with an anguish he hadn't felt since his mother died. He'd blamed himself for Sissy's illness. He'd blamed his father for not taking care of Mom. He even blamed Mom for giving up. But he shouldn't have blamed God. He'd messed up, but he didn't know if claiming it before God would be enough. Yet it had to be. He had nothing else to offer.

Gradually, calm came over him and his jumbled thoughts began to clear. Before him stood a long ridge. An injured Darcy would have gone around it, but he saw no breaks in the elevation. She couldn't have climbed it, could she? He walked in both directions, hoping to find her huddled at the bottom.

Nothing.

He could barely see twenty feet ahead. The snow had piled to his ankles. Soon it would be dark. The flashlight wouldn't last long.

He turned it on.

Nothing.

He shook it, tried repeatedly, but it wouldn't light. The dry cells must be too cold. He tucked the icy cylinder next to his body under sweater and jacket. If it warmed, it might work. Might. In the meantime, dusk was falling quickly. He had to find her now.

The melting snow ran into his eyes. His trousers were soaked through and he began to ache from the cold.

"Darcy," he called out.

The forest gave back only silence.

He could have been wrong all along. He thought she made the holes, but it might have been something else, something natural, and she'd gone another direction entirely.

Please, God.

Once again, God wasn't answering. He remembered his mother gasping for breath, asking him to come near. She'd pressed the ring, his grandmother's ring, into his hand and told him she was going home to Jesus. He'd cried and begged her to stay with him, but in the dark hours before dawn she died.

Jack pulled out the ring. He'd almost given it to Darcy. He'd almost proposed, but he'd been too afraid. Then he let foolish pride stand between them. They didn't need to fly on Sunday, but he'd been too pigheaded to listen. He should have. He should have answered every invitation. He should have talked to God sooner.

He should have asked her to marry him. If he had, they'd be together now, not lost in the Canadian wilderness.

"Help me," he called out to God.

He had no idea where to turn.

Something urged him forward, to the top of the hill, but again he found nothing.

"Why won't You help me? Why won't You answer?" he

cried. The words died in the thick air, muffled by the snow. He dropped to his knees.

"Jack?"

He almost didn't hear the faint voice. *Could it be?* God was speaking directly to him? He started shaking. His hearing must be going.

"Jack?" Again, a little louder and directly below.

Not God. *Darcy!*

A rush of energy propelled him to his feet and down the slope.

"Darcy? Darcy?" He sang her name as he slipped and slid to the bottom.

He couldn't see a thing down there. In frustration, he yanked the dead flashlight from his waistband. *Work, please.* He pressed the switch and on came the beam, shining brightly at the glistening snow-covered ground. And Darcy.

"Jack." She trembled, her lips bluish, and tried hard to smile.

His knees gave way. *Darcy. Darcy.* He dropped the flashlight and it flickered out. He'd found her. He hugged her, shaking as he brushed the snow from the thick sweater. He then wrapped her in his jacket and held her close.

"Home," she murmured.

"Yes, home." Relief brought even more spasms as he tried to hold back the emotion. He would never let her go. Not ever. "Thank God. You were right all along. God does listen. He does answer prayers. He led me to you. I'll never doubt again."

She wrapped her arms around him, and he gave up trying to hold back the emotion. He didn't care about being tough anymore. He was going to say what he should have said months ago.

"I love you. I love you so much."

Chapter Eighteen

"**Y**ou do?" Darcy's joy that Jack had returned to God almost overwhelmed those three important words, but once they sunk in they extinguished the pain for precious moments.

He pulled back slightly. "This is news to you? Some newspaper reporter you make."

She began giggling. Jack had found her. Jack loved her. She couldn't be close enough to him. Wild emotions raced through her at full throttle. "I love you. I love you. I've always loved you." Her mad confession degenerated into tears.

He buried her words in a kiss, tender yet desperate. "Don't you ever leave me again, Darcy Shea," he said between kisses. "No note, not even a word to let me know where you were going."

A laugh bubbled up. She'd said the very same thing to him after the last crash. "I won't. I promise."

"I don't ever want to lose you again. Ever."

"Me either." Ever. She clung to his snow-coated sweater and let the tears flow. No she wouldn't leave him again. Jack had given her dream wings.

"Don't cry." He wiped the tears and melting snow from her cheeks. "Please don't cry, Miss Optimism."

His use of her pet name only made her cry harder. She

shouldn't have gone off on her own, trying to be the heroine. She should have listened to Jack. She should have been more careful straining the oil. So many mistakes. So much false pride.

"I—I thought I'd get help. I thought the mining settlement was close. According to the map..." She hiccupped. "The map. I lost it. I lost the map when I fell. There's no moon and it's snowing and we don't have a map and it's cold and how will we ever get home?"

"Don't worry." His breath felt so hot on her cheek. His arms were so strong. "Together we'll find a way."

She gathered herself, ashamed that she'd lost faith. Of course they would. Hadn't she known that the moment she lifted up her prayers? "The most important thing is we're together. Jack, you are everything to me."

"And you to me."

The tenderness of his kiss resuscitated a deep longing for family and home—and evening walks and picnics and fishing in the creek. How foolishly she'd cast those treasures away. How much she'd give to have them back again.

She shook involuntarily. Then again. Then her teeth started chattering.

Jack rubbed her hands. "You're freezing. We need a fire."

"N-n-no m-matches."

He hunted around in the snow. "If I can find the flashlight, we'll go back to the camp."

The camp. Yes, the camp. "N-n-near m-my legs." The pain came back, dull and aching this time. "S-s-stuck. C-can't move."

"Don't worry, I'll get them free, once I can see."

It would hurt terribly, but she could endure anything, now that Jack was here.

"Aha. Found it."

She heard a click but saw nothing.

"Dead." He sounded discouraged.

She reached for him but felt nothing. Frostbite. "I-I'm a lot o-of t-t-trouble."

"Not at all. Let's get your legs freed. It's going to hurt."

Jack tucked the flashlight against his body again, hoping for some life from the batteries. It wouldn't be much, not enough to get them back to the camp—and that meant problems. Big problems.

New moon. Hypothermia. No way to start a fire. Odds were, they wouldn't survive the night. Before morning they would slip quietly into unconsciousness and death if he didn't figure out a way to start a fire. He wished he'd thought to bring matches.

"I'm going to touch your leg now."

He felt along her limb to where it was wedged in the V between two four-inch trunks. The toe of her boot had caught under a fallen log, and her ankle was twisted at a bad angle. She should be screaming with pain. The cold must have numbed it. And her.

Without giving her a chance to prepare herself, he yanked her boot from under the log and lifted her leg out. She screamed. *Good, still some feeling left.*

"Oh, my," she gasped.

Her teeth weren't chattering anymore. He didn't have long. He needed to make a fire now. But how, without matches? *Think, Hunter, think.*

"I don't suppose you have a piece of flint on you?" he asked. Together with the steel of the hatchet, he could strike a spark and start a fire.

She didn't answer right away, and he thought he'd lost her.

"Darcy?" He touched her cheek.

"No, I don't. Is there a rock nearby?"

How would he know? He couldn't see more than shadows. "Sorry." He rubbed his temples. How to start a fire?

She shifted slightly. "We need something that will create a spark, right? Something electrical, perhaps? Like the flashlight?"

"There's not enough energy in it to create a spark."

"The lamp?"

"Not hot enough to catch anything on fire."

"F-filament?"

The filament? Would it get hot enough? Maybe. It was their best and only chance. "We need some dry fiber."

"C-cotton."

"Perfect. I still have mine in my pocket." While the flashlight warmed, he cleared snow from a patch of ground and cut some kindling with the hatchet. Darcy's hatchet. If they got home alive, he'd have it mounted. "Now the tricky part. Are you still with me, Miss Optimism?"

She giggled softly, and he fished out the flashlight. He had to break the glass off the bulb without damaging the filament, all in the dark. He lightly tapped and the glass came off.

"Don't hurt yourself," Darcy cautioned.

He inwardly smiled. It felt good to have someone worry and fuss over him. "All right, I need you to blow on the kindling when the cotton ignites."

She shifted into position.

"Ready?" His finger hesitated on the switch. "We only have one chance."

"Let's pray first," she suggested.

Though he'd never heard of praying for a mechanical device, Jack agreed. Together they held the flashlight cylinder and asked God to give them the fire they needed. That amazing calm returned, and Jack knew that whatever happened, God was with them.

He pressed the switch. At first nothing happened, but then a glow began, faint at first, but then growing as the fibers smoked and caught fire. He blew gently, transferring the flame to the kindling. Darcy blew until the twigs ignited. Within moments, they had fire.

Darcy cheered, clapping her hands. The fire grew and soon illuminated her in a golden glow. Jack's chest tightened. They would survive. Together. He'd never felt like this for anyone. Now he understood what Sissy meant. Love was definitely worth the risk.

Neither slept that night. Darcy suffered through thawing her fingers and toes, but being with Jack made the burning pain bearable. They fed the fire and melted snow for drinking water in the metal flashlight cylinder. And they talked on and on until morning, clearing up the questions that stood between them.

Jack explained that the engines had died because the carburetors iced, not due to anything she had done. Darcy asked him to forgive her for thinking he'd been drinking at Mrs. Lawrence's saloon.

"I would have thought the same," he said, his face solemn in the firelight. "You couldn't know I vowed never to touch the stuff. You see, my father is a drunkard." He cringed slightly when he said it, and Darcy knew he feared her reaction.

"So is my Aunt Meg's husband," she whispered.

"Aunt Meg?"

"Not the one in Buffalo. Aunt Meg is Papa's sister. That's why he supports temperance so strongly."

"Now I understand why he doesn't like me."

She was puzzled. "He doesn't know you went to Mrs. Lawrence's."

"It's a small town. That sort of news spreads."

"That doesn't mean Papa dislikes you. He might seem forbidding, but he's all bluster and no bite. He'll like you once he gets to know you. Mum's in your corner already."

"She is?" He sounded shocked.

"She thought the way you rescued me from the plane wreck was quite heroic."

He laughed. "She's not going to think much of this rescue."

By morning they'd covered every member of their families and every minor like and dislike. They laughed. They talked quietly. They held hands and dreamed of future flights.

"If the transatlantic record falls," Jack said after they'd drunk another cylinder of water, "let's go for your North Pole flight."

"Really?" He'd said *let's,* as in the two of them. "But, this time I'm the pilot."

He grinned. "The pilot goes with the plane. If you own the plane, you can be the pilot."

She flexed her hand. The feeling was coming back. "All right. I'll settle for copilot."

He leaned close again. "Me, too."

They sealed the bargain with a kiss.

"Oh," she cried, breaking away. "Look." The eastern horizon had begun to lighten, and when Darcy looked overhead, she saw stars, millions upon millions of stars.

Within the hour, the forest creatures began their day gathering food. The rustling, cheeping and occasional scolding gladdened Darcy's soul. She was terribly hungry and weak, but they'd survived the night. Somehow they'd make it home. She knew it.

Jack found the map resting against a birch tree, and using the compass, determined their approximate location. He sat beside her with a grunt. "I'd say we're a good ten miles from the coast."

"Ten miles?" How would she walk that far? Nevertheless, she said, "I can make it."

Jack lifted the hatchet. "First I make you a new crutch." He hesitated a moment. "I wish I had brought the sandwich that you started to eat."

She wrinkled her nose. Even in starvation she couldn't stomach that. "It was soaked in gasoline."

"Rest," he ordered, rising.

But how could she? While Jack looked for the perfect branch from which to craft a crutch, Darcy surveyed their surroundings. Last night's snow was already melting. It was only an inch thick and in some places the twigs and dead leaves and plants poked through. Plants. Darcy looked closely. If she wasn't mistaken, that was wintergreen. She broke off a leaf and sniffed. Sure enough. She chewed on it. It didn't fill the stomach but it helped.

She'd gathered handfuls by the time Jack returned with the crutch.

He pounded it on the ground. "This'll last a good twenty, thirty miles."

"I sure hope it's not twenty miles to the mining camp."

"Ten, twelve at most. We'll take it slow, and I'll help you over the hills." He handed her the crutch and held out a hand to assist her to her feet.

"First, eat." She held out the wintergreen. "It's mint. Try it."

He took a leaf and chewed. His eyebrows shot up. "So it is. Where'd you learn about edible plants?"

"Papa's expedition books."

He munched on a handful. "I'll have to thank your father. After we walk to the mine."

A familiar screech drew Darcy's attention upward. A dozen

white, black and gray birds floated above them. "We won't have very far to go, maybe one or two miles."

"Impossible. The location of the stream, the terrain; it all indicates we're here." He pointed to the map.

"Then how do you explain the seagulls?"

Jack followed her outstretched arm. "What do gulls have to do with where we're located?"

"Gulls mean we must be near the coast. Near Lake Superior." As if to confirm her statement, a long low moan reached their ears. Darcy pushed to one knee. "A steam horn."

"A ship's horn." Jack looked around. "That direction." He pointed to the next ridge.

"Well, help me up."

Instead, Jack scooped her into his arms. "Hold on tight."

"You'll hurt yourself."

"Stop nagging." But he was grinning.

She laughed, bouncing against his chest. They reached the top of the hill, and he stopped. She felt something release in him.

"What is it?"

He let her down, making sure she had her crutch for balance. There before them spread the deep blue of Lake Superior. Far below sat the mining settlement, smoke trailing from the shacks' chimneys. A steamboat moored at the pier, taking on ore. The descent would be difficult, but they'd survive.

"We're going home." She positioned the crutch under her right arm, but before she could move he drew her close. "There's something I've been wanting to do for a long time, something I should have done long ago. Give me your hand."

She lifted her right hand.

"No, the other one."

Darcy caught her breath. Her *left* hand. *Was he? Could it possibly be?* She started to tremble.

"Darcy Opal Shea, I know it's lousy timing and I should have asked you sooner, but there's no one else I want to spend my life loving."

The spasms started the moment he used her full name and accelerated with each successive word.

He gazed deep into her eyes. "Will you fly with me across the Atlantic or to the North Pole or just to the next town? Will you navigate the rest of our lives?"

He wanted her to navigate. And not just aeroplanes but an entire life together. Her throat ached as she blinked back tears.

He steadied, his voice clear and true. "Will you share every takeoff and landing, no matter how many or few, for the rest of our lives? Will you marry me, Darcy?"

She couldn't restrain the sobs any longer. They choked out of her punctuated by hiccups. "Yes, yes, a thousand times yes."

Then he slipped a sapphire-studded band on her left ring finger. "My grandmother's. She and my grandfather spent nearly fifty years together before he passed. Please wear this as a token of my love."

"I will." She touched it, feeling the power of fifty years of marriage. "It's beautiful, Jack."

"Understand that I want to marry you properly, in your church, if they will have me."

"Of course, of course. Oh, Jack, we welcome you with open arms." She hugged him close and thanked God for answering even the prayers she didn't know to ask. Jack had made peace with God. They would walk forward in faith. God's plan was truly more glorious than anything she could ever have imagined.

He pulled back a little, terribly serious. "And we will need your father's blessing. I hope you're willing to wait."

Wait for Papa? Oh, dear. What would he think of Jack

after this failed flight? Would he forbid their marriage? If so, how long before she convinced him? Darcy wanted to marry now, but Jack was adamant. She'd have to wait.

Chapter Nineteen

A week, a boat ride and a doctor visit later, Jack and Darcy headed south. After crossing the Straits of Mackinaw by ferry, they boarded the train to Pearlman. Darcy's knee had only been severely strained, and though she had to use crutches, she'd soon return to normal life.

Yet nothing would ever be normal again. As each mile clicked past, Darcy's elation turned to trepidation. By now everyone in Pearlman must be worried, wondering what had happened. Her parents. Would Papa accept Jack? And the investors. The Kensingtons. It just got worse and worse.

Jack, too, had grown silent, his brow creased.

"Try not to look so happy," she teased.

Though he smiled briefly, he didn't explain, and her tension increased. She gnawed on her fingernails. They'd spent so much of other people's money with no hope of return. Every cent of the investment lay in ruins in the wilderness.

"I wish we could sneak into town without anyone noticing," Darcy said after they left the Grand Rapids station.

"I don't think that's going to be possible."

"I know," she sighed. "I don't know how we're going to repay everyone, but I'll do my part. Do you think a story on the flight would sell?"

"Not likely, considering the way it ended."

The thought of how much Blake and Beattie had spent brought tears to her eyes. She'd have to face them, but it wasn't going to be pleasant. She could lose her dearest friend.

Jack patted her hand. "Don't worry. Every investor knew the risk going in. The venture always had a very real chance of failure."

Failure. The word still stung. "But I'm sure they hoped for success."

"Of course, but even if we'd won the prize, it wouldn't have paid the whole bill."

Darcy's eyes widened. Fifty thousand dollars wasn't enough? "How much did you lay out for this flight, Jack Hunter?"

He slouched a little lower in the seat. "I haven't exactly totaled it up. It might be a little more than we had subscribed, though. We were supposed to make it back on the lectures."

Darcy took in that dismal news as the farmland passed by the train window. "That's a sorry way to start out married life."

His hesitation told her everything she needed to know. "Second thoughts, Miss Shea?"

"Don't think you can slip out of this that easily."

He smiled weakly. "I hope your father feels the same way."

Darcy wanted to reassure him, but she had no idea what Papa would say. As the train creaked and rattled along the rails, her thoughts dwelled on the future.

"What if..." She hesitated to say aloud that Papa might refuse. "What if we need to wait? Where will we live?"

"I'll go back to Buffalo and reopen the flight school."

"And I'll finish my lessons and get my license." That covered the next three months, but then what? She couldn't stay with Perpetua forever.

The train left the Belvidere station. They were getting close. Darcy squeezed Jack's hand, but she knew he couldn't protect her from the storm to come.

"Oh, Jack, why don't we go straight to Buffalo? I don't want to see their disappointment. I don't want to tell them we failed, that we wasted their money. Oh, dear. I hope they don't know about the crash."

"No chance of that, I'm afraid," he said, "considering I sent a cable from Sault Ste. Marie."

"Oh, no," she groaned, burying her head in her hands.

He actually laughed.

"It's not you they're going to string up," she cried. "I'm the one from Pearlman. I'm the one who said it could be done. I'm the one who got people to invest, who convinced my parents. Oh, dear."

"Pearlman!" the conductor called out.

She felt ill. "I'm going to faint."

"Take deep breaths," Jack said, rubbing her back. "You'll be fine."

"No I won't," she sobbed. "I can't face them. I can't face Papa. Can't we just go on to Buffalo?"

"Don't have the money. I'm afraid you're going to have to face the music."

The train screeched to a halt, and ironically, Darcy heard music. Sousa, to be precise. She raised her head. "What's that?"

Jack was grinning. "I never knew you were so yellow, Darcy Shea. All this time you had me convinced you could handle anything, but throw a few local townspeople your way, and you fall apart."

"Wait. Listen." Darcy leaned over Jack trying to see, but their car was too far back. "What's going on?"

"You two getting off?" asked the conductor. "We don't have all day."

"Yes, sir," said Jack, helping Darcy to her feet while he fetched her crutches. "We're definitely getting off."

No getting out of this. She'd have to apologize to every craftsman who helped rebuild the plane, every merchant who donated materials, to Blake, Beattie, her parents and a hundred other people. She'd repay every cent, if it took the rest of her life.

Jack helped her down the aisle and lifted her onto the platform. The music was louder. She raised her head and blinked at the astonishing sight before her.

Practically all of Pearlman stood on the platform clapping and hooting. The civic band blared an off-key Sousa march. A huge banner hung from the station and proclaimed CONGRATULATIONS ON RECORD FLIGHT. Red, white and blue bunting. Cakes, pies and bowls of punch. It looked like Independence Day.

Devlin took their photograph with a bright flash, and Darcy blinked, spots before her eyes. "What is all this?"

"Looks like a celebration," said Jack.

"I know, but why?"

Beatrice rushed toward her, arms outstretched. She wore the same ridiculously flowered hat she'd had on the day Jack first flew into town.

"Darcy, Jack, welcome home," she said, giving Darcy a kiss on the cheek. "I'm glad you're safe. I have such news."

"Me, too."

"I want to hear everything, but I'm just bursting to tell you. I'm going to have a baby." Beattie practically hopped up and down. "Blake is so excited. He's told everyone in town at least a hundred times. I want a boy, but he'd like a little girl."

Darcy hugged her friend, all the time eyeing that congratulatory banner. "But Beattie, what is all this hullabaloo about? There must be some mistake. We didn't set any record."

"Yes, you did." Papa beamed at her and clapped Jack on the

back. "Longest over-water flight in North America. Between two countries, too. Congratulations." He gave her a bear hug and whispered, "I'm proud of you, Darcy."

She could have cried. It was preposterous, and quite likely incorrect, but as in gifts, it wasn't in good taste to question the giver.

"Thank you, Papa."

That hug was quickly followed by one from Mum, Amelia with baby John, her nieces and nephew, Prudy, Terchie and everyone she'd ever known in Pearlman, all offering outlandish accolades for the failed flight.

Jack stood to the side, feeling awash in this tide of congratulations. Sure, Blake had offered a handshake and a startling proposition, but the rush of goodwill was directed at Darcy. He was just incidental. At least her father hadn't had him hauled off to jail. Yet. That might change when Jack asked for Darcy's hand.

He looked to the station to see if any law enforcement was waiting, and that's when he saw her. Sissy. In a wheelchair and smiling broadly. The sun glinted off her hair.

Jack stumbled forward. Sissy hadn't left St. Anne's since her accident. How had she known about the test flight? Not from him. And how had she gotten here?

Then he saw how. George Carrman stood behind Sissy pushing her wheelchair. The doctor. Darcy had said Carrman worked at St. Anne's, but Jack hadn't made the connection until now. This was the man Sissy loved.

An icicle stabbed Jack's heart. Everything that had seemed so right moments before dived into the ground.

"Jackie," his sister called out, arms held wide.

He went to her of course, knelt and embraced her. "Sissy."

She laughed, clear and sparkling as a spring stream. "You're going to have to stop calling me that. I'm a grown woman, you know. I'm so proud of you, Jack."

"How," he stammered, standing back up, "did you know?"

"Blake Kensington wired George, and we decided on the spur of the moment. Isn't it glorious? Oh, Jackie, I saw such sights. Cities and farms and cattle and little towns and streetlights at night and—oh, I can't tell you everything."

Stunned, Jack realized his sister reveled in what he'd taken for granted. She glowed, alive with excitement.

"But that's not the best of all," she said mysteriously, a conspiratorial smile on her face.

Carrman stepped forward. The man was actually shaking. "M-Mr. Hunter, I'd like to ask your permission to marry Cecelia."

Jack's jaw dropped.

"It's fine with Dad," Sissy said.

Jack tensed. "Our father has no right to grant permission." He glanced at the crowd, looking for the bum.

"He's not here. I saw him in Buffalo when he came to visit."

Jack's joy twisted into pain. "I don't know why you still see him, after all he's done."

"He took care of me, Jackie," she said quietly. "Long ago, he set up a trust for my care and your schooling. Yes, he stumbled. We all do at one time or another, but God will forgive us if we can forgive others. Dad's hurting, Jack. He's confused and lost and doesn't know where to turn. Mom was his rock, and without her he fell. But I still believe that somehow, someday, he'll find his way. God hasn't given up on him, and I won't either."

Deep down, Jack knew what she said was true. After all, God hadn't given up on him after years of denial. Jack had lost his way, and the combination of Darcy's faith and a little forest miracle brought him around.

"Do we have your blessing?" Sissy squeezed Carrman's hand and smiled at the man with such joy that Jack couldn't break her heart.

"I will love and care for your sister all her life," Carrman said. "She will want for nothing. I'll treat her like the angel she is."

He gazed at Sissy with a love that Jack recognized. It was the way he felt about Darcy.

Sissy laughed. "Oh, do stop being so formal, George. We love each other, and that's all that matters."

That was all that mattered. For Sissy and for Jack.

"Of course," Jack said after clearing the clot from his throat. He shook George's hand. "I'll hold you to that promise."

"Yes, sir."

"Call me Jack." He gazed at his sister. She'd never looked happier or lovelier. "There's someone I want you to meet."

Sissy's smile widened. "Darcy. You're going to marry her, aren't you?"

Jack blinked. "You know?"

"Oh, Jackie, it's been written all over you for months."

Jack didn't realize he'd been so transparent. "I hope you don't want Grandmother's ring."

"You gave it to her?" she squealed in delight. "Oh, Jack, when? How? Tell me everything. Maybe we can have a double ceremony."

"A double ceremony?" said Darcy, joining them.

"A double ceremony?" echoed her father.

Jack's gut wound tighter than a locked propeller. Why was doing the right thing so difficult? "Sir. Mr. Shea. We, that is, *I* would like to ask your blessing to marry your daughter Darcy. She's accepted."

Mr. Shea's eyebrows rose. "Is that so?"

"Yes, Papa, I love him."

Her father looked at her a long moment. "He hasn't even come to supper."

Jack swallowed. He couldn't let Darcy take the brunt of this. "I'd be pleased to join you. Any time." He was bungling this. What on earth had happened to the cool, charming Jack Hunter? He was acting like a schoolboy.

Darcy threaded her fingers through his, giving him strength.

Mr. Shea stared at him. "And how do you plan to support her?"

"Jack is going to run the Buffalo flight school," Darcy said before Jack could open his mouth, "and I'll help."

"You will?" Jack didn't remember agreeing to that.

"I see." Mr. Shea tapped a finger to his lips. "I don't suppose I have much choice in the matter. Darcy tends to do exactly as she pleases. I hope you know what you're getting into, young man."

Darcy hopped up and down. "Then we have your blessing? Thank you, Papa." She threw her arms around her father.

Mr. Shea extricated himself with a few pats to her back and "there now"s. He then stuck out his hand. "Welcome to the family, son."

Son. No one had called him son in almost twenty years. He could have burst from happiness. Not only did the Sheas welcome him, but Darcy soon fell into conversation with Sissy. He supposed it was odd that the two women in his life had been battered up a bit, but both were strong. Both had survived and were the better for it.

After George took Sissy back to the Kensingtons and Jack accepted the Sheas' dinner invitation, Jack asked Darcy what she thought of his sister marrying George Carrman.

"He's a good, honorable man, and perfectly suited to her," Darcy said. "She's wonderful, Jack."

"Yes, she is," Jack said. "Just like you."

Darcy cocked her head. "You're silly with love. In a year you'll feel differently."

"Never," he professed. "But we do have something to discuss."

Her grip tightened on his arm. "What is it?"

"Do you still want to live in Buffalo?"

"What are you getting at, Jack Hunter?"

"Blake Kensington wants to start an airfield here. Thought I might be just the one to do it."

She grinned. "You'd be perfect."

"Then you don't object to staying in Pearlman?"

She looked round at the fields and the town, with its regular, clapboard buildings and tidy yards. "Pearlman is where we began. It may not be where we end, but it seems as good a place as any to take our next step."

"Is that so?" Jack scooped her from the platform. "I thought you didn't have the courage to face all these people."

"I'm a lot stronger than you think."

"I guess I have a lot to learn about women."

Darcy tilted her head in that unbelievably alluring way. "Then it's a good thing I have a lifetime to teach you."

* * * * *

Dear Reader,

While visiting the Frontiers of Flight museum in Dallas, I happened upon an exhibit honoring women aviators. I had no idea so many women were involved in the dangerous early days of aviation. That exhibit piqued my curiosity and ultimately led to this story of Darcy and Jack.

Though Darcy's story is fictional, the events surrounding the first transatlantic flight are based on fact. On May 31, 1919 one of the Curtiss flying boats crossed the Atlantic Ocean from Newfoundland to England with a stop at the Azores. John Alcock and Arthur Brown completed the first nonstop transatlantic crossing a couple weeks later. More information on the early days of flight can be found through links on my website or in books and articles at your local library.

I love to hear from readers. You can reach me through my website at *www.christineelizabethjohnson.com*.

Christine Johnson

QUESTIONS FOR DISCUSSION

1. Darcy often acts impulsively, placing her own desires first. How does that affect her relationship with Jack? With her father?

2. Rejection and disappointment are part of life, yet Darcy perseveres when her desire to fly is thwarted. From whom or what does she find the strength to go on?

3. How does Darcy's relationship with her family affect her choices?

4. How do the people closest to us affect our life choices?

5. At what point does Darcy realize she forgot to include God in her decisions?

6. Other than Jack, who helps Darcy achieve her dream of flying? Do you have someone in your life who has served as mentor or inspired you?

7. Forgiveness is one of the most powerful gifts we can give to another and to ourselves. Who did Jack have trouble forgiving? Did it affect his relationship with Darcy?

8. Does Jack risk too much in his pursuit of the transatlantic record flight? Does Darcy?

9. Jack battles twin desires: to protect Darcy and to let her spread her wings. How does Darcy's eagerness to go along with Jack's plans feed into his decision?

10. What does Darcy learn from taking on the challenge of caring for her nieces and nephew? Have you ever faced something that took you out of your comfort zone? What helped you get through it?

11. How does Jack's response to the children surprise Darcy? How does it change their relationship?

12. In times of crisis, it's natural to turn to God, yet He desires a deeper relationship. Will Jack and Darcy move forward into that deeper relationship with the Lord? What in the story leads you to believe that?

13. For much of the story, Jack and Darcy work against each other, even though they ultimately want the same thing. Are there any areas in your life where you're working against someone, when working together would bring the desired result more quickly?

14. When Jack's faith was shaken in childhood, he turned from God, yet the Lord remained faithful. How has God shown steadfast patience in your life?

15. In the world's eyes, Jack and Darcy's transatlantic attempt would be called a failure, yet they consider it a success. Why?

Love Inspired.
HISTORICAL

TITLES AVAILABLE NEXT MONTH

Available December 7, 2010

LIHCNM1110

REQUEST YOUR FREE BOOKS!

2 FREE INSPIRATIONAL NOVELS
PLUS 2
FREE
MYSTERY GIFTS

Love Inspired.
HISTORICAL
INSPIRATIONAL HISTORICAL ROMANCE

YES! Please send me 2 FREE Love Inspired® Historical novels and my 2 FREE mystery gifts (gifts are worth about $10). After receiving them, if I don't wish to receive any more books, I can return the shipping statement marked "cancel". If I don't cancel, I will receive 4 brand-new novels every other month and be billed just $4.24 per book in the U.S. or $4.74 per book in Canada. That's a saving of over 20% off the cover price. It's quite a bargain! Shipping and handling is just 50¢ per book.* I understand that accepting the 2 free books and gifts places me under no obligation to buy anything. I can always return a shipment and cancel at any time. Even if I never buy another book, the two free books and gifts are mine to keep forever.

102/302 IDN E7QD

Name	(PLEASE PRINT)	
Address		Apt. #
City	State/Prov.	Zip/Postal Code

Signature (if under 18, a parent or guardian must sign)

Mail to Steeple Hill Reader Service:
IN U.S.A.: P.O. Box 1867, Buffalo, NY 14240-1867
IN CANADA: P.O. Box 609, Fort Erie, Ontario L2A 5X3

Not valid for current subscribers to Love Inspired Historical books.

Want to try two free books from another series?
Call 1-800-873-8635 or visit www.morefreebooks.com.

* Terms and prices subject to change without notice. Prices do not include applicable taxes. Sales tax applicable in N.Y. Canadian residents will be charged applicable provincial taxes and GST. Offer not valid in Quebec. This offer is limited to one order per household. All orders subject to approval. Credit or debit balances in a customer's account(s) may be offset by any other outstanding balance owed by or to the customer. Please allow 4 to 6 weeks for delivery. Offer available while quantities last.

Your Privacy: Steeple Hill Books is committed to protecting your privacy. Our Privacy Policy is available online at www.SteepleHill.com or upon request from the Reader Service. From time to time we make our lists of customers available to reputable third parties who may have a product or service of interest to you. If you would prefer we not share your name and address, please check here. ☐

Help us get it right—We strive for accurate, respectful and relevant communications. To clarify or modify your communication preferences, visit us at www.ReaderService.com/consumerschoice.

LIH10R